Time to Die

Stephen Puleston

ABOUT THE AUTHOR

Stephen Puleston was born and educated in Anglesey, North Wales. He graduated in theology before training as a lawyer. Dead and Gone is his ninth novel in the Inspector Drake series

www.stephenpuleston.co.uk
Facebook:stephenpulestoncrimewriter

OTHER NOVELS
Inspector Drake Mysteries
Brass in Pocket
Worse than Dead
Against the Tide
Dead on your Feet
A Time to Kill
Written in Blood
Nowhere to Hide
A Cold Dark Heart
Dead and Gone
Prequel Novella– Ebook only - Devil's Kitchen

Inspector Marco Novels
Speechless
Another Good Killing
Somebody Told Me
Times Like These
Dead of Night
Prequel Novella– Ebook only -Dead Smart

Copyright © 2022 Puleston Publishing Limited
All rights reserved.

ISBN: 9798852377166

In memory of my mother
Gwenno Puleston

Chapter 1

They threw the body over the cliff a few minutes after midnight. There was no scream, no shout of terror. The only discernible sound was the thud of bone against the jagged edges of the cliffside and the rocks below.

The older of the two men standing at the edge of the precipice took a small step and peered down into the darkness. He wanted to check: be certain that at the bottom of the cliff was a dead body. But he knew he needn't clamber down and feel for a pulse.

The beach below them was popular with locals and tourists. The path around the island frequented by energetic walkers passed nearby. It was only a matter of time until a dog walker or local taking a morning stroll would discover the body.

He stepped back and re-joined his companion. They stood staring over the bay. In the distance the lights from the decommissioned nuclear power plant lit up the night sky. Out of sight in a small bay over to their left was the village of Cemaes, its residents happily tucked up in bed. The older man smiled to himself, enjoying the prospect of the turmoil that would be unleashed in the morning, once the man's body had been discovered.

The younger man dipped a hand into a pocket of his fleece and pulled out a packet of cigarettes. He kept a hand over the cigarette at his lips as his companion fumbled with a lighter. He drew a deep lungful of smoke and exhaled in one long breath. 'He cried like a baby, didn't he?'

The older man chortled his agreement recalling the man's desperate pleas when they had dragged him off his motorcycle. It hadn't taken long for both to overpower him, get his hands tied behind his back and then fasten three layers of duct tape securely over his mouth. Then there had been whimpering and a terrified look in his eyes.

Behind them was an ancient church and whilst he wasn't a religious man – despite his mother being a devout

Catholic – he couldn't quite detach himself from the mystery of religion. A visit to a church would bring back all the memories of childhood and an incensed-filled service. It always tickled his nostrils and he recalled his mother scolding him at the merest attempt of a cough. He'd seen photographs of the church on Facebook. Perhaps in the future people would visit the spot, not to walk the coastal path or gaze in awe at the stained-glass windows, but to gawp at the location of their handiwork that evening.

'There's some great places to fish off the coast here,' the younger man said.

'I know.'

'Friend of mine's got a boat, well, shares in one anyway. He's promised to take me out.' He drew smoke from the dying embers of the cigarette into his lungs.

'Take the stub with you.'

The younger man hesitated for a moment, but his companion's voice left no room to challenge. He extinguished the cigarette and slipped the stub into the packet. The older man nodded, just the once, and looked out over the beach, then over the bay and away into the distance.

A gentle wind picked up and feathered their faces with a salty residue. The younger man turned to his companion. 'Will anyone miss him?'

'Not a chance – it was his time to die.'

They burst into laughter and turned away from the cliff edge.

Chapter 2

Detective Inspector Ian Drake had only a short drive from his home in Felinheli to Llangefni police station for the training session that morning. His normal commute to work would have taken him along the A55, the main dual carriageway that stretched across the North Wales coast, to the Northern Division headquarters of the Wales Police Service at Colwyn Bay. The road was like an artery, essential for the day-to-day activity of the people living in North Wales. Lorries trundling their way to and from the port of Holyhead towards the conurbations of England and beyond into Europe filled the road at all times of the day.

Not having a long commute meant a few more precious minutes with Annie, his partner, before setting out for work. Although autumn was fast approaching there was still enough warmth in the air for them to sit out on the balcony looking out over the Menai Strait, enjoying a leisurely breakfast. She told him about her day. She would leave at the same time as he did and make her way to the history department at Bangor University. Drake knew how much she enjoyed her work and although the University term hadn't started she had lectures to prepare, research to be completed and, imminently, freshers to be handled.

'What time will you be back tonight?' Annie said.

'I'll be back before you,' Drake chuckled.

'Well, I suppose there's a first time for everything.'

'Seriously, the training I'm doing shouldn't take long. It's been rescheduled so many times the superintendent was most insistent that nothing would prevent this course taking place. So I'll be finished by four o'clock.'

'And how is Superintendent Hobbs these days?'

Drake raised his eyebrows. 'Nothing changes. I can't work the man out. You'd expect a superintendent role would need someone with a bit of personality. But no one likes him, nobody trusts him.'

'I'd like to meet him some time.'

'No, you wouldn't. He's got small piggy eyes and—'

'Now you're being unkind.'

Drake fell silent, acknowledging that Annie was probably right. But it didn't change his view of Superintendent Hobbs.

They retreated back into the house. Drake pulled on the jacket of his dark grey suit. It was one of several he kept regularly dry cleaned. A sombre paisley tie in a purple shade was knotted tightly to the collar of a double cuffed white shirt. He stared at himself in the mirror by the front door. He tilted his head up before moving it sideways trying to convince himself there were no bags under his eyes. Then he drew in his stomach.

Annie joined him and smiled. 'Not going to seed just yet.'

She didn't wait for him to reply before kissing him on the lips and adding. 'Perhaps we can go for a walk before dinner. Help you work off some of that imaginary flab. And remember that your mother is visiting – so don't be late.'

Annie teasing him was so different from the strained, argumentative attitude his former wife could take. But he quickly brushed away any recollection of his previous life and all the baggage associated with it.

He leaned down and kissed Annie. 'I won't be late.'

After a short drive he crossed the Britannia Bridge over the Menai Strait onto Anglesey. Then he powered the car towards Llangefni, the market town of the island, and a few minutes later he signalled left for the slip road. He threaded his way through the industrial estates on the outskirts, eventually pulling up outside the purpose-built police station. Aerials and masts sprouted from the roof, a testament to the high-tech world of modern policing.

Once he was through the security gate, he parked his BMW X3 and walked over to the rear entrance of the building. Another security keypad faced him. Numbers were important for Drake. The daily regime of completing a sudoku had become part of the routines that curbed his obsessions. And when his OCD had been troubling, numbers regularly featured. Sian, his ex-wife, had complained bitterly when he had to check the front and rear doors of their home by pressing the handle of each five times before going to bed.

He looked down at the keypad and brusquely tapped in the number, brushing away the memories of his compulsions into a dark corner of his mind.

Drake reached the training suite and pushed open the door. Several young officers had congregated around a table with coffee- and tea-making facilities and plates of biscuits. Drake spotted Brooks, the detective inspector from Wrexham, who was to take the first session, deep in conversation with Superintendent Hobbs. Neither man looked over at Drake, who made his way over to join Sara Morgan, the detective sergeant on his team. Hobbs had insisted that Sara attend despite a busy workload.

'Morning boss,' Sara said, before taking a mouthful of tea. A couple of biscuits were perched on the side of the saucer. 'Are you having coffee?'

Drake shook his head. 'Have you spoken to the superintendent?'

'No, but he sort of nodded in my direction.'

Sara crunched on the last of her custard creams and finished her drink. Drake noticed movement from the other side of the room and saw Superintendent Hobbs make his way over towards the desks set out for the trainers. The young officers began taking their seats, leaving their empty coffee or tea cups on the table at the back of the room.

Drake peered over at Superintendent Hobbs, but there was no invitation to join him at the front of the room – simply a nod of acknowledgement. So Drake and Sara found two chairs and sat, content to wait for the first of their sessions to start. 'Better switch off our mobiles,' Drake said.

They both fumbled with their handsets.

'Good morning.' Superintendent Hobbs began the introductions. He went through the usual housekeeping routine of making certain mobiles were switched off, that everyone knew where the toilets were and, in the case of emergency, where the exits were located. Then he ran through the order of the day explaining that he hoped all the constables attending would benefit greatly from the expertise to be shared by both Inspector Drake and his counterpart from Wrexham.

Policing a town like Wrexham had changed a lot over the years. At one time the town had a big Polish community which had created difficulties in itself. And Wrexham and its nearby towns of Queensferry and Shotton lining the Dee estuary faced regular challenges from drug dealers of the cities of England stretching their tentacles through their county lines operations into the small towns and villages of North Wales.

Half an hour into Detective Inspector Brooks' initial training session a young uniformed officer entered and scanned the room. Then he marched over to Drake and Sara.

He leaned over and whispered in Drake's ear, 'There's an urgent call for you, sir.'

Drake thought about the session he was supposed to deliver later that day and the promise he'd made to Annie that he'd be home promptly. They were going for a walk before dinner. The words 'urgent call' surely meant the carefully structured plan for the day had already been consigned to history.

He followed the officer out and through into the main operations room of the station where the young constable pointed at a phone. Drake picked up the handset. It was area control and he listened carefully to the message. He said nothing. He didn't have to, but once he had finished the call he switched on his mobile and it came alive with messages.

He trooped back to the training suite and, opening the

door, he gesticulated at Sara to join him.

'What's up, sir?' Sara said.

'There's a body. On a beach on the other side of the island. We are leaving now.'

Drake gave Sara his mobile as they trotted over to his car. She punched the postcode from the message on his mobile into the satnav as he made his way out of the secure police compound. He headed for the A55, assuming that travelling west and then north would be the quickest way to reach Cemaes, a village on the northern edge of the island.

He listened to Sara's one-way conversation with area control. The body of a single male had been found on a beach near Cemaes. The CSI team were en route but the pathologist wasn't expected until later that morning.

As Sara fiddled with the satnav Drake lost patience. 'Is there any quicker way to reach Cemaes than to travel along the A55 and then north? Because if there is we need to find it now before we get to the dual carriageway.'

'We could go through Llanerchymedd and Llanfechell but it's through narrow country roads. It's a bit shorter.'

Drake reached the bridge that crossed the dual carriageway. On the other side was the roundabout with the slip road onto the A55. 'To hell with that, we'll take the A55. Get area control to warn traffic – I don't want to be pulled up by some traffic cop.'

Seconds later Drake was accelerating down the slip road. He sped into the outside lane, the speedometer registering ninety miles an hour. Luckily the road was quiet and the car hurtled west.

Drake took a junction off the A55 signposted for the nuclear power station and once he was clear of the traffic lights at Valley he powered the car northwards. He paid little attention to the speed limits other than within the villages. He slowed as he drove down the hill into Cemaes, advertised as the most northerly village in Wales. The satnav told them to skirt round the village, following a road that bypassed the centre. At a junction a marked police vehicle prevented further access to what looked like an unclassified road. Drake stopped and flashed his warrant card at the uniformed officer.

'You need to drive down for a mile or so. A car park by an old church has been requisitioned for the CSI team and our vehicles. And other officers have warned all the neighbours they can't leave their homes this morning.'

Drake nodded. It sounded as though someone had been in charge first thing making certain that access to the crime scene was unhindered. He thanked the officer and drove away. The road was narrow and after the short journey he pulled into the car park and spotted two other officers.

'Where is the crime scene?' Drake said, not bothering with introductions. The older of the two constables led Drake to the side of the car park and gesticulated down towards a beach. 'A man from Cemaes was walking his dog this morning and he spotted the body on the rocks by the bottom of a large white sea stack. The beach is called Porth Padrig. A couple of officers and a probationary constable are down there at the moment. We've tried to make sure that nobody gets access along the coastal path.'

Drake nodded. He turned to Sara. 'Any update from the CSIs?'

Sara shook her head. 'I'll try area control again.' She dialled the number.

Drake scanned the surroundings. In the middle distance he spotted two properties, one of which had scaffolding surrounding it. All of the neighbouring homeowners would need to be spoken to – house-to-house enquiries completed, witnesses traced.

'What time was the body found?' Drake said.

'An hour and a half ago, I guess.'

'Guessing isn't good enough, get me the exact time.' Every second, every minute after the discovery of a body was part of that golden time every detective valued. An identity to be established, family to be informed and evidence collected.

Sara finished the call. 'They've just come into Cemaes.'

'Excellent.'

The officer standing to one side added. 'I just checked with area control, sir. They received the 999 call at nine-fifteen from a Mr Oldfield who lives in the village.'

Drake thanked the officer after she shared details of Oldfield's address and turned to Sara. 'Let's go down to the scene.'

The footpath across the headland was regularly tramped by the look of the hard, flattened soil, and well maintained from the evidence of the trimmed hedges. He spotted two officers either side of the imposing sea stack in the middle of the beach and between them a bundle of what looked like clothes. Drake increased his pace, Sara following behind along the narrow path. Drake heard the crime scene support vehicles approaching as he stopped by an opening in the hedge that allowed access to the beach below.

Drake peered down the rock-strewn path leading to the pebbled beach. It was going to ruin his brogues, might even tear or damage his suit trousers. He smothered any reluctance his mind might throw up and started down, taking care with his footfall, occasionally looking back at Sara who nodded her confirmation that she was managing just fine.

The police constable looked far too young to be wearing a uniform. Drake doubted she was no more than a few years older than his eldest daughter, Helen.

'Good morning, sir.'

The name badge on her uniform said Jones.

'Morning, has anything happened whilst you've been here?'

Jones looked nonplussed.

'Any rubberneckers? Anybody walking on the beach? Boats in the bay?'

Jones shook her head.

Drake walked over to the body.

It was a man who looked to be mid-forties, duct tape pulled tightly over his mouth. His jeans looked an expensive brand and underneath the red fleece he wore a green gingham shirt. He hadn't been out for an evening stroll by the look of his tan leather shoes. He was lying face up towards the morning sky and the day's sunshine. On his left wrist Drake spotted an Omega watch.

He looked up instinctively, suspecting that the man had been pushed to his death from the cliff above. Why had his killer – or maybe killers – decided on this spot? The CSIs would tell him in due course how much of a fall it was, but Drake was certain it was enough to have killed a man.

Hearing the CSI team approaching Drake moved to one side and greeted Mike Foulds.

'Morning, Mike.'

'What have we got?'

'The body was found this morning by an early morning walker. It looks as though he was pushed from the cliff.'

Foulds pitched his head up instinctively trying to measure the height of the fall. 'I guess you need an identification.'

'Nobody has touched the body. I've only just arrived.'

Foulds got to work, directing initial photographs before snapping on a pair of latex gloves to match the one-piece hazmat suit that had taken him a couple of minutes to wriggle into. It didn't take him long before he extracted a wallet from the rear trouser pocket. He flicked through it with expert fingers and pulled out a driving licence.

'Jason Ackroyd,' Foulds said. 'And there's an address in the village.'

Sara scribbled down the details.

'Thanks, Mike. Let me know when you've finished.'

Drake turned to Sara. 'Let's see if he has a family.'

Chapter 3

Drake rang the doorbell of the Ackroyd property several times before sharing an exasperated look with Sara. After banging on the door he stepped back and glanced around the property. 'Call area control and tell them we need a family liaison officer down here. We haven't got time to waste waiting around.'

Sara nodded her agreement and made the call as they made their way back to the car. Drake negotiated the narrow streets of Cemaes, crossing a bridge before the satnav instructed him to take a sharp right down towards a promenade that swept along the opposite side of the bay from where he had been earlier that morning. Drake drove at low speed, conscious that one or two cars would cause a jam in the narrow street. The young officer had told them that Henry Oldfield's property had colourful lapped cladding and a flagpole. Drake spotted a Union flag and the flag of Wales fluttering in unison.

Drake pulled into the drive and brought his BMW to a halt next to a Range Rover. It certainly wasn't new, but from the personalised number plate – 'HO', followed by four numbers – Drake guessed it might well be more valuable than the vehicle itself.

Henry Oldfield stuck his hand out towards Drake after opening the door. He didn't give the warrant cards Drake and Sara offered any attention and ushered them into his house.

'I've been expecting you. Damned unfortunate business this morning. Do you know who he was?'

'The CSI team are at the scene. We'll be able to make an announcement in due course about the identity of the victim.'

Oldfield seemed content with Drake's platitude. They entered a lounge at the side of the property which offered glorious views over the bay and the village that curled around it.

'What a wonderful view,' Sara observed, standing near the window.

'That's why we bought this place. My late wife loved sitting in here. She loved wildlife and never tired of entertaining me with the different birds she'd spotted.'

Drake got straight down to business. 'I shall be leading the team investigating the suspicious death.'

Oldfield nodded enthusiastically.

Drake continued. 'I understand that you discovered the body this morning. What can you tell me?'

Oldfield settled back into his chair and composed himself. 'Most mornings I take a walk with Toby my Labrador, down into the village and then over the bridge before crossing the promenade on the opposite side of the river that empties into the bay. If it's inclement of course, then of course I don't bother but I go well equipped so even if I'm caught in a shower it's not the end of the world.'

Drake nodded and attempted a smile of encouragement even though he was beginning to sense his own irritation building.

'And once I've built up a good pace the path at the end of the promenade takes me over towards Porth Padrig – I do hate it when my fellow English compatriots use that name: 'White Lady Bay'. There are so many wonderful Welsh place names.'

Drake was warming to Mr Oldfield and silently complimented him on his Welsh pronunciation.

'It's from the prom that the path gets a bit tricky. Some of it is part of the Anglesey Coastal Path but I've become well accustomed to the route and it takes me down to Porth Padrig. I love just walking on the pebble beach. Sometimes if I'm feeling really energetic I'll extend the walk up along the headland. But that jolly well didn't happen this morning.' Oldfield paused, gathering his thoughts and his composure. 'It was when I reached the stack in the middle of the bay that

I saw the body.' The tone of his voice lowered as if to emphasise the seriousness.

'How near did you get to him?' Drake said.

'As soon as I saw that it was a body I stopped rigid. God knows, I've seen enough of these crime dramas on the television to know all about contaminating a crime scene, so I just got my mobile phone out and called 999 immediately. No hesitation, I knew it was the right thing to do.'

'Did you see anybody else on your walk this morning? Did you meet any other regular walkers?'

'No to both of the above. There was nothing unremarkable at all, Detective Inspector Drake. It was just me, Toby and the elements.'

'Any boats out in the harbour?'

Oldfield shook his head.

'Did you see anybody on the adjacent fields to your walk? Farmers going about their work, visitors in cars etcetera.'

Oldfield frowned as though he hadn't contemplated the two questions Drake posed, and ploughed through his mind as though trying to bring the recollections fresh to the forefront of his thoughts.

'A lot of people walk in the surrounding area. And the path is popular but nearly all will be later in the day. When I ventured out first thing in the morning the place was quiet. And as for farmers and other vehicles I didn't notice anything. Sometimes, during the summer I will take a longer walk around the headlands following the Anglesey Coastal Path. And lots of visitors enjoy the sunshine and the spectacular scenery we have here on the island. But this morning I didn't see anyone, sorry, Inspector.'

'And did you wait until the officers arrived?'

'Of course, absolutely. And Toby didn't get anywhere near the body. I had my mobile ready to take a photograph of anybody on the beach or nearby. I took a video of the crime scene after I'd first arrived. I hope you don't think I'm some sort of voyeur. I can email it to you, of course. It was always intended for use by the Wales Police Service. I do so admire all the work you do to keep us safe.'

Sara made her first contribution. 'Are there any other regular walkers from the village you see using that path?'

'I can give you the name of a woman who organises walking groups.'

'That'll be helpful, thank you.'

Drake got up, announcing that they had to return to the crime scene.

Oldfield led them to the front door and found his mobile on a hall cupboard. He dictated the contact details for the woman he had promised and Sara entered the details in her mobile. Before leaving, Drake gave Oldfield his business card, which he clutched carefully before retreating back into the house. 'And do send me the original footage you took this morning. It would be inappropriate if you were to show that to anyone. And we will need a sample of your DNA in order to eliminate you from our enquiries. It's all very straightforward I assure you.'

Oldfield nodded his head enthusiastically, his eyes widening slightly.

'What did you make of him?' Sara said after they'd closed the car doors.

Drake fired the car engine into life. 'Nice enough bloke, I suppose, although he is a bit overbearing. Taking a video could well be misconstrued.'

Drake headed out of the drive and back down into the village. He returned to the car park he had used earlier that morning. Three crime scene support vehicles as well as two marked police cars were parked near a BMW like his own which he knew belonged to Lee Kings the pathologist.

'Lee took his time getting here,' Drake said.

They left the vehicle and from the vantage point of the car park they spotted the fluttering yellow crime scene tape marking the outer perimeter of the scene. Doing a minute search in each of the fields surrounding the path and the headland would demand more than the CSIs present.

Walking down the path again Sara was ahead of Drake which gave him an opportunity to walk more gingerly, realising he couldn't resist taking care to avoid tearing the hem of his trousers. Ahead of them Mike Foulds and Lee Kings emerged together from the beach.

Kings blew out a mouthful of air as he greeted Drake. 'That's a bit of a climb.'

Foulds looked over at Drake. 'The one good thing is that we're going to have lots of time before the tide turns against us.'

'Good. We've spoken with the eyewitness this morning. He was the only one on the beach that early. He does it most mornings and he called 999 once he realised there was a body. He stayed until the officers arrived.'

'At least nobody else might have contaminated the crime scene,' Foulds said.

'How long has he been dead, Lee?' Drake said.

'I can be more certain when I do the post-mortem tomorrow. I took body temperature and rigor mortis is still present so my preliminary assessment would be within the last twelve hours.'

Drake nodded. 'So Mr Oldfield discovers the body at about quarter past nine. That takes the time of death to no later than nine-fifteen pm last night.'

Kings began to say something, but Drake added. 'I won't hold you to that. At least it gives us something to work with for now. Any obvious cause of death?'

'Apart from falling from a great height and smashing his body into rocks? I'll be able to give you a more accurate cause of death tomorrow.'

'We'll need more officers to conduct a detailed search of all these fields immediately surrounding the crime scene,' Foulds said. 'All we can do, for now, are the nearest fields. But after that you'll have to organise with Superintendent

Hobbs for a full team. It could be a massive exercise gathering all the possible forensics. And so much might have been contaminated by the weather. I don't think it rained last night but, Christ knows we could lose so much valuable evidence if we don't get enough support.'

'I agree. I'll contact the super.'

Drake and Sara retraced their steps back to the car park followed by Lee Kings. Foulds was already on an adjacent field directing the activity of his investigators. They'd reached Drake's car when his mobile rang. He didn't recognise the number.

'Detective Inspector Ian Drake,' he answered formally.

'Ian, it's Tony Parry. We need to talk, urgently.'

Chapter 4

Drake had last worked with Detective Inspector Tony Parry several years ago. He was tough and uncompromising with his junior officers but an effective detective. Parry's recent unsuccessful application for promotion to a chief inspector's role had only made him more determined and single-minded.

'What do you think he wants?' Sara said as Drake accelerated out of Cemaes, heading south for the A55.

'He didn't say but he emphasised it was urgent.'

Sara fumbled for her mobile. 'I'll call area control. They may have more information on Ackroyd's family.'

Drake listened to her one-sided conversation. Eventually she finished and announced. 'There's a Mrs Ackroyd and a family liaison officer should be with her.'

'Good. We'll speak to her once we've finished with Tony Parry.'

Drake had insisted Parry travel to Llangefni, despite his suggestion they meet in Caernarfon. Drake retraced their route back to Llangefni police station. At least it would give him the opportunity of talking to Superintendent Hobbs, getting him to agree to allocate more manpower for the search to accompany the crime scene investigators' activity.

One of the civilian members of staff at the station directed Drake to an office on the top floor. Detective Inspector Tony Parry was deep in conversation with a uniformed sergeant when Drake entered the room. They finished talking and the sergeant left. Then he waved Drake and Sara to the visitor chairs. Parry's thick curly hair cascaded over each ear. He tugged a hand through it before tightening the navy tie with discreet white stripes to his collar.

'Why the urgency, Tony?' Drake said.

'You found Jason Ackroyd's body this morning. I picked up the details on the system.'

'That's right. There was duct tape over his mouth and it

looks as though he was thrown off a cliff and onto rocks below. The body is a mess.'

'Jesus, I thought so.' Parry ran a hand over his face. His gaze darted around the room. Then he closed his eyes as though he were in pain. 'That is really fucking bad news.'

'What the hell are you talking about?'

'Jason Ackroyd was a witness in a big trial coming to court in a couple of weeks. In fact, he was more than that – he was one of the crucial witnesses.'

'What case is that?' Drake sat back, pleased that they had an early focus to the inquiry.

'We have been investigating two brothers who run a scaffolding business for months, years even. They are real toe rags. We've suspected them of being involved in various burglaries over the years but we could never make any prosecution stick. I could really fucking swear at some of these CPS lawyers and at the system.'

'What makes this one different?' Sara said.

Parry blew out a mouthful of breath, expressing his exasperation. 'All the evidence fits together. We've got good eyewitness testimony from the homeowners and from traders at the car boot sale who saw them flogging items they pinched from the house. And Jason Ackroyd knew the homeowners and could identify the pieces of antiques they'd stolen. He runs a second-hand car business and he hires out vans and lorries. And Jesus, this is a mess.'

'Can the case proceed without his evidence?'

'It'll mean a review of everything. And it's Mr Personality – Andy Thorsen – as the senior Crown prosecutor. He's a bundle of laughs.'

'But he's a good lawyer,' Drake said.

Parry waved a hand in the air. 'Yeah of course, I know. We had these two bastards bang to rights.'

'We're going to see Mrs Ackroyd this afternoon. What can you tell me about her?' Drake said.

'They're not short of a bob or two – expensive cars,

luxury holidays et cetera.'

'You'd better send me a summary of the case against the two brothers – what are they called?'

'Haddock, as in the fish. Simon and Tim. I'll email you. Christ almighty, I hate it when this happens. Might be different if he'd had a heart attack, dropped dead on the golf course but he's been fucking murdered. I'll set up a meeting with Andy Thorsen and Superintendent Hobbs for tomorrow. The Haddock brothers have got an army of fancy lawyers so be careful.'

Drake got up, nodding to Sara that they needed to leave. 'I'll keep you posted.' The Haddock brothers were now their prime suspects and he and the team had work to do.

Drake pulled up into the drive of Ackroyd's home and noticed the burnt orange Range Rover Evoque – a two-door convertible version. Next to it was a silver Ford Fiesta.

'No prizes for guessing which one belongs to the family liaison officer,' Sara said.

'That orange colour certainly makes a statement.'

They left the car and walked up the drive. A video camera high up on the wall above the front door recorded their movements. Annie had suggested they install one at home – another of those things on his home life to-do list. Loud chimes sounded once Drake had pushed the doorbell.

'Hello, sir,' the family liaison officer said once she'd opened the door. 'She's in the conservatory. I have warned her to expect you.'

Drake nodded. At the rear of the property the conservatory looked out over a carefully manicured garden. At the bottom was a timber lapped summerhouse, a decking area outside abutting the recently cut lawn, its border edges neatly strimmed.

Mrs Ackroyd sat on a leather recliner gazing nowhere in particular. She got to her feet and reached out a hand. The handshake was limp and her eye contact feeble.

Drake never liked being the officer having to break bad news. Family liaison officers were specially trained to deal with sharing news of a death. Offering condolences and support was much easier.

'Mrs Ackroyd, please accept my condolences. I shall be the senior investigating officer in charge of the inquiry into your husband's death.'

Mrs Ackroyd slumped back into the recliner. Behind Drake the family liaison officer found two chairs and Drake and Sara sat down. On the granite tiles to the left of Mrs Ackroyd's chair a slice of lemon lay forlornly at the bottom of a tall glass. Mrs Ackroyd wouldn't be the first to find solace with a decent slug of gin after losing her husband.

'Mrs Ackroyd,' Drake began.

'Call me Vicky.'

'Vicky, when did you last see your husband?'

She turned to look at Drake as though she couldn't quite understand the question. She frowned. 'It was... I can't be certain. Yesterday, some time. He was working in the garage. He is so busy. I was going out with friends last night, so I got home early and changed.'

'Did you see him before you went out?'

She shook her head.

'Then when did you last see him?'

She frowned.

Being unable to recall when she had last seen her husband troubled Drake. Surely she could remember?

Ackroyd shook herself out of her malaise. 'Of course, stupid of me. He came in just as I was going out. It was about six-thirty. We chatted for a few minutes. He told me he was going out with some friends. They were doing their usual pub crawl before ending the night at an Indian restaurant for a curry.'

'Can you give us the names of his friends?'

'One is called Les Jones. The other is Phil Rhodes and I've got his address somewhere.'

Sara made her first contribution. 'And we'll need the names and contact details of the friends with you last night.' Ackroyd gave her a sharp incredulous look. Sara continued. 'It's all routine I assure you. We do this for all family members in an investigation of this sort.'

'Do you have to? They can't possibly be involved and I don't want them contacted. All they can tell you is the name of the restaurant where we had our meal – and that they had too much to drink.'

'I do understand, Vicky but it's entirely routine. All they will be doing is confirming exactly what you're telling us.'

'I don't want them involved.' Ackroyd raised her voice insistently.

Vicky Ackroyd's reluctance was understandable but downright refusal was perplexing. Drake said as firmly as was justified, 'I must insist you tell us their names and give us appropriate contact details.'

Vicky Ackroyd narrowed her eyes as she stared at Drake. 'It was Marion and Ruth if you must know.' She pouted and returned to staring out of the window.

Drake sat back in his chair pondering Vicky Ackroyd's reluctance to share the details of her two friends. He wondered what else she might be hiding. And what else they had to discover about her husband.

'Did you speak to your husband last night or text him?'

'I spoke to him – it must have been quite late because he sounded drunk, and his voice was slurred.'

'What did you talk about?'

'Nothing in particular. He complained about the curry being too hot. And his motorcycle is missing.'

'Why would he have taken it out last evening?'

'I've got no idea. He loved riding it.'

It was the beginning of an explanation for some of Ackroyd's movements. Drake pondered what had made him leave the house late at night. It must have been important.

'We have to ask this Vicky but are you aware of anyone who might want to kill your husband?'

She spun her head around and gave Drake a questioning look. 'Who do you think?' She laced the comment with venom. 'It's those Haddock brothers.'

'I take it you're referring to Simon and Tim Haddock.'

'Of course I am. I told Jason not to get involved. I told him they were dangerous. I need another drink.'

Vicky got to her feet and walked over to the kitchen area to one side of the conservatory. Ice cubes clinked into the glass followed by a generous shot of gin and then tonic bubbling up inside. She took a deep slurp before returning to a chair.

'Do you think they could have been responsible for killing your husband?'

'Of course I bloody do. They've been terrorising us for weeks – ever since they realised Jason was going to be giving evidence against them.'

'What do you mean by terrorising?'

'Exactly that. Excrement was left in the car showroom. And dead cats were thrown into our back garden and two cars on the forecourt were badly scratched. Afterwards Jason installed CCTV cameras covering the front of the showroom. But even that didn't stop them. Then they started sending us anonymous letters.'

'We'll need to see those,' Drake said.

'That useless Detective Inspector Tony Parry knows all about this. He did absolutely nothing. It's as though our safety counted for nothing for him. Jason gave him the letters.'

'I can assure you, Vicky, that all officers of the Wales Police Service take public safety very seriously indeed. Anybody else with a grudge against your husband? Had he fallen out with clients or former partners?'

Vicky Ackroyd shook her head but didn't turn her gaze away.

They spent a few minutes explaining exactly what would now happen. A family liaison officer would accompany her to identify the body. She didn't look convinced when Drake told her that she'd be kept fully informed about progress on the investigation. Reluctantly she shared the contact details for her friends and Phil Rhodes and once they had finished, Drake and Sara left. The FLO followed them out as they walked to Drake's car.

'Something odd about her,' the FLO said as they reached Drake's vehicle. 'When I took the call this morning I got here in good time and for the last twenty minutes or so of the journey to the village I spotted Vicky's Evoque in the distance in front of me. But I got caught behind a tractor. She made a song and dance when I arrived of pretending to have just woken up.'

'Thanks. Keep me posted,' Drake said. He wondered why Vicky might lie. People often did for the oddest of motives but her husband had just been killed and that made him uneasy.

The FLO nodded.

Drake thanked the officer as the message from Annie reached his mobile. 'Where are you? You're late. You promised not to be! Your mother is here.'

Chapter 5

Drake's mum would certainly not have approved of the speed he was travelling on the journey back to Felinheli. He was delayed by having to detour to drop Sara at the Llangefni police station but once he was back on the A55 he hammered the car towards the Britannia Bridge. He reprimanded himself for having completely forgotten about the arrangements for his mum and her partner, or friend – he wasn't quite certain how best to describe Elfed – to visit that evening. He should have texted Annie during the day suggesting she contact his mother to cancel. It would be easy enough to rearrange as she only lived a few miles outside Caernarfon. And both Annie and his mum, Mair, knew all about the demands on his time, especially on the first day of a new inquiry.

He parked behind Elfed's car and hurried up to the front door, letting himself in. He glanced at his watch, knowing he was at least an hour later than he should have been.

The sound of conversation from the first floor living room filtered down the staircase. Annie must have been busy from the strong smell of garlic and herbs that filled the air. He had promised himself after meeting Annie and falling in love with her that things would be different in the future. He would put their relationship first. He would try not to let his work dominate everything. But that evening it felt as though he had failed.

He walked upstairs to the first floor, announcing his arrival as he did so. Annie gave him a stern look which soon mellowed into concern as she looked into his eyes before kissing him on the lips.

'Sorry I'm late,' Drake said. 'I've started a new inquiry this morning. We've been all over the place.'

'There was a report on the news,' Elfed said. 'About a body on a beach near Cemaes. Is that the case you're on?'

Drake nodded. 'A walker found the body first thing this

morning on Porth Padrig beach. The victim is a local man. I can't tell you any more than that for now.'

'There was even some footage from a television crew that'd been able to requisition a boat. They were bobbing up and down in the bay. It all made me feel quite seasick.'

'The journalists take an interest in getting every single possible angle for a story.'

Drake sat on the sofa next to his mum. She put a hand over his and squeezed. 'How are you, Ian?' She didn't wait for him to answer. 'Don't work too hard.'

They exchanged small talk and pleasantries for the next few minutes whilst Annie organised the final preparation for their meal. Mair Drake wanted to know everything about Helen and Megan, how they were doing at school, what their favourite subjects were and reminding Drake she hadn't seen them for some time. Drake was well accustomed to this gentle scolding which was only made worse by Annie piping up. 'Perhaps we can plan to do something with you and Elfed when they're staying with us next.'

'That would be lovely,' Mair said.

'We've booked that cruise we were talking about,' Elfed announced through a barely concealed smile.

It would be Drake's mum's first cruise. Losing his father at a comparatively young age Drake often felt his mum had lost out on the things that couples in their seventies did. Her relationship with Elfed gave her an opportunity to enjoy herself. He hoped she would enjoy the break.

Annie asked him to open a bottle of wine. He did as he was told and moments later she waved a hand towards Mair and Elfed, inviting them come to the table.

The coq au vin had been in the oven for too long, Annie explained by way of an apology, darting an accusing glance at Drake.

'It looks and smells delicious,' Elfed said. Drake's mum complimented Annie on the meal as she tucked into a plateful.

Drake realised how hungry he felt when the plate was in front of him and that he had eaten little during the day. He had left most of the tasteless tuna sandwich from the canteen at the Llangefni police station.

He tried to switch off but his mind kept returning to the sight of Jason Ackroyd lying on the beach. And then to the conversation with Vicky Ackroyd. She was upset, of course, at his death and grief could impact on people in different ways, but her reluctance to share with him the names of her friends was worrying. And by lying to them she had created suspicion which meant they still had a lot to learn about Mr and Mrs Ackroyd.

After clearing away the dessert dishes – lemon meringue pie was one of Annie's favourites – Drake was responsible for making coffee. The coffee machine buzzed into life and went through its preliminary setup routine. Then he made the right selection and delivered everyone's preference before sitting at the table.

Mair had told Annie they had something to discuss with them and he mulled over how he could prompt his mum to open the conversation. Deciding to allow her to do so meant the occasional pause developed around the table.

It struck Drake that his mum and Elfed were doing everything possible to avoid raising the topic they had come to discuss. They asked Annie about her work. They sounded interested in learning about a new course she was launching. Occasionally Annie gave Drake a self-conscious glance that told him she knew exactly what was on his mind, so she kept her replies brief.

'I'd love another coffee,' Elfed said.

Drake's mum nodded her agreement.

'Give me a minute.' Drake said.

Drake fussed over coffees, making one for himself but not for Annie, who'd declined.

Once his mum had turned half a teaspoon of sugar into her drink she looked up at Drake. 'I wanted you and Annie to be the first to know. Elfed and I have decided to get married.'

'Oh, I see,' Drake said until he realised his bland emotionless response really wasn't good enough. He got up, strode over to his mother and kissed her on the cheeks. 'Congratulations, this is wonderful news.' Then he warmly shook Elfed's hand.

'How exciting. I'm really pleased for both of you,' Annie said.

She followed Drake's example by kissing Mair and then Elfed too.

'Well, this is unexpected,' Drake said once everyone had retaken their seats. 'What does Susan make of it?'

Susan, his sister, would react very differently, of that Drake was certain.

'I haven't spoken with her yet,' Mair said looking into her coffee cup. 'Once I've spoken to her and told her about our plans, I was hoping you could call her.'

'Of course, Mam. But don't delay making the call.'

'That's what I've told your mother,' Elfed said. 'I think she finds the prospect of speaking to Susan a bit daunting. Your sister isn't...'

'The easiest?' Annie said.

'Now that I've spoken to you both it's going to be a lot easier talking to Susan. I can't remember when I last spoke to George. It was probably on one of the boy's birthdays.'

Susan's husband George didn't hide his lack of interest in the life of his mother-in-law and brother-in-law. He adopted an affronted posture whenever they spoke Welsh within his hearing and his income as an accountant in one of the big firms in Cardiff had given him enough wherewithal to spoil his two sons. Susan's reaction had been unfiltered disgust when her mother had initially started a relationship with Elfed. The mere thought that she might be sharing a bed with another man appeared too much for Susan to tolerate.

Elfed continued the conversation, clearly aware of

Mair's discomfort. 'We've booked a room at the Portmeirion Hotel for the ceremony in a couple of weeks. We are going to invite a few people to the reception afterwards.'

'And the cruise is, of course, the honeymoon,' Annie smiled.

Elfed grinned back.

'And I wanted you to contact Huw,' Mair said. 'I would like him to come.'

Now it was Drake's turn to try and remember when he had last spoken to his half-brother, Huw. Discovering his father had a son from a relationship when he was a young man had come as a complete surprise to Drake when he had been in the middle of an investigation. Susan had reacted with customary suspicion and reluctance to have anything to do with the man that she somehow perceived as a gold-digger.

'Of course, I'll make contact with him unless you want to speak to him direct?'

'No, I think it will be better if you spoke to him.'

'I'll tell Sian too. I'll make certain that Helen and Megan will be with me that weekend.'

'That'll be lovely. I am so looking forward to it.'

Drake looked at his mother, sharing the happiness showing on her face.

Chapter 6

Sara returned from her early morning run, perspiration dripping from her face. She checked her times, pleased her pace was reasonable. She had recently joined a group that ran regularly but committing to exercise on specific days of the week was difficult in her job.

She quite enjoyed running on her own. It gave her an opportunity to clear her mind, especially first thing in the morning. Showered and dressed, she wolfed down a hurried breakfast and an instant coffee. Not the sort Inspector Drake would drink at all. She checked the time on her watch and was satisfied she could reach the mortuary promptly.

Post-mortems were the part of an inquiry she hated. The sight of a dead body on a table could turn her stomach. Trying not to retch was the hardest challenge she faced. She overcame her squeamishness by realising how important it was for a senior investigating officer to attend. One day she might well be a detective inspector in charge of her own inquiry.

She left the house and drove down to the A55; her mind settled into analysing the events of the day before. A body on the beach had attracted attention from the media – images of Mike Foulds staring angrily out to sea featured on a television report. At least there hadn't been a helicopter overhead sending footage of the activity on the beach – after all, this was North Wales not New York.

This morning work would begin on digging into the life of Jason Ackroyd. And contacting his drinking buddies to confirm the details of the pub crawl.

Sara drew up in the car park near the mortuary – no sign of Drake's BMW X3 so she sat and waited. She tuned into BBC Radio Wales and the main story was about utility bills and their effect on ordinary families. Sara counted herself lucky she had a reasonable salary and could afford, just, the increasing gas and electricity bills. A brief piece mentioned the murder of Jason Ackroyd with a number for anyone with information to contact the Wales Police Service.

Drake drove into the car park and she left the car to join him.

'Sorry I'm late, traffic was awful.'

'I was listening to the news. There's an appeal for anyone with information about the Jason Ackroyd killing to use that new number public relations organised.'

'There'll be a lot of time wasters then.'

They walked over to the entrance to the mortuary and once they'd signed the health and safety forms the assistant showed them through. Lee Kings was waiting for them.

'Good morning, I'm glad you're punctual.'

'Morning Lee,' Drake said.

Sara added her greeting. Rendering herself taciturn was the by product of her ability to deal with the post-mortem.

'Let's get started,' Kings said as he drew the white sheet off the body of Jason Ackroyd. He stared down at the corpse with the concentration and interest of a man devoted to his work.

'This is the body of Jason Ackroyd. He is a forty-five-year-old Caucasian, slightly overweight and otherwise appearing to be in good health.' Kings dictated as he worked. He began with an investigation of the arms and fingers before moving to the shoulders dictating in minute detail anything of significance. Then he moved to the feet and legs. He would be at the part, very soon, that Sara found challenging.

He reached for the large scalpel from the tray of instruments at his side and completed the deep 'Y' incision, opening up the skin over the torso. He stood back for a moment examining the remains of Ackroyd's body. Then he found the pliers that would snap open the torso. One body part after another was removed and placed in trays alongside the trolley.

Kings maintained a relentless commentary on his work,

expressing his opinion when needed. Sara coughed loudly when he switched on the saw that would slice open Ackroyd's head. She put a hand to her mouth, looked away until he had finished.

It didn't seem to be affecting Drake. And she envied him for that. It was the single-minded determination she admired in him, that made him a good detective.

Once Ackroyd's brain had been removed and carefully examined, Kings turned to both officers. 'Heart and lungs all seem reasonably healthy for a man of his age. Once I have his medical notes I can review everything. The skull was fractured in several places and brain damage would have been so severe it would have killed him without doubt. I've had X-rays and an MRI scan undertaken.'

'That normal?' Drake said.

'X-ray, yes, but MRI scan, no. I want to be completely satisfied about the bruising you see all around the legs and on his back. And the duct tape covering his mouth was removed by one of your CSIs. We might find a piece of DNA on it.'

'So, cause of death, Lee?'

'He suffered catastrophic injuries to his body. His skull was fractured – once I've done more on the brain we should be able to confirm the extent of the injuries but I'm almost certain it would have been enough to kill him. The legs and arms have also been badly bruised.'

'Were the fatal injuries caused before he was pushed off the cliff?' Drake said.

'I can't say, sorry. But they could well have been caused as a result of being pushed off the cliff.'

Sara made her first contribution. 'And what about the time of death?'

'I don't think I can add very much from what I said yesterday. Working back from the time I first saw the body I would say he was killed between nine and twelve hours before that. There was still some evidence of rigor in the body. As you probably know that doesn't leave for eighteen hours. That fact, and the temperature of the body when I saw him on the beach yesterday.'

'Thank you.'

'Any suspects? Angry widow?'

'He was a crucial eyewitness in a big upcoming trial,' Drake said. 'So our attention is on the defendants in that case but we need the evidence.'

'Sounds clear-cut then – open and shut case.'

'I wish things were that easy.'

Sara left with Drake a few moments later and was pleased to be outside in the fresh air. She took a massive lungful as though she were emerging from a deep dive.

'You never get used to it,' Drake said. 'It took me ages to get accustomed to the sight and smell of a post-mortem.'

'I don't know how the medics do it.'

They made for their cars, and then headquarters.

Drake strolled into the Incident Room as two civilian staff finished erecting the board that would become a crucial part of the inquiry. Gareth Winder and Luned Thomas, the two detectives on Drake's team, sat at their desks and each looked up at Drake and Sara as they entered, announcing in unison, 'Morning, boss.'

Winder took a photograph lying on his desk and pinned it to the board. It was an image of Jason Ackroyd.

'Thanks Gareth,' Drake said. 'Jason Ackroyd was found dead at Porth Padrig yesterday morning. His mouth had been covered in duct tape and the pathologist says that he died from catastrophic injuries to his body consistent with a fall from the cliff. We believe he may have been thrown or pushed from the cliff above a sea stack that stands in the middle of the beach.'

'The CSIs have emailed me some photographs of the crime scene,' Luned said.

Drake waved a hand at her inviting her to add them to the board.

She sat down once they had all been pinned to one side of Ackroyd's face. The sea stack was recognisable from its imposing position.

'I want a large-scale map added to the board in due course,' Drake said. 'The beach is near the village of Cemaes. A local man doing his usual morning walk discovered the body. Time of death was between nine pm and midnight the day before.'

'What do we know about Ackroyd, sir?' Winder said.

'We spoke to his wife yesterday. Apparently, he went out with two of his friends the night before on a pub crawl and then for an Indian meal. Gareth, I want you to get the preliminary work done on the background to Mr and Mrs Ackroyd. Vicky Ackroyd was evasive when we spoke to her, and she was reluctant to give us the names of the two women she'd been with the night before. Comments by the FLO suggests she wasn't entirely truthful about when she had returned home. So track down any CCTV cameras. She's got a very distinctive convertible Range Rover Evoque.'

'I didn't trust her.' Sara sounded troubled. 'There was something about her. She was upset, right enough, but...'

'Woman's intuition?' Winder said.

'Don't be such a chauvinist,' Luned said.

Drake raised his voice slightly. 'Sara, you're with me this morning. We'll interview the two men Ackroyd had been drinking with.' He sat down on one of the chairs. 'Yesterday afternoon we had a meeting with Detective Inspector Tony Parry who told us Jason Ackroyd was a crucial witness in an important forthcoming case in the Crown Court.'

Winder whistled under his breath. 'And the defendants?'

'Simon and Tim Haddock. Print their photographs from the system and put them onto the board. They are persons of interest for now. Apparently, Tony Parry and his team have been gunning for the Haddock brothers for a long time. And I've got a review meeting with DI Parry and the super as well as Andy Thorsen the Crown prosecutor this afternoon. We're not going to take any chances with the Haddock brothers.'

Drake looked over at Winder and Luned. 'Gareth, I want you to get over to Cemaes and see if you could find any CCTV and Luned do some preliminary work on the Ackroyd's finances.'

Drake got up and jerked his head at Sara. 'Let's go.'

Chapter 7

Once Drake took the slip road off the A55 after crossing the Britannia Bridge he indicated right and headed north. Sara punched in the postcode for Phil Rhodes' home and the system bleeped directions. The journey didn't take long and Drake pulled into an estate of comfortable bungalows. It was the sort of property people from the small towns of North Wales aspired to. He parked by the pavement and looked over at Rhodes' home. A weed-free drive led past a small garden to the front door.

'Do we know anything about Phil Rhodes?' Sara said.

'Nothing,' Drake replied. 'Let's hope he can tell us something about Jason Ackroyd.'

The car bleeped as Drake locked it and they made for the front door. It opened as they approached.

'Are you the cops?' A tall thin man with a narrow, long face stood in the doorway. He didn't wait for a reply. 'I suppose you've called about Jason.' He turned on his heel, implicitly inviting Drake and Sara to follow him. He led them to a sitting room that looked out over the front garden.

'Do you want a coffee or something?' Rhodes sounded disinterested.

'No thanks,' Drake said firmly. 'We've come to talk to you about Jason Ackroyd. I'm in charge of the inquiry into his murder.'

Rhodes sank into a chair. Wordlessly he nodded at a sofa for Drake and Sara to sit.

'I can't believe he's gone. Dead like that.'

'Did you know him well?'

Rhodes hesitated for a moment. 'Yeah, I suppose I did. We were drinking mates. He was a good guy. Always good for a laugh. I can't believe anybody would have it in for him.'

'You were with him that evening, before he was killed.'

'It was the three of us. Jason, Les Jones and me. We're

just ordinary guys who went for a drink occasionally and then had an Indian at that place in Amlwch.'

'Did Jason complain about any threats or feeling his life was at risk?'

Rhodes paused. 'He was looking forward to giving evidence against the Haddock brothers. Those two bastards had burgled a place owned by Jason's friends. And when he visited the Haddock's yard he saw some antiques that belonged to his friends that had been stolen during the burglary. There they were as bold as brass moving the stuff they'd nicked.'

'Did he mention any threats at all?' Drake focused on the reply trying to interpret Rhodes' body language and facial expressions.

'He said there had been some crap, literally, at the forecourt of the garage he owned. He laughed it off. I don't think he took it seriously at the time.'

A mobile on the coffee table bleeped and Rhodes scooped it up and as he read the message darted a glance at Drake. 'That was Les, asking if I'd heard from you.'

Sara responded. 'We were going to see him next.'

'He'll be working. So you won't catch him at home.'

'Where does he work?'

'He's a general manager at one of the big caravan parks.'

Drake got to his feet. 'Tell him we are on our way and you can come too.'

Rhodes looked surprised and hesitated for a moment. Then he scrambled to his feet and joined Drake and Luned as they left the bungalow.

Rhodes led the way and the journey didn't take long. Soon Drake followed Rhodes over a recently tarmacked road through carefully manicured lawns towards a large detached old farmhouse. A sign above the doorway said 'Mountain View Restaurant and Bar' and, as its name suggested, in the distance Drake spotted the mountains of Snowdonia.

Another sign directed business visitors to a small car park at the rear. Drake followed Rhodes and joined him as he parked in one of the visitor slots.

Rhodes led the way into the premises and threaded his way through the corridors. Les Jones was sitting by his desk and scrambled to his feet when he noticed he had company.

'This is Detective Inspector Ian Drake and—' Rhodes said.

'Detective Sergeant Sara Morgan,' Sara said.

'Are you in charge of the investigation into Jason's death?' Jones said.

Drake nodded. 'We need to discuss with both of you Jason's movements on the night he died.'

Jones waved at the visitor chairs. Rhodes sat, as did Drake and Sara, who produced a pad.

'It was like any of the other nights when we go out on the piss. We have a few beers and then end up in an Indian restaurant. We probably went to half a dozen pubs. We drank too much, talked a lot of shit – mostly about football. I'm a diehard Liverpool supporter and Jason supports, I mean supported, Everton.'

'Do you have the names of the pubs you visited?' Sara said.

Jones reeled off the details, occasionally looking over at Rhodes inviting confirmation. 'Will you need to contact all the publicans to check we were there?'

'It's all routine,' Sara replied formally. 'And the name of the Indian restaurant?'

She jotted down the reply.

Drake looked over at Jones. 'Do you know of any reason for anyone to wish Jason Ackroyd dead? Did he mention any enemies, people with a grudge against him, people who might have threatened to kill him?'

'I'm sure he was nervous about giving evidence against Simon and Tim Haddock – although he kept saying that he was looking forward to seeing them behind bars.'

'Did he complain of any money worries?'

Both men chortled in unison. Jones expanded. 'Jason was loaded. He worked on some big construction site in London years ago where he made a fortune.'

Their comments chimed with Drake's recollection of Ackroyd's expensive-looking attire and watch. 'What time did you get to the restaurant at the end of the evening?' Drake said

'I can't be certain. Half ten maybe,' Jones said.

Rhodes nodded. 'We'd had a skin full by then. Nothing like a vindaloo after eight pints of lager.'

'When did you leave?'

Jones looked over at Rhodes. The look on his face was a noncommittal reply.

'It was about midnight. My wife came to collect me. I wouldn't have been able to drive home, that's for certain,' Jones said.

Rhodes nodded. 'My son picked me up. But Jason had left by then.'

'Did Jason use his motorcycle?'

Both men shook their heads. Rhodes replied. 'He got a taxi home.'

'So Mrs Ackroyd wasn't his taxi service that evening?'

Both men sniggered. Jones was the first reply. 'I think you'll find Mrs Ackroyd was otherwise engaged.'

'What Les means is that she was playing away from home.'

Drake introduced a steely edge to his voice, intended to emphasise to both men he was deadly serious. 'Would you clarify that statement, please?'

'It's hardly a secret that Jason and Vicky had a sort of 'arrangement',' Rhodes emphasised the last word.

'You need to talk to Sam Chandler about his relationship with Vicky,' Jones said, looking over at Rhodes, who grinned back.

Jones added, 'And Jason had been having a fling with a

woman who worked at his accountants.'
'Do you have a name?'
'I think it was Vanessa Grant.'

Chapter 8

Winder often wondered how inquiries had ever been successful in an age before CCTV. It had become an essential tool. Innocent parties could be excluded quickly, alibis offered expeditiously checked and the fingers of guilt pointed at the right people.

But his first task before the journey to Cemaes was requisitioning the financial checks on Jason and Vicky Ackroyd. He knew that they wouldn't have to wait long for the relevant details. Banks and other institutions always responded quickly to requests.

Once he'd completed the standard formalities, he drove over to Cemaes. A filling station and convenience store on the outskirts of the village proved to be a constructive place to begin his search. They nearly always had cameras inside. He parked and called into the convenience store first.

After persuading an assistant that he really had to speak to the manager, a man in his fifties with greasy hair and a crumpled grey shirt appeared. 'I'm Detective Constable Gareth Winder. I'm part of the team investigating the murder of Jason Ackroyd.'

'Yeah, that was tragic. Who did it? Jas used to come in here quite often. Bottle of milk, pack of chocolate – the usual sort of stuff.'

'Do you have CCTV in the shop?'

'Of course. Do you want it?' The man's voice sounded excited at the potential for being involved.

'Does the coverage include outside the shop?'

'No, but the garage next door has got cameras too.'

'What's the name of the manager there?'

'You want to speak to Don. But he won't arrive at work for another half an hour.'

'I'll need you to send me the footage from your CCTV camera from six pm on the evening before Jason's body was found.'

'Yeah, of course.'

Winder handed the man one of his cards and repeated how urgent it was.

He retraced the steps to his vehicle and headed into the village. He parked and found the narrow street with shops, hairdressers and a post office. A bakery was located on a side street, he recalled from a previous case. and that meant the potential for a doughnut or something similar, and maybe even a coffee.

Winder kept tilting his head upwards hoping to spot randomly fixed CCTV cameras. His efforts were rewarded when he noticed, high up on the gable of the community centre, two cameras each one covering opposite lengths of the street. He took the steps up to the front door and pushed open the darkly stained mahogany doors, which groaned in protest. He read a sign advertising a display by the local flower arranging club.

The sound of activity from beyond another door took his attention and, on entering the main hall, he saw tables lining the edge and a dozen people, maybe more, fussing around making final adjustments to their displays, drinking out of plastic cups and gossiping. Winder stopped at one of the tables and asked if there was somebody from the community centre present. A woman with long silver-grey hair sounded annoyed at the interruption and waved a hand at the door telling him to ask for Mavis upstairs.

He took the stairs to the first floor. He heard the voice of a woman, clearly on the phone judging by the one-sided conversation, and walked over the well-polished parquet flooring towards the door to her room. Mavis' hair had benefited from a recent visit to the hairdresser by the look of the tight curls and the immaculate cut. She gave Winder a startled look. Then she abruptly finished the call and turned to Winder.

'The flower celebration is downstairs in the main hall.'

Winder stepped into her room and pushed out his

warrant card. 'I'm Detective Constable Gareth Winder of the Wales Police Service. I'm one of the officers investigating the death of Jason Ackroyd.'

Realising he was on official business Mavis got to her feet as though she were about to salute him. 'I don't know what I can do to help. There are certainly lots of police officers in and around Cemaes at the moment.'

'That'll be the house-to-house team. I notice there are CCTV cameras on the building outside.'

'Of course, of course.' Mavis sat back in her chair. 'The trustees of the hall really complained about the cost but we had a break-in and some kids causing damage so in the end they spent the money.'

'I'll need all of your footage for the evening before Mr Ackroyd's death.' Winder reminded her of the exact date and times.

Mavis nodded enthusiastically. Winder added in his most kindly tone, 'And I'll need that today.' He found his card and after placing it on her desk tapped it firmly.

'I'll do it right away.'

Winder left the community hall and headed back downstairs and outside. He'd tracked down two helpful CCTV cameras so it was about time he rewarded himself.

He found the bakery on the side street. There was a handwritten bilingual menu on a large blackboard above baskets containing selections of various breads. He didn't remember this sophisticated atmosphere from his previous visit.

The two shop assistants stared a little too long at him and he heard them whispering about cops and the body on the beach as he took his coffee and doughnut to a small seating area. He checked his emails in between mouthfuls of soft chewy cake and sweet coffee. An email from the manager of the convenience store had attached the footage as promised.

Once he'd finished, Winder left the bakery and headed

over the bridge that crossed a narrow gorge with a stream that emptied into the harbour. He caught sight of uniformed officers undertaking the house-to-house enquiries – something he'd done regularly before promotion to work as a detective. Winder saw a large pub with a paved area abutting the pavement. He stopped to scan for any sign of a camera outside but saw none, and to his right the road led into a small estate of bungalows. Uniformed officers undertaking house-to-house enquiries would establish if any homeowners had CCTV footage. Winder was in and out of the public house within a few minutes, having established that their CCTV only covered the inside. He retraced his steps back into the village meeting the sergeant in charge of the house-to-house team who confirmed that, so far, none of the homeowners had CCTV cameras. He decided that after speaking to the manager of the garage he'd return to headquarters. Hopefully by then the footage from Mavis at the community hall would have arrived. He could spend the rest of the day in front of his monitor.

A few minutes later he pulled into the filling station and parked in the spot marked – Reserved Staff. A tall man with a pronounced Adam's apple stood behind a cashier serving a customer and jerked a hand towards a door nearby. Winder walked over and as he reached it, it eased open and the man stretched out a hand.

'I'm Don, the manager,' he managed in his most important sounding voice.

'Detective Constable Gareth Winder.' Winder flashed his warrant card out of courtesy. Don paid no attention and led Winder through into what he described as his office. It had one chair and a small narrow desk with a monitor split into two images. Shelves reached up to the ceiling were filled with brochures and box files.

'The manager of the shop told me you have CCTV coverage of your forecourt.' Winder nodded at the screen.

'I knew Jason. He wasn't a friend or anything but I

knew him well enough to pass the time of day. Used to come in here. It's important to support local businesses and he always went out of his way to do that.'

'Can you tell me what your CCTV footage records?'

'I'll show you.'

An image filled the screen from the first camera. Don explained that it covered most of the forecourt from the direction of the shop and counter. The images of the cars filling with petrol and beyond it in the road filled the monitor. The second camera recorded the forecourt exclusively.

'I'll need you to send me the footage from both cameras.' Winder said staring at the monitor. He gave Don his email address, telling the manager he needed the footage urgently. Winder left and, pleased with his progress, headed back for headquarters.

Luned was sitting at a desk when Winder arrived back in the Incident Room. He booted up his computer and listened to Luned sharing her work on the Ackroyds' financial details.

'How did you get on?' Luned said.

'I'm waiting for different chunks of footage from Cemaes. Hopefully we'll have something that will help.' Winder added.

Clicking into his computer, it pleased Winder that all three sets of CCTV footage promised earlier were attached to emails in his inbox. He started with the file from the convenience store and once he'd opened it, he found himself watching customers entering the shop and activity in the road outside. He ran it on at an enhanced speed wanting to identify if there was any record of Jason Ackroyd visiting the premises but he was disappointed.

Then Winder turned to the coverage from the community hall. There was a lot of activity and until they had a specific focus it was difficult to know what information to gather. The village's main street led up towards the large roundabout and the Ackroyd's home was on the road heading south. It was little after seven-thirty pm on the evening before Ackroyd's body was discovered that Winder spotted Jason Ackroyd sauntering down the road. He paused the coverage and jotted down the time. Quickly he found the footage for the camera covering the opposite direction. He saw Ackroyd meeting and talking with two other men. He watched them walking down into the village. At least they now had the beginnings of timeline for Jason Ackroyd.

Speeding up the replay of the CCTV footage from the service station created an almost cartoon effect and Winder realised he had to slow down or he might miss something. Cars and trucks passed on the road. Vehicles and motorcycles pulled into the services, filling up with fuel before driving out. All regular and mundane. He noticed a flatbed truck driving on the road outside and something about the livery made Winder pause the footage. Rewinding it gave him a buzz of achievement when he read the name: 'Haddock Brothers Scaffolding'. He jotted down the vehicle registration number and completed the standard request to the DVLA, the government agency responsible for vehicle registrations, for full details of all vehicles owned by the Haddock brothers.

As soon as Drake entered the Incident Room, he could tell Winder had something on his mind from the excited look on his face. But before a catch-up with the rest of his team he needed coffee. And it had to be brewed just as he liked it. He detoured to the bathroom on the way to the kitchen, scrubbing his hands and splashing his face with water. It had been a long day and he felt grimy.

He measured the correct amount of grounds, let the kettle boil for the required time before filling the cafetière and waiting, again, for the correct interval for the coffee to brew. Then he filled a mug and went back to the Incident

Room. He headed over to the board, placing his drink on a free desk after taking a couple of sips. It tasted good, it was a fresh pack after all.

'We've spoken with Jason Ackroyd's drinking buddies from the night he was killed. They regularly went out on a pub crawl finishing in an Indian restaurant where one of them at least enjoyed a vindaloo.'

Sara added, 'The wife of one of the men and the son of another came to collect them and Jason Ackroyd took a taxi home.'

'What was interesting is that both men made clear that Mrs Ackroyd is having an affair with a bloke called Sam Chandler. So we need to find out as much as we can about him. Where he lives et cetera et cetera. And they both said that Jason Ackroyd was having an affair with a Vanessa Grant. Or at least they thought he was. Again let's find out as much as we possibly can about her too. We'll need to interview her.'

'They really were playing happy families weren't they,' Winder smirked.

Drake turned to Luned. 'Anything on Ackroyd's finances?'

'From the preliminary bank statements there were no financial worries. Both have substantial deposits.'

'Good, get the profiles finished. There just might be something unusual.'

'I've made progress with footage from the CCTV's in Cemaes,' Winder said. 'I spotted Jason Ackroyd walking down the high street and meeting two men at about seven-thirty on the evening before his body was found.'

'One of his friends said that they'd had a couple of drinks in Cemaes before moving to Amlwch for the evening,' Sara said.

'But I also discovered a flatbed truck with Haddock Brothers Scaffolding on it going towards the village at eleven-fifteen pm.'

Drake put his coffee mug back on the table after taking a mouthful. Progress on the second day of the investigation was positive, especially as it pointed firmly to their prime suspects. 'Excellent.' He glanced at his watch, at least he had progress to report to the imminent meeting with Superintendent Hobbs and DI Parry and Thorsen the Crown prosecutor. 'We'll pay the Haddock brothers a visit once I've finished my meeting.'

He scanned three determined faces that shared his resolve to interview both men, both prime suspects.

Chapter 9

Drake made his way through the corridors of headquarters to the senior management suite in good time for his meeting. Andy Thorsen was already sitting in the reception area, waiting to see Superintendent Hobbs.

'Ian,' Thorsen managed, barely moving his lips.

'Good to see you, Andy,' Drake replied before turning to Hobbs' secretary.

'DI Parry shouldn't be long,' she said replying to Drake's unasked question.

Moments later Tony Parry arrived, tightening and adjusting his tie. 'Sorry I'm late.'

Drake listened to Hobbs' secretary announcing to him on the phone that everyone was present. Then she ushered them through and they sat around the conference table to one side of Hobbs' office. After exchanging the usual greetings Hobbs began. 'The murder of Jason Ackroyd has a direct impact on the case where DI Parry is the senior investigating officer and as a result everyone needs to be fully appraised of the position in both the inquiry and the court case. So, DI Drake please give us a summary of where you are with your inquiry.'

Drake nodded before looking over at his colleague and the Crown prosecutor.

'We've established that Jason Ackroyd was out drinking with two of his pals the evening of his death. We've spoken to his friends and my team are checking their version of events but there is nothing to suggest his friends had reason to kill him.'

Tony Parry interjected. 'I got the impression from Jason Ackroyd that he was one for a good time. He loved his beer and a decent Indian too.'

'Both men told us that Mrs Ackroyd was having a relationship with another man. She was very reluctant to give us details of the friends she was with that evening. And we believe she lied to us about when she got home.'

Andy Thorsen sounded a note of caution. 'Do you suspect she could be involved in her husband's murder?'

'I'm keeping an open mind about it.'

'I'm looking very carefully at the possibility Mrs Ackroyd could give evidence against the Haddock brothers. After all she knew the people they burgled. And she might be able to give evidence to build a picture that might convict both men.'

'I'm sure the defence will have something to say about that,' Parry chortled.

'One of Ackroyd's friends told us that Jason Ackroyd had seen some stolen antiques at the Haddock brothers' yard.'

'It was more than just that,' Parry added. 'Jason Ackroyd arrived at the Haddock brothers' yard one morning because they hadn't returned a van they'd hired from him. He knew they had a dodgy reputation so he was worried that the van might have been damaged. So he parks and walks into the yard. Both brothers were off-loading furniture and antiques into the unit they've got. Ackroyd thought he recognised a couple of the pieces as belonging to his friends Mr and Mrs O'Rourke. He tried to sound flippant making some comment about the Haddock brothers going into the antique business. It was then that they got aggressive and bundled him out of the yard.'

'Any of the Haddock employees there?'

'Yes, and they all said that Jason Ackroyd came into the yard shouting and swearing and swinging a tyre iron.'

'I've already had the Haddock brothers' solicitors on the phone. They are this aggressive outfit in Liverpool. They are threatening to make an application to have the case dismissed on the basis that Ackroyd's murder fatally weakens their case.'

'They won't succeed, surely?' Drake said.

'Not a hope in hell. They were just rattling my cage. I

told them exactly where to go.'

Hobbs took back control of the conversation. 'It doesn't help that Ackroyd was one of the important witnesses in the case.'

'Mrs Ackroyd made reference to death threats she and Jason had received,' Drake said.

'Not again.' Tony Parry groaned.

'Do you know about these?' Hobbs said.

'Of course, Superintendent. My team have investigated them in detail. We've spent hours on it. In fact it deflected us from other work. We couldn't make any link to the Haddock brothers at all.'

'I don't think Mrs Ackroyd shares your confidence that everything has been done,' Drake said.

'I think it's important we get a perspective here,' Thorsen added in his usual monotone. 'Jason Ackroyd's evidence was central to the case against the Haddock brothers. I don't think it's fatal but I'm reviewing the paperwork with the prosecuting barrister. If there's anything at all I should be aware of, even at this early stage of your investigation into Ackroyd's death, I need to be kept fully informed.'

'This is only the first full day but we've already established that Mr and Mrs Ackroyd's personal life isn't straightforward. And we've discovered CCTV footage of a flatbed truck owned by the Haddock brothers seen in Cemaes on the evening Ackroyd was killed.'

'Thank Christ for that,' Tony Parry exclaimed.

'I'm going to talk to the Haddock brothers later this afternoon.'

'I'll need a full report,' Hobbs said. 'From everything I've read they need to be locked up for a long time. I hope we'll get enough evidence to pin the murder of Jason Ackroyd on them.'

Drake retraced his steps to the Incident Room, knowing that everything pointed to the Haddock brothers having the perfect motive for the death of Jason Ackroyd. But was the connection to both men too obvious, too convenient?

Drake expected Pencoed Industrial Estate to be a thriving collection of small workshops and local artisans. Instead, it was a dilapidated affair on a road behind a large supermarket near Bangor. At the end of the short access road, Drake spotted scaffolding planks and poles stacked against the tall, galvanised perimeter fencing.

A blacksmith's yard occupied the first small unit they passed, the car park in front of it a mass of discarded blackening steel. Shutters covered the doors and windows of the second unit, weeds the only occupants of the drive.

'Place is a mess,' Sara said as Drake pulled into the premises the Haddock brothers occupied. Two shipping containers sat at the far end next to three small Mini-type vehicles. The air filled with the sound of steel poles clanking against each other once they left Drake's car. Two men paid them no attention and carried on filling a flatbed truck. They made their way over towards the office.

Drake pushed open the door and a warm muggy smell assaulted his nostrils. A makeshift kitchen with an ancient oven and a battered microwave filled one corner. A sliced loaf spilled its contents over a worktop near a toaster.

'If you're looking for the boss he's in the other trailer.' One of the men sitting by the table shouted over at Drake.

Drake retreated and made for the second trailer.

This time the atmosphere inside was neat and ordered. Behind a glass panel to his left a woman sat in front of a desk. Box files and folders lined the wall behind her. Drake caught her attention and she slid back a glass section of the panel.

'What do you want?'

'We want to speak to Simon and Tim.'

She nodded down a makeshift corridor to Drake's right. 'Try the office.'

The door at the end was flimsy and Drake didn't bother knocking, guessing the occupants had heard his footfall. Both men looked up as he entered. He flashed his warrant card; Sara by his side did the same.

'Simon and Timothy Haddock?' Drake said.

'Yeah, and who wants to know?'

'I'm Detective Inspector Ian Drake and this is my colleague Detective Sergeant Morgan. I'm in charge of the inquiry into the murder of Jason Ackroyd.'

The older of the two men, Simon, mid-forties give or take, curled his fingers around a chipped mug in front of him. The younger brother, Tim, sat in front of the desk rolling a cigarette. Both men gave Drake and Sara lingering, challenging stares.

'What the fuck has that got to do with us?' Simon said.

'Just because your lot are trying to fit us up you think you can come here and accuse us of murder. Well you can just fuck right off,' Tim added.

First rule of policing was to keep calm, Drake thought. Tony Parry had warned in his email with a summary of the case against both brothers that Tim was the psycho of the two.

'We are aware, of course, that Jason Ackroyd was giving evidence in the forthcoming trial against you.'

'What trial?' Tim laughed. 'Case won't go ahead now. Our brief has told us that the case will collapse. The judge will throw it out dead quick.'

Drake detected on Simon's face the merest hint of irritation with his brother.

'There's no chance the case against us was going to succeed anyway,' Simon said taking control of the conversation. 'We've pleaded not guilty because we didn't do nothing. We've got the best lawyers defending us and they've told us that we'd have been a guaranteed not guilty verdict.'

It was what the Haddock brothers wanted to hear. Their

reaction was typical of crooks with an inflated opinion of themselves. The outcome of court proceedings was never guaranteed. 'You must be pleased Jason Ackroyd can't give evidence against you,' Drake said.

Neither man responded.

'His evidence was important to the case.'

'The case is full of shit,' Tim said.

'I don't think the judge will see it that way.'

'We are the innocent victims of police harassment. We had nothing at all to do with any of those burglaries.'

I'll be sure to give Detective Inspector Tony Parry your regards, Drake thought.

'Do you know where Jason Ackroyd lives?' Drake decided on a fishing expedition.

'Of course we don't,' Simon said.

'But you must know where he has a business.'

'He has a second-hand car lot and a garage,' Tim added.

'You've seen the reports on the news – Jason's body was found on a beach near Cemaes yesterday.'

'So what?'

'Cemaes is a pretty village with a nice beach. Have you ever been there?'

Simon turned to Tim. 'Don't answer. He's just trying to get under your skin.' Then he looked over at Drake. 'Time for you to piss off.'

Drake didn't move – just stared at Simon Haddock. 'I want you to tell me exactly where you were on the evening Jason Ackroyd was killed. Both of you have got the perfect motive for wanting him dead.'

Simon Haddock got to his feet. 'I've had enough of all this police intimidation. I was at home watching telly with the wife. We had nothing to do with Jason Ackroyd's death.'

Tim Haddock gave Drake a snide half smile. 'I was at home too, if you must know, Mr Policeman.'

Drake turned to Sara who nodded confirmation that she had jotted down the replies in her notebook. Even though it wasn't an interview under caution it was a straightforward answer by two persons of interest in a murder inquiry to a simple question.

'When we arrived there were a number of flatbed trucks parked in the yard. Are they all yours?'

Simon Haddock gave an uneasy frown. 'Of course they are all our business vehicles. In case it has escaped your notice we run a successful scaffolding business.'

Drake turned to Sara who already had open on her mobile an image of the flatbed truck pictured driving through Cemaes.

'One of your vehicles, registration number RK16 HAD, was seen driving through Cemaes at about the time Jason Ackroyd was killed. Would you like to revise your answer to the previous questions about where you were that night?'

'Donna!' Simon screamed.

Seconds later Drake heard footsteps along the corridor leading to the office door and the woman he had seen previously burst in.

'Which of the fucking toe rags I have employed took RK16 HAD the night before last?'

'I've no idea, Simon.'

'Then bloody well find out.'

Simon beamed at Drake. 'One of the lads must have taken the truck without our consent. We'll let you know who it was but for now get lost.'

'We'll need your details in case we need to contact you again.'

Simon reached for a business card on the desk and scooped two together. He jerked a hand towards Drake. 'Now bugger off.'

Drake sat in the supermarket café wondering whether the chicken in the sandwich he had just eaten really was chicken. He had his doubts. The meat tasted plasticky, the lettuce flaccid and the bread soggy. The soft drink was long finished, and he toyed with the idea of a coffee but the colour of the version served at the checkout was a brownish shade of dishwater. So, he passed.

'What did you make of the Haddock brothers,' Sara said.

'They have the perfect motive for killing Jason Ackroyd. DI Parry and Andy Thorsen are terrified the case against both men will collapse without Ackroyd's evidence. I wouldn't trust anything they tell us. Let's get back to the Incident Room.'

Half an hour later Drake drew the car to a halt in the car park. His mind had been playing over and over the conversation with the Haddock brothers. He trusted Tony Parry's judgement but there was no escaping the conclusion that the inquiry into the Haddock brothers was having an effect on him. Simon and Tim Haddock were the sort of criminals who had nine lives and would frustrate the attempts of the WPS to bring them to justice.

He walked over to the main entrance and then up to the Incident Room.

He anticipated being at his desk late into the evening. The first days of a murder inquiry were always the same – they demanded his full-on attention. He'd text Annie as soon as he'd finished with updating the team. She would understand.

Winder and Luned broke off from staring intently at their monitors when he entered.

'How did you get on, boss?' Winder said.

Drake reached the board, the image of Jason Ackroyd pinned in the middle.

'Denied everything of course. We got their mobile numbers, though, so you can requisition a full triangulation search for both men. We might just get lucky and find that we can place them in Cemaes on the night of the murder.'

'That would really mean they'd had their chips.' Sara managed a weak smile.

'Why do I get the feeling that's not going to be the last fishy joke in this case. And in the morning, Gareth and Luned you go and see the wives of the Haddock brothers. They were offered as the alibis. Sara and I will go and see Mrs Ackroyd's buddies.'

Drake had a summary from DI Parry to read and the preliminary reports from the house-to-house team to read before leaving. And he had to message Annie. Before heading for his office he looked over at three officers all with intense, determined faces.

Chapter 10

Drake collected Sara the following morning from the police station in Bangor where she'd parked. She punched the postcode into the satnav as they exited the car park. The directions took them back over the Menai Bridge, which had given its name to the town where Ruth Salier lived. The disembodied voice took them along a narrow street with parked cars making free-flowing traffic impossible. Drake had to wait for over twenty minutes as a van disgorged a disabled passenger. The waiting annoyed Drake and he found himself tapping the steering wheel knowing he should be more generous.

He drew into an elevated parking slot high above Ruth Salier's house. They left the car and walked down a few steps to the rear door. A woman in her forties opened it. She had neatly trimmed auburn hair, clear blue eyes and an open expression. 'Yes? How can I help you?'

Drake held up his warrant card. 'I'm Detective Inspector Ian Drake and this is Detective Sergeant Sara Morgan. We're investigating the murder of Jason Ackroyd. I wonder if you can spare some time.'

'I'm sorry, I'm really sorry but I can't.'

'Is now a difficult time? We could call back.'

'No, I mean there's nothing I can say. I've spoken to my husband about this and we don't want to be involved.'

Sara used her most reasonable tone. 'As you were with Mrs Ackroyd on the evening her husband was killed we just wanted to ask you to confirm the details.'

Sally started to close the door. 'Like I said, I've got nothing to say.' Then she closed the door and Drake and Sara stood, nonplussed, staring at it. They retreated up the steps for Drake's car.

'Interesting,' Sara said.

'My guess is that Mrs Ackroyd has been talking to her. Which means she has something to hide about the night

Jason Ackroyd was killed. His drinking buddies knew all about Sam Chandler and I wonder why Ruth Salier didn't want to cooperate.'

Once they were in the car Drake fired the engine into life and prayed that there wouldn't be another delay along the road. The satnav directions took them out of the town and northwards towards the village of Benllech for the home of Marion Walker, the second of Vicky Ackroyd's friends. Doubts gathered in Drake's mind that Marion Walker would be prepared to talk to them after the brush off from Ruth Salier. They couldn't force anyone to give evidence, but Salier's behaviour was unusual.

'Let's hope Marion Walker is going to be more cooperative,' Sara said as Drake drove down the street of carefully maintained bungalows.

They pulled up. Drake led the way down the driveway. He rang the doorbell but he didn't hear any chime inside and no sound of movement. From the rear garden he heard activity so he ventured to open a side gate. The latch opened easily enough, and he walked through to the rear of the property. A pond had pride of place alongside a carefully manicured, landscaped garden. Energetic clipping of a Griselinia hedge accounted for the sound he had heard earlier. He called over. 'Mrs Walker?'

Nothing. She carried on clipping.

'She's got ear buds,' Sara said.

Drake walked over to Mrs Walker and got her attention although it startled her and she stepped back in surprise. Then she took out the buds from her ears.

'I'm sorry to startle you,' Drake said stepping back allowing Marion Walker to retake her personal space. 'I'm Detective Inspector Ian Drake and this is my colleague Detective Sergeant Sara Morgan.' Both Drake and Sara produced their warrant cards and Marion Walker gave them a good long look. 'We are investigating the murder of Jason Ackroyd.'

Marion Walker nodded slowly. 'I've been expecting you.'

At least she was answering the questions and appeared to be prepared to cooperate. After Ruth Salier's obstructiveness, Drake took this to be a minor victory.

She placed the pruning secateurs on the ground near the hedge and took off her gloves. She led Drake and Sara back towards the table on the patio.

Then she turned to both officers. 'I'm good friends with Vicky Ackroyd and I know her husband Jason, not as well as Vicky I'm bound to say.'

'I understand you were out with Vicky on the night her husband was killed.'

It was a statement and a question, inviting Marion Walker's confirmation.

'That's correct. I joined Vicky and Ruth and all three of us went out to a local restaurant, quite early in the evening. We had a nice meal, but I can't remember what we talked about. Families and children and a lot of rubbish, as you do.'

Drake made a mental note for someone to call the establishment and check the booking. 'Were you with Vicky Ackroyd throughout the entire evening?'

'Our table was booked for seven and I guess we'd finished by about nine-thirty. I didn't keep track of time, Inspector.'

'And the name of the restaurant?'

Sara sounded intrigued. 'Did you go on anywhere else together? A nightcap in the pub or something?'

'No. We did not.'

The woman's clipped formality was sure to irk Sara in due course Drake knew. She was sharing with them just enough to discharge her duty as a good citizen.

'How much do you know about Vicky's personal life?'

'What do you mean?'

'Were there other men in her life?'

Sara's bluntness surprised Drake but he guessed she

wanted to gauge Walker's reaction.

'It's not for me to judge.'

So there were other men. Drake silently complemented Sara.

'Did she ever mention their names?'

'I am sure you can ask her.'

'How often do you go out socially?'

Walker paused. 'I cannot possibly see how…'

Sara deployed her most reasonable voice. 'It's no more than background. Everything helps us and we are determined to find Jason's killer.'

'Yes, of course. We meet up more often in the summer. Vicky has this yacht and we go cruising along the coast.'

She shook her head when Sara asked if they'd visited the yacht on the night Jason was killed. 'Did you go directly home after the meal?'

'Yes.'

'And Ruth Salier?'

'I can't possibly say. She certainly left the same time as I did.'

'Did Vicky Ackroyd say where she was going after she left you?'

'No, she did not.'

Drake took back the momentum of the conversation. 'Did you believe Vicky Ackroyd was going home?'

Marion Walker managed a troubled look as she paused. 'She didn't say anything directly to the contrary.'

'Were Vicky and Jason happily married?'

Marion Walker shrugged.

'Surely you would have some idea as one of her good friends. Perhaps she talked about difficulties at home. Things that were more than simple domestic tiffs.'

'None of us are perfect, Detective Inspector, as you must well know. Occasionally she might complain about Jason but I had no reason to believe that they were not, as you put it, "happily married".'

Standing on the patio by the wooden table wasn't the best place to be conducting an interview but there was no invitation to step inside for a coffee or tea and Drake wasn't going to suggest they do that. He sensed the momentum might be lost.

'Was Jason having an affair?'

'I do not know.' Walker resumed the simple one-line answers.

'Did Vicky Ackroyd ever mention to you that she believed he was having an affair?'

'Am I being treated as a witness? Because this is beginning to feel quite intimidating. You're asking me questions about a close friend and I'm not able to answer them directly. And are you treating Vicky as a suspect? That would be utterly preposterous.'

'Mrs Walker, let me make this clear,' Drake's tone displayed his impatience. 'I'm investigating a murder. I've got a killer to catch and I don't much appreciate your obstructive attitude. We believe Mr and Mrs Ackroyd were both having affairs and that they had an open marriage or relationship – call it what you will. So I'd really value your cooperation.'

Marion Walker pinched lips together, stared first at Drake then Sara. Squeezing out the truth was clearly painful. 'Vicky knew that Jason was seeing a woman who worked in some firm of accountants. She didn't tell us her name.'

'And Vicky was having an affair?'

'Really, Inspector, I don't think this is relevant to your inquiry at all.'

'I'll decide what's relevant, Mrs Walker.'

'Vicky liked to try out new people. She had been seeing a man called Sam Chandler. I can't possibly tell you whether it was current – she hasn't mentioned him for a while. I switched off when she mentioned different men. That's all I know so if you don't mind, I have things to do.'

At least she had confirmed their suspicions about Vicky

Ackroyd. Now they had a name and that felt like progress which pleased Drake despite the time it had taken to get Walker's cooperation.

Chapter 11

Winder indicated left and drove into an estate of shabby bungalows. Simon Haddock's property was at the end of the potholed road and Winder didn't have to search for a number as he guessed which property it was from the collection of dilapidated vehicles filling the small drive as well as the front garden. None looked roadworthy and Winder wondered whether it was worth their while running a check to make certain that all had been declared as off-road.

'It looks a mess,' Luned said.

Winder parked by the pavement near the property.

'I thought scaffolding contractors were supposed to make a lot of money?'

'Who told you that?'

'A friend of mine is a builder. He's forever complaining about the cost of scaffolding.'

Winder led the way up the concrete path towards the front door. He pressed the doorbell and before the chimes had finished he heard the sound of frantic barking. And then a woman's voice attempting to silence the animal. She wasn't successful. A few seconds elapsed until the noise died down and the door was opened.

Winder and Luned flashed their warrant cards into the face of the woman standing at the threshold. She gave them a brief examination.

'Mrs Haddock?' Winder said.

'Tina, yeah, what do you want?'

'May we come in?'

She pushed the door open and Winder and Luned followed her into a sitting room that looked over the mangled remains of an old Land Rover. The room was far too warm, and the heavy smell of unwashed clothes hung heavily in the air.

It didn't seem to affect Tina Haddock, who sat down on one of the sofas after brushing aside some discarded clothes.

Her blonde hair had been tied behind her head and she had thin spectacles perched on the bridge of her nose. Winder guessed that a healthy diet of five portions of fruit and veg a day didn't feature in Tina Haddock's household by her pasty complexion. It was difficult to make out her age – Winder guessed she was probably younger than she appeared.

Winder sat with Luned on the sofa opposite Tina Haddock.

'We're part of the team investigating the murder of Jason Ackroyd.'

Tina looked over blankly.

'Did your husband mention it?' Luned said.

'Yeah, sort of. Somebody been to see him.'

'And are you aware of the fact that Jason Ackroyd was an important witness in the pending trial against your husband on burglary charges?'

'Yeah, sort of.'

'Where were you two nights ago?' Winder decided to waste no further time.

'I was here. Where else would I be?'

'And was your husband with you all the time?'

'Yeah, of course he was. We had a takeaway curry. Chicken tikka masala, it's my favourite with lots of naan bread and that fancy Indian beer.'

It took another few minutes to extract the full details of the restaurant and the timing of its delivery from Tina. It would be something else to check in due course.

'And was your husband with you all night?'

'Yeah, of course he was. Don't be stupid, where else would he be. He couldn't have driven safely anyway – too much to drink.'

Luned contributed by asking Tina Haddock about any other family members. There were no children and no other adults living in the house – nobody else to confirm Simon's alibi.

Once he was satisfied that Tina Haddock couldn't add

anything further Winder got up, nodded at Luned and thanked Mrs Haddock. 'You've been most helpful Tina.'

A couple of minutes later Winder was driving out of the estate. 'She was away with the fairies.'

'Something wasn't right about her.' Luned said.

'We need to check with some of her neighbours if any of them had seen activity late in the evening of the night Ackroyd was killed.'

Luned nodded.

'Now you'd better punch in the postcode for the address for the second Mrs Haddock.'

The satnav told Winder the journey would take eighteen minutes but by the time he had spent twenty-five he still hadn't been able to find the property. A local man walking his dog gave them the directions they needed.

Scaffolding poles and scaffolding planks as well as builders' bags half full of sand and building materials were dotted around the driveway of Tim Haddock's home. It was an old, detached property that had probably belonged to the nearby Nonconformist chapel years ago. Garish multicoloured signs advertised the former place of worship as an alternative centre for yoga and relaxation events.

There was no sign of an excitable domestic pet and the woman who opened the door scanned them with clear, determined eyes that barely dwelt on their warrant cards. She was expecting them. There was no invitation to step inside.

'What do you want?'

'We are investigating the death of Jason Ackroyd. The detective inspector in charge of our team interviewed your husband yesterday. As I'm sure you're aware,' Winder said believing she knew everything about her husband and why they were there, but she didn't react. 'Your husband is facing serious charges of burglary and Jason Ackroyd was a crucial witness in that case against him.'

'And you've immediately come to the conclusion that my husband killed him.'

'Where were you two nights ago?'

'I was here, as was my husband. He was here all night. We watched television. We had a chicken stew which I prepared earlier that afternoon and a glass of Pinot Grigio, if you must know. My husband works very hard.' She began closing the door. 'I don't think I have anything further to add.'

The door closed in Winder and Luned's faces. They stood there for a few seconds until Winder turned to Luned. 'Somehow I can't see Mrs Tina Haddock and Mrs Haddock number two meeting socially for coffee.'

They retraced their steps to the vehicle. Inside Luned was the first to speak. 'At least we got formal confirmation of the alibis offered by both wives. For what it's worth.'

'Exactly, I think we need to ask around the neighbours. I'll see if I can dig out any CCTV locally. I don't think I believe a thing either woman told us.'

Drake pulled into the headquarters car park as his mobile rang. He didn't recognise the number that appeared on the screen on the dashboard. He parked before taking the call. 'Detective Inspector Drake.'

'Inspector, this is Jack Oldfield calling from the *Northern Gazette*. I'm going to be running a feature article on gangland murders and the impact of county lines drug operations on the villages and small communities of North Wales with a particular interest on Anglesey. As the senior investigating officer in charge of the Jason Ackroyd murder inquiry, do you have a comment?'

Any decent journalist would know that all enquiries would have to go through Northern Division's public relations department. And how had this hack got Drake's number?

'Contact public relations. I can't comment.'

'But I've got a tight deadline. I really hoped you might be able to help. And I'm sure the communities of Anglesey would appreciate knowing that senior officers of the Wales Police Service were taking everything about Jason's Ackroyd violent murder seriously.'

'Call public relations.' Drake finished the call and turned to Sara sitting in the passenger seat. 'I wonder if he's any relation to that Oldfield who found the body. If they're related and he's shared that video there'll be hell to pay.'

They left the car and headed for the Incident Room.

Drake shared a greeting with Gareth Winder and Luned Thomas as he made for his office. Sara shrugged off her jacket and hung it over the back of her chair. Drake let his computer boot up and walked out, pleased when he realised the images of Simon and Tim Haddock had been pinned to the board to the right of a photograph of Jason Ackroyd. To his left was the image of a man Drake didn't recognise. As he turned to face his team Winder piped up.

'That's Sam Chandler, sir.'

'Good, he's got to be a person of interest. He was having an affair with Mrs Ackroyd, and while that doesn't give him a motive in itself perhaps he just wanted Jason Ackroyd out the way. So let's do a full financial search on Mr Chandler.'

'How did you get on with the Haddock brothers' wives?' Sara said.

'They are a pair of charming individuals,' Winder said.

Luned murmured her agreement.

Winder continued. 'Both women stated that their husbands were in all night. We'll ask some of the neighbours if they recall anyone leaving the Haddock homes late in the evening.'

Drake turned back to the board. 'We've had the preliminary results from house-to-house enquiries but I'm still waiting for forensic results. So for now let's concentrate on the Haddock brothers as significant persons of interest. Vicky Ackroyd lied to us about when she arrived home. But she must have known we'd discover she was having an affair with Sam Chandler.'

'People do stupid things, boss,' Sara said.

'I found the name of the accountancy business where Vanessa Grant works – she was the woman both of Jason Ackroyd's friends thought he was having an affair with,' Luned said.

Drake turned to look at the team. 'Good. We'll talk to her tomorrow. In the meantime you can do some digging around into her background.'

'Do we treat her as a person of interest?' Luned said.

'We'll talk to her first.'

'Somebody of considerable strength or maybe two people would have been needed to throw Jason Ackroyd's body off the cliff,' Sara said. 'The pathologist couldn't confirm if he was dead before he went off the cliff. So that means he might have struggled. A woman acting alone couldn't have done it and that might rule out Vicky Ackroyd or Vanessa Grant unless they were acting together.'

'We need evidence. For the rest of the afternoon, I want to check all the house-to-house reports,' Drake said before heading for his office.

He started with the location of the burned out remains of Ackroyd's motorcycle that had been spotted in an industrial estate in Amlwch, the nearest town to Cemaes. Drake scanned the photographs wondering why it had ended up there. Had Ackroyd been killed there or had the motorcycle simply been dumped there? Drake spent time reading statements from the officers who had enquired around the estate but they had nothing useful to add.

Drake recalled Vicky telling him that her husband had enjoyed riding the machine. She had no explanation for him leaving the house after he had arrived home from his pub crawl. There were no reports of Ackroyd's motorcycle being spotted travelling to Amlwch and no traffic cameras to record his journey.

He read his notes from the initial conversation with

Vicky Ackroyd and the details she had volunteered about her phone call to her husband. He was drunk and had slurred she had said which made leaving the house even more inexplicable. There must have been a good reason for it, Drake thought as he turned to the details of the calls to and from Ackroyd's mobile. There had been several during the evening before he was killed as well as more from two numbers they hadn't been able to trace at about the time Vicky had called him. Who had been the mysterious callers?

It was the end of the afternoon before Drake left his room and headed for the board in the Incident Room. He pinned to it a photograph of the motorcycle he had printed out moments earlier. Then he turned to his team.

'Someone called Ackroyd the night he was killed. He took his motorcycle – later found burned out – so there must have been a good reason for him to leave his home. Get the PR department to issue a statement appealing for anyone who saw Ackroyd's motorcycle travelling to Amlwch to come forward.'

'I'll email them now,' Sara said.

'Have you made any progress on the house-to-house?'

Luned responded first. 'There's a report of campers in the field near the cliff above the beach where Ackroyd was found. One of the eye witnesses said they looked a young pair – boy and girl.'

'But there was no one there when we arrived first thing.'

'They must have left.'

'Get a more detailed description and as much detail as possible – cars, bikes ... they must have travelled there from somewhere. Did they have permission from the farmer?'

'The house-to-house officers checked that and apparently not. Do you want the PR department to mention the campers?'

Drake paused for a moment. The last thing he wanted was to warn the killers there might be a witness. 'Tell them to make it bland – no specifics, just an appeal for campers and caravaners in the area.'

Drake read the time on the clock on the wall and knew he was already late. 'Let's make progress tomorrow with everything – someone knows who those campers are and someone called Ackroyd on the night he was killed. All we have to do is find them.'

Chapter 12

A mixture of emotions clattered around Drake's mind as he took the short journey from headquarters to his former home. Regret about his failings as a husband and father when his compulsions had driven him to work long hours, ignoring his family. A sense of contentment that his relationship with Annie was on a sounder footing than his marriage had ever been. And with his mother getting remarried, it was about time he and Annie discussed their future. A twinge of apprehension chastised him for that.

The convoluted personal life of Jason Ackroyd and his wife Vicky hardly seemed an advert for the benefits of marriage. Drake's mum clearly wanted to make the commitment to Elfed and as he parked he wondered how he would feel seeing his mother getting married. Although his father wasn't around, he still had his memories and that was all that counted.

He walked up to the front door and Sian opened without delay.

'You've put on weight, Ian.'

'Sorry I'm late.'

'I should think so too. As I told you this morning the girls aren't here. They are with friends.' She pushed open the door, inviting him in, and they walked through into the kitchen.

He turned down her offer of tea or coffee, taking a glass of water instead.

'What's this about anyway?'

'I saw Mam with Elfed recently. She wanted me to tell you that they are going to get married.'

'What? at their age?'

'I thought you'd be happy for her.'

'Are they doing it for tax reasons? Do they want to save Inheritance Tax?'

'Don't be cynical. Sounds like Robin talking,' Drake

scolded her by referencing Sian's new partner, a local accountant that completed the accounts for Sian's medical practice.

'But, I mean, at their age.'

'They're going to get married in a couple of weeks' time. It is going to be a very low-key affair. They've booked a registrar to officiate at the Town Hall building in Portmeirion.'

'I'm assuming that I'm not invited – I wouldn't expect to be. After all...'

'Mam wants Helen and Megan to be present.'

'Well, it might clash...'

'She was very insistent.'

Sian gave Drake an impatient glare. 'I'm sure Robin and I can rearrange.'

Drake took a sip of his water, scanning the contents of the kitchen as he did so. Sian had replaced the electric kettle and there was a new toaster. Otherwise, the room was unchanged.

Sian continued. 'And how are you these days?'

'Well, busy of course.'

'Are you the SIO on that murder case in Cemaes?'

Drake nodded.

'It sounds horrific.'

Drake finished his water and didn't overstay his welcome. Any enduring emotion he had towards the house had long since dissipated – it was Sian's home and Helen and Megan's too.

Sian seemed pleased when he left – no peck on the cheek or lingering eye contact. He drove away without looking back and called his brother to confirm the arrangements for their meeting. Warning Annie at breakfast why he expected to be late returning home had been met with a nod of understanding.

Discovering he had a brother he knew nothing about until after his father's death had thrown up so many unanswered questions. And a child his father had no contact with when he was growing up – how did his father feel about not having known his son? What had been said by Drake's grandparents at the time? Were they ashamed of a child born out of wedlock or pleased? Drake suspected his grandparents had been too old-fashioned to have accepted the position. They would probably have acted as though it had not happened. But not knowing always felt like a gaping chasm in his mind. And one that would never be answered. It made Drake angry that things had gone unsaid for so long.

The pub where Huw had suggested they meet was a regular haunt for Drake's brother. A widower with grown-up children, he exuded a veneer of loneliness whenever Drake met him. And being a few years older than Drake there was never that bond a similar generation could create. But Drake enjoyed his company, and they sat in a corner, Drake with a lemonade, Huw with a pint of beer. His brother smiled broadly when Drake shared the news with him.

'I'm really pleased for her. Our father went too young.'

Drake had lost count of the times people had said that to him. He knew it all too well. A sense of something unfulfilled, missed conversations, love not shared. But he reflected on the positive memories he had of his father – ones that he had been able to share with Huw.

'She was very insistent that she wants you to be present at the wedding.'

'I shall be delighted to attend. I'll look forward to it.'

Once the drinks were finished Drake excused himself and headed for his car. He felt that a new chapter was starting in his life and his mother's. The loss he felt after losing his father would never go away but Elfed loved his mother and Drake looked forward to sharing his own life with him. He texted Annie – *Seen Sian and Huw. On my way home xxx*

Chapter 13

'Have you told anyone?'

'Of course I haven't. Don't be stupid, Paul,' Zoe whispered.

'What shall we do?'

'How should I know. I'm terrified. Mum asked me today what was wrong.'

'My dad's the same. But he's complained that I've been acting strange for a while so I didn't pay any attention. We should meet – usual place later.'

Zoe finished the call. The house was quiet. Her mother was still at work and her father wouldn't get back until much later. She couldn't talk to them about what had happened. They had banned her from seeing Paul. He was older than her and her mother and father both thought he wasn't suitable. They'd be shocked if she told them where she had really been the night she was supposed to have been staying with a friend. It hadn't been her first time of course. But it was special. Paul had been sensitive and took time to make sure she was comfortable. In a tent! But they'd had fun and now every minute of enjoyment had been ruined.

If only Paul had stayed in the tent. If only he hadn't been so bloody inquisitive, downright nosy. Zoe told herself that nobody knew they were involved so she was fretting about nothing.

She made herself some sweet tea and two rounds of toast smothered in butter and lemon curd, her favourite. She sat by the television in the sitting room trying to take in the evening news but she couldn't concentrate on any of it. And when the Welsh news started she stared at the TV fearing another reference to Jason Ackroyd's death and its appeal for witnesses. The first one she had seen felt like a stab to her heart.

She couldn't stay in the house even though she wasn't meeting Paul for another hour. Maybe a walk would clear her mind, help her to think straight. So she pulled on a pair of trainers and an old fleece over her denim shirt and T-shirt. She walked out of the house and down into the countryside along the lanes near her home. She kept up a good pace and soon she unzipped the fleece, allowing it to drape at her side. The warmth of the summer sun had disappeared now that autumn was approaching and the weather forecasts, the only part of the news bulletins she remembered, were predicting cooler temperatures over the next few days.

The walk didn't help. Tension still dragged at her chest, almost suffocating her. Pleased that her mother hadn't arrived home Zoe kicked off her walking trainers and replaced them with a more fashionable pair. She chose her light denim jacket instead of the fleece and headed out to meet Paul. He collected her at their usual spot before taking them to their regular haunt, a pub where the landlord didn't harass her for proof of her age when she bought a drink. The small back room of the pub was their special place.

'I can't believe this is happening,' Zoe said.

'The cops were at the campsite yesterday talking to the manager.'

'Why were they there?'

'How would I know?'

'Do they think you could be involved?'

'Don't be stupid, Zoe. Nobody knows we were there.'

'Somebody must have seen the tent. Maybe even the people who did this…Have you still got those photographs?'

'I haven't deleted them from my phone. I keep meaning to do it but…'

'I can't think straight either. Jason Ackroyd was killed. I mean he was murdered. And we were there. Do you think the manager was responsible?'

'I've tried asking around. Hoping somebody could tell me why the cops called but everybody was very secretive.'

'You mustn't do that.'

'Everyone is talking about it. I was just joining in.'

'You must be careful.'

'The staff are always gossiping. So it is not going to be difficult to find out what's happening.'

'Don't draw attention to yourself – it's not going to help.'

Paul took a long swig of his drink, Zoe did likewise.

They sat in silence for a moment.

'I think we should go to the police with the photographs,' Paul's voice was calm but it couldn't conceal the dread on his face.

Zoe leaned forward, grasped his hand. 'Don't be stupid. My parents would know then that I'd been with you. They would go mental.'

'But someone has been killed.'

'And we might be next. They could kill us. If they know we've got photographs we don't stand a chance. Mum said that Dad thought Ackroyd was giving evidence against a couple of gangsters and he reckons they killed him.'

'Your dad can be full of bullshit, sometimes. He drinks too much in the pub.'

'Don't you dare criticise my dad. You were the stupid one who went out of the tent and started taking photographs. Why the hell did you do that?'

Paul didn't reply, took another swig of his beer.

Something triggered another recollection in Zoe's mind. She turned to Paul. 'What did you do with that...'

Paul's lips parted slightly in apprehension as he realised what Zoe was asking.

'I threw it... into a hedge.'

'Christ, if the police find that condom they could get DNA from it. I've seen it on the telly. Then they'd track us down. They can get DNA evidence from anything these days.'

Paul attempted reassurance. 'But nobody from my family has been in trouble with the cops. Even if they found our DNA there's nothing they can do.'

'I am really scared, Paul.'

Chapter 14

Annie had been satisfied with Drake's perfunctory summary of his conversations with Sian and Huw the previous evening and over breakfast around the kitchen table the following morning she had reminded him he needed to make certain he could book time off for his mother's wedding. Drake hesitated, finishing his toast, slurping on a coffee, but Annie wanted a commitment. Something he couldn't get out of.

'You know what it's like when I'm in the middle of an inquiry.'

'It's important for your mother. You need to tell Superintendent Hobbs it's a family event you can't get out of. Surely any developments in the case can be dealt with by Sara in your absence.'

'It's not that easy.'

'Ian, I know how much your work means to you. I have been supportive.'

'I know that.'

'But sometimes family commitments simply have to take priority.'

Annie was right. But he couldn't see any prospect of the case being solved before his mother's wedding and what if something happened on the morning of her special day? He would have to do everything possible to crack the case despite the abundance of suspects. He put the trepidation to one side, rehearsing in his mind the opening sentences with Superintendent Hobbs.

He asked about Annie's day. She narrowed her eyes slightly, a gentle scolding that distracting her wasn't going to work but, knowing she had made her point, she let it pass.

'I've got quite a full day. The new professor has instigated some new initiatives. And it's all very positive stuff.'

Drake got up and made to leave, kissing her on the lips before dragging on his jacket and promising to text when he had an idea what time he'd be home.

He had just joined the A55 stream of traffic heading eastwards when his mobile rang. He glanced at the screen on the dashboard – it said 'Kings Path'. He took the call knowing it was Lee Kings, the pathologist.

'I need you to call in. There's something I want to discuss with you about Jason Ackroyd's death.'

'Is it urgent?' Drake thought about the need to have a meeting with Superintendent Hobbs and his prearranged meeting with Jason Ackroyd's girlfriend that morning.

'If you're on your way to work call to see me first.'

Drake didn't have an opportunity of asking for further clarification before the line went dead. He accelerated into the outside lane.

It wasn't long until he pulled into the car park at the hospital and walked over towards the mortuary entrance.

Denver, the assistant, was waiting for him and jumped to his feet rather self-consciously thrusting a health and safety form at Drake.

'Do you think I should read these in detail?' Drake said.

It stretched Denver's powers of conversation to reply. He allowed his bottom lip to slip while filling his face with a puzzled look.

Drake pushed open the door in reception and paced down for the mortuary room itself.

'Good morning, Ian,' Kings sounded enthusiastic. 'Let's go to my office.'

Kings ushered Drake down a short corridor. Nothing much had changed in Kings' office from the last time Drake had visited. A large pot plant stood in one corner and there was an antiseptic feel – clean and neat and tidy – just as Drake would have expected from a doctor.

Kings waved a hand towards a chair in front of his desk. He sat down and drew himself near to the clutter-free desk.

'As I mentioned to you, I took the precaution of having an MRI scan undertaken.'

Drake nodded.

'There were enough fractures to the bones and spine from that, so I wanted to be certain that I'd interpreted everything correctly. But the MRI threw up something which troubled me. I was looking for evidence that the fractures corresponded with a fall and collision with jagged rocks. And I found all those.'

'But?' Drake sensed a 'but' was coming.

'That's where it gets interesting.'

Typical pathologist, Drake thought, getting pleasure from dissecting and interpreting a dead body.

Kings continued. 'Let me show you.' He swivelled the thirty-inch monitor on his desk to share with Drake exactly what he was talking about. Using the cursor he circled a section at the base of Ackroyd's spine. 'This fracture struck me as rather odd. It was neat and not really what I was expecting from a body falling from the cliff.'

'Are you suggesting he was killed elsewhere and that his body was then dumped over the cliff?'

Kings shook his head. 'I can't tell you that. Forensics might be able to. I was more exercised about the possibility there might be another explanation behind the cause of death. I sent the scan to a colleague of mine who is a forensic pathologist. He is an expert on injuries caused in battlefield and he is also experienced in undertaking specialist reports on gangland killings.'

Now Kings had Drake's entire attention.

'He's promised to send me a detailed report in due course, but his preliminary opinion was that Jason Ackroyd's spine had been snapped in a very specific way, probably immediately before he was thrown over the cliff to his death. It's a technique known as a Russian omelette.'

'And what the hell does that involve?'

Kings lent back. 'It involves crossing the legs of the victim and pinning him to the ground chest down. Once that's done the legs are pushed up toward the person's back and the killer then sits on the victim to fold and break the base of the spine. It's usually fatal.'

'It sounds like a nasty way to die.'

'Nothing pleasant about dying. But I should tell you that the killer should be of substantial weight.'

'So, we can probably rule out Mrs Ackroyd who hardly meets that definition. Unless, of course, she was assisted by somebody.'

'I suppose it's possible one person could have been responsible but in my professional judgement it probably needed two, one in order to subdue Ackroyd before he was killed.'

'Why is it called Russian omelette?' Drake immediately thought it sounded menacing as though it might have a military connection, but it confirmed what the team had already discussed – that Ackroyd hadn't been killed by a lone killer.

'I have no idea and I dare say that time wasted on Google will give you the answer.'

Superintendent Hobbs wasn't available for a meeting with Drake until the end of the day, which suited Drake perfectly. He could finalise a formal update that he hoped would include a report from the forensic pathologist. And it all meant that his meeting's coda would be an off-the-cuff comment that his mother was getting remarried and that whatever was happening Sara would be in charge that day.

He read the important emails in his inbox after adjusting the photographs of both his daughters alongside the phone on his desk. Old-fashioned landlines were almost obsolete as everything seemed to be done on a mobile.

Once he was satisfied his administrative tasks were complete he walked out into the Incident Room and made for the board. 'Has anybody heard of a Russian omelette?'

He turned to face three frowning faces.

'I've just seen Lee Kings who reckons there is a possibility Jason Ackroyd had his spine cracked using that method of killing. He completed an MRI scan and picked up a fracture that didn't fit with the other injuries Ackroyd sustained.'

'Are we looking for a bodybuilder or somebody experienced in the martial arts?' Winder said. 'Or even someone with a military background?'

'For the time being we keep an open mind. It seems likely that two people may have been involved. One to keep Ackroyd subdued while the other snapped his spine in two.' Drake looked over at Winder and Luned. 'I want both of you to go and interview Sam Chandler, Mrs Ackroyd's boyfriend. She's probably primed him on what to say. Sara and I will go and visit Mr Ackroyd's girlfriend.'

Drake returned to his office, pulled his jacket off the wooden coat hanger before leaving, signalling to Sara for her to join him. The satnav told them that it would take them thirty-five minutes to reach their destination in an address in Bangor. 'Do we know anything about Vanessa Grant?'

'Nothing much, boss. She works in an accountant's office.'

'Let's hope we can make sense of Ackroyd's tangled web of relationships.'

Drake made good progress and took a slip road off the A55 before he reached the Britannia Bridge, allowing the satnav to direct him to a new estate of detached properties. Once he had arrived he pulled up and cast a glance out of the windscreen, spotting the number of the property he wanted.

Drake knew that somebody was home from the movements he had seen inside as they walked up the path towards the front door. He became unnerved by the delay in opening the door. It was Mr Grant who opened it eventually.

He looked at Drake. 'Yes.'

The unexpected aggression in his voice confirmed for Drake he knew two police officers were standing at his front door. Drake thrust out his warrant card. 'Detective Inspector Ian Drake the Wales Police Service and this is my colleague Detective Sergeant Sara Morgan. We need to speak to Mrs Vanessa Grant.'

'What's this about?'

'We'd prefer to speak to Mrs Grant if you don't mind.'

'I'm afraid my wife hasn't slept well. She takes sleeping tablets and sometimes they aren't effective. Perhaps it could wait until another time.'

'No, it can't. May we come in?' Drake took a step towards the threshold, entering Mr Grant's personal space.

He said nothing for a moment but then realised resistance was futile. He stepped back, beckoning Drake and Sara into a sitting room with an ostentatious wave.

He shouted his wife's name up the stairs before making certain Drake and Sara sat in one of the sofas in the immaculately tidy room. Grant closed the door and Drake heard his footsteps climbing the stairs and then a brief muffled conversation. It was another few minutes before Vanessa Grant entered the room and sat on the sofa in the window alongside her husband.

She was thin with carefully styled blonde hair that almost tickled either side of her jaw. Make-up and lipstick were important for Mrs Grant from the generous quantities she used on her face.

'We would like to speak to you alone, if possible, Mrs Grant,' Drake said.

'We don't have any secrets, not now,' Vanessa Grant said. Her voice was flat and emotionless. Her husband reached out a hand and squeezed hers. Drake was certain he saw her recoil for a fraction of a second.

'I'm the senior investigating officer in charge of the murder of Jason Ackroyd. I understand you had a relationship with him.'

'That was a mistake. It came to an end sometime ago and Bill,' she gave her husband the slightest of nods, no smile or any emotion shown, 'has been very forgiving.'

Sara used a soft tone when she asked, 'I'm sure this must be very difficult for you, Mrs Grant, and for both of you in the circumstances. But I'm sure you realise why we must ask you these questions?'

Drake expected some sort of recognition of the work they had to do but nothing on the face of either suggested they did.

'When did you last see Jason Ackroyd?' Sara said.

'I don't remember.'

'Where were you on the night he was murdered?' Sara added the day and date.

'We were both here if you must know,' Grant said. 'We had pizza and a glass of wine and watched a film.'

Vanessa Grant detached her hand from her husband's.

Sara continued although Drake doubted she was going to get any success.

'How long did you have a relationship with Mr Ackroyd?'

'It was... it's not something I want to talk about. It was too long. Now if you don't mind I need to get to work.'

Drake and Sara each deposited a business card on the coffee table before they got up and left. After returning to the car Sara turned to Drake. 'What did you make of that boss?'

'Something isn't right in that relationship. All that make-up might be hiding some bruises – you know what domestic abusers are like.'

'And he got us to sit staring into the window with a light streaming in so that we couldn't see her face in detail. I don't like that man.'

'Bill Grant has just promoted himself to person of interest. I wonder how Luned and Gareth are getting on with Sam Chandler?'

Chapter 15

Drake turned into the car park at headquarters as his mobile rang. He recognised Mike Foulds' number.

'I need to see you. We're making progress with the forensics from the scene of the crime at the beach.'

'I'm just parking. Give me five minutes.'

Drake turned to Sara. 'Let's go and see what Mike has to say.'

The forensic department was in the bowels of Northern Division headquarters. Looking at the investigators beavering away at their desks, they appeared the picture of serenity.

Foulds had been a crime scene manager for many years and Drake always valued his judgement. It was difficult to imagine working a crime scene without his expertise. Foulds waved at Drake and Sara for them to enter his office when he spotted them through the glass partition. Inside Drake approved of the uncluttered, orderly environment.

'Sit down,' Foulds said, tipping his head at two of the visitor chairs.

'I've got some news for you too,' Drake said. 'I spoke to the pathologist this morning and he's convinced Jason Ackroyd's killer used a technique called Russian omelette to bend and snap his spine.'

'Sounds like something out of a Netflix action film. Why is it called the Russian omelette?'

'I asked the same. Kings didn't know.'

'I'll google it.'

'So what have you got for us?'

'We've completed our forensic examination of the paths and fields surrounding the crime scene. I was amazed how much rubbish there was around the place. It's in the middle of nowhere after all. I can't believe people discard so much detritus in the countryside.'

'So were you able to gather any DNA from rubbish you

collected?'

'We are working our way through it. We gathered empty Coke cans, food packaging, including sandwiches and crisp packets. We'll go through everything of course, but I wouldn't hold out much chance of successfully recovering fingerprints or other DNA from that sort of material.'

'Lee Kings reckoned two people were involved in the killing. Apparently, a Russian omelette would take someone of some weight to be able to complete the manoeuvre effectively.'

'Somebody had been camping in one of the fields not far from the path near where Ackroyd was thrown over the cliff. We've got photographs of where we think the tent would have been pitched – it'll be included in the report in due course.'

Drake nodded. 'We've had reports of two people camping near the cliff. A young pair.'

'And we found a used condom near an area of flattened grass. It had been discarded into the gorse and brambles along the field boundary.'

'And that should give you DNA?' Drake sounded positive.

'A degraded semen sample isn't the best for providing DNA. Ideally the sample would be one that hadn't been lying around in the fields for hours or days.'

'So let's assume the user had been playing happy families and after discarding the condom realises what had happened on the cliff nearby. There is a possibility the condom might have been discarded within a few hours of Jason Ackroyd's death.'

'You're making a lot of assumptions here, Ian.'

'We know a young pair were camping so it's hardly guesswork.'

'We'll have to send the sample for testing.'

'And what about the outside of the condom,' Sara said. 'You only mentioned the semen but there must be the possibility of gathering evidence from the outside.'

'I've told the lab to undertake a complete test.'

Drake dragged from his memory the protocols for requesting a familial search. His mind had already dismissed the possibility that any DNA recovered couldn't possibly be the killer or killers. The circumstances of the death, the method by which Ackroyd had been disposed of suggested someone who wouldn't take the risk of leaving a used condom around. And that meant the sample belonged to a third party, a potential witness who needed to be interviewed. If DNA evidence existed, it might be possible to track a family member who might lead them to the person responsible for the semen sample. Progress.

Now he had more than just the pathologist's report to discuss with Superintendent Hobbs later that afternoon.

Drake and Sara detoured to the kitchen on their way back to the Incident Room. Drake flicked on the kettle while Sara took out two mugs from the cupboard.

'Maybe they were locals camping out,' Sara said.

'Or holidaymakers.'

'And if they saw or heard what happened they must be frightened.'

'There's no guarantee they saw what happened. But we need to find them.'

Sara nodded her understanding.

Once the kettle boiled Drake allowed it to cool for the requisite time whilst Sara dunked a teabag into a mug of hot water. Then he filled the cafetière and set another time on his mobile for it to brew correctly. He took it and a mug to the Incident Room where he sat with Sara looking at the board where a red pin on a map of Cemaes and the surrounding area showed the location where Jason Ackroyd's body had been found. After the alarm bleeped he plunged the cafetière and poured his drink – it had the usual chocolatey taste and nutty aroma he enjoyed.

Drake had taken a couple of mouthfuls when Luned and Winder returned.

'How did you get on?' Drake said.

'Sam Chandler is a really objectionable individual,' Luned said. 'He made my skin crawl.'

'So what did he have to tell you?'

Although Winder was her superior in terms of experience and length of service, he allowed Luned to summarise.

'He didn't make any secret at all of the fact that he was having a relationship with Vicky Ackroyd. He was all winks and nudges alluding to the intimate sexual nature of their friendship.'

'Did he confirm she had been with him on the night Jason Ackroyd was killed?'

'That's when he got weird. He got all secretive and refused to confirm what he had been doing that night – told us it was none of our business. He started spouting the law about what his rights were. And that he wasn't a suspect nor a person of interest.'

'Well, he is now,' Sara said.

Luned continued. 'I cannot understand why he didn't tell us if she'd been with him that night. It would give her an alibi.'

'But she's already told us she had returned home. So if he confirms she was with him why the hell would she lie to us?' Sara said.

'I want a full search done against Sam Chandler – finances, background all the usual stuff. We need to know everything about him.'

Drake stood up and walked over towards the board. 'The pathologist reckons Ackroyd's injuries to his spine were caused by a method called a Russian omelette. It requires someone, maybe two people, to snap his spine.'

'Sounds horrific,' Luned added.

Drake was about to continue when his mobile rang.

'DI Drake.'

'Main reception, sir, there's a man here says he wants to speak to you. He is employed by the Haddock Brothers scaffolding contractors.'

Chapter 16

Owain Hughes had a warm, kindly face, wide ruddy cheeks and a small mouth. He also filled one of the chairs in a room off reception and his scratched and calloused hands matched his bulk. His eyes darted between Sara and Drake sitting opposite him.

'The boss told me I had to come in.'

'Did he tell you why?'

'Something about the flatbed truck I was driving.'

Drake kept direct eye contact with this young man. Having a witness turn up at the instigation of two persons of interest was always going to arouse suspicion.

Sara had the details of the vehicle on a notepad and she had made a screenshot of the image from the CCTV footage recovered. 'The vehicle in question is a flatbed truck owned by the Haddock brothers with registration number RK16 HAD.'

Hughes nodded energetically. 'Yeah, that's right.'

'Is that the vehicle that you normally drive?' Drake said.

'I don't drive normally. I am one of the lads who helps with the scaffolding erection.'

'How long have you worked for the Haddock brothers?'

'Five years or so.'

'Do you enjoy working for them?' Drake saw no reason to miss this opportunity of digging into the Haddock brothers' business.

'It's a job I suppose. They pay okay and we finish early Friday afternoon – about four normally, except last week when we worked late.'

'How often do you take the trucks home at night?'

'Doesn't happen. The boss doesn't like it.'

'Do the other employees enjoy working for them?'

'They're a good bunch of lads. I've got some good mates. We have a bit of a laugh sometimes.'

'Is there a big turnover of employees?'

Hughes frowned.

'I mean, do the employees often leave to be replaced by new staff?'

Hughes shook his head. 'Some of the younger lads can't stick it but three or four of us have been with the company a while.'

'Where do you live?'

'Rhos y Bol.'

'That's not far from Cemaes is it?'

Another shake of his head.

'Owain, did Simon or Tim actually explain to you why we wanted to talk to you?' Drake tried to sound his fatherly best. 'A man called Jason Ackroyd was killed near Cemaes recently and on the night before his body was found we have been able to identify the flatbed truck RK16 HAD driving into Cemaes.'

The pace of Hughes' blinking had increased significantly during Drake's question.

'That was me yeah, yeah.'

'If you didn't normally drive that particular vehicle why were you using it that night?'

'That's different. It wasn't the same. I was picking up a couple of the lads the following morning and the foreman thought it was easier if I took the truck with me.'

'Even though your boss doesn't like the employees taking the trucks home.'

'That's different,' Hughes said, flustered. 'We had this job... it was local. I mean it made sense for me to pick up the other lads in the morning.'

'Who were the other lads?'

'I think it was Harri and Daz.'

'Can you give me their full names and addresses?'

A terrified look descended on Hughes' face.

'As you were picking up Harri and Daz you must have known where they live.'

'I don't know the addresses. I know how to get there.' He stood up. 'The boss wants me back at work. He told me not to stay long.'

Then he rushed for the door. Drake and Sara watched as he jogged down the stairs out of reception towards the car park.

'Someone else lying through their teeth,' Sara said.

Superintendent Hobbs checked the time on his monitor. He would never want to keep Detective Inspector Drake waiting but an update to policy changes had to be completed for the senior management in Cardiff. His life was a never-ending cycle of preparing reports, reviewing case files and managing staff.

The public relations department had already sent him a draft of a press release. It included a reference to contact by a journalist known for his work investigating gangland activities. Nothing suggested Jason Ackroyd was involved with organised crime so he had made certain the press release was simple – an invitation for members of the public to contact the helpline number with any information.

One of the innovations he had been most proud of in his time at Northern Division headquarters was the introduction of a dedicated helpline for major incidents like this – another feather in his cap. An achievement to add to his CV. He turned his attention to the preliminary report Drake had provided after the discovery of the body.

In addition Hobbs had asked to be kept fully informed of the progress of the existing prosecution against the Haddock brothers. Detective Inspector Tony Parry had been as good as his word in forwarding updates and Hobbs was expecting a copy of the written opinion from the barrister reviewing the case. They had been prime suspects in other burglaries too. Parry's frustration at the inability to prosecute was clear. His conviction that the Haddock brothers were responsible for Ackroyd's murder made Hobbs realise they had to get evidence. No mistakes could be tolerated.

Unless Drake's investigation unearthed startling new evidence pointing in a different direction Hobbs wanted to focus on the Haddock brothers. Drake had an annoying habit of being too focused on his own priorities in an inquiry. He really had to learn to be more of a team player.

Hobbs scanned his own desk, knowing how meticulous Drake could be. He tidied a pot used for spare ball points and pencils, although he preferred the reassuring quality of a Cross fountain pen.

When his secretary announced that Detective Inspector Drake had arrived Hobbs told her to show him in. 'Good afternoon, Detective Inspector,' Hobbs said formally. No first names in his world.

'Sir,' Drake said, sitting uninvited in one of the visitor chairs.

'You wanted to update me on the Jason Ackroyd inquiry. I'll need a proper briefing memo afterwards of course. Is there anything urgent?'

'I had a meeting this morning with the pathologist. I thought I should bring his report to your attention immediately. When Lee Kings discovered a fracture that troubled him on the MRI scan he consulted another pathologist experienced in forensic work and also from post-mortems from gangland killings.'

Hobbs sat back, wondering what exactly was coming next.

'The specialist pathologist took the view that the injury suffered by Jason Ackroyd is consistent with a Russian omelette.'

'What?' Hobbs spluttered.

'I haven't had an opportunity to google it yet, sir. But it involves snapping the spine in two. Obviously, there's no blood involved and it would need someone of substantial weight to actually complete the manoeuvre.'

'Are both Haddock brothers well built?'

Drake nodded.

'Excellent.'

'And in all probability a single person could not have perpetrated the manoeuvre alone.'

'And that again points to the Haddock brothers.'

'Or two other people, sir.'

'Do you doubt that these men were involved?'

'We need evidence, sir. They are experienced criminals so I'm taking no chances. We need to be able to lock them up.'

'I agree. When am I going to see this report?'

'I'll forward it as soon as I receive it.' Drake paused. 'We've been able to establish that Mr and Mrs Ackroyd had relationships with different people. Detective Sergeant Morgan and myself interviewed a woman who had been having an affair with Jason Ackroyd. We are treating her and her husband as persons of interest at the moment as well as a man with whom Mrs Ackroyd was having a relationship.'

'What a tangled web they lived, but I hardly think this was a crime of passion, do you, Inspector? A Russian omelette is hardly something a jilted lover or cuckolded husband would use, don't you agree?'

'Yes, but we can't rule out anybody at this stage.'

'No, of course, absolutely.'

'One final thing sir, eyewitnesses saw a young pair camping in a field near the cliff. I've asked the PR department to issue a general appeal for campers or caravanners in the area with any information to come forward. And I've spoken with Mike Foulds who tells me that they recovered a used condom from the field next to the crime scene. He believes forensics can recover DNA evidence which might point us towards a witness or someone who is a potential person of interest.'

'Good, it looks as though you're making progress.'

'I've also had contact from a journalist – he seems to be poking around trying to establish links between this murder and gangland activity.'

'Public relations told me about him. They can deal with him for now.'

'Are you considering a press conference?'

'I don't think we'll benefit by arranging one for now.' Hobbs reached for his fountain pen, a clear sign the meeting was at an end.

Drake stood up and lingered. 'I thought I should tell you that I do have one imminent personal matter which I cannot get out of. My mother is remarrying shortly. It will only mean my absence for perhaps part of one Saturday and I'm sure that Detective Sergeant Morgan will be able to manage without me.'

'Remarrying you say.' Hobbs trawled his memory recalling that Drake's father's death had had an impact on the inspector.

Drake turned and took a step towards the door. 'And I was hoping that you might authorise a familial DNA search in the event that the results from the used condom are negative. As you know sir the UK has one of the most extensive DNA databases.'

'I agree. Keep me informed.'

Drake drew the door closed softly behind him and Hobbs got back to another two hours' work.

Chapter 17

Drake didn't expect a Mercedes coupe to be parked in the drive when he arrived home. He assumed it was one of Annie's work colleagues, so he drew up by the pavement. Mulling over the events of the day driving home meant he was ready to relax with Annie, enjoy a meal and a glass of wine or a bottle of beer. He didn't relish making small talk to one of the lecturers in her department.

He let himself into the house and the sound of casual conversation from the first floor sitting room-cum-kitchen surprised him. By the time he reached the top of the stairs he recognised his sister's voice and that surprised him even more. She hadn't called him – perhaps she had spoken to Annie instead although they weren't that friendly.

It meant only one thing. His mum and Susan had discussed her plans.

'We've got a surprise visitor,' Annie said.

Both women got up from the sofa and, after kissing Annie, Drake hugged his sister. 'Good to see you, Susan. I didn't know you were planning a visit.'

'It was a last-minute thing – a bit impulsive.'

'It's not like you.' Drake sounded softly critical.

'Susan's going to stay the night,' Annie said.

Drake didn't respond immediately. He loosened his tie and shrugged off his jacket which he placed over the back of a kitchen table chair. He got a cold Peroni from the fridge and joined both women in the seating area. A half empty bottle of Pinot Grigio sat on the coffee table.

'I didn't recognise the car,' Drake said.

'George bought it for me. One of those tax-deductible things.'

'How is George?'

'He is just fine.' Susan changed the topic too quickly. 'I wanted to talk to you about all this nonsense with Mum.'

She reached for her glass and took a generous mouthful

from her glass. Drake shared a glance with Annie. He detected the merest suggestion of worry in her eyes as though she couldn't make out if there was something to be concerned about.

Susan continued. 'She called me. She told me about her plans to get married to Elfed. I don't know what to think. I mean how well do you know him?'

Susan's question sounded familiar. She'd doubted her half-brother Huw's motives when she became aware of his existence. Drake had eventually persuaded her that Huw was only interested in getting to know his family.

'What has Mum told you about him?'

'She told me they had been discussing it for some time. She described Elfed as a bit of a romantic. At that age? Is he pressurising her? And once they've married what will happen to the farm? Is he going to move in?'

Drake hadn't dwelt on the consequences of his mother's marriage to Elfed. He had a home of his own and the farm and the land was in his mother's name. As Elfed wasn't going to be financially dependent on his mother he hadn't given the financial concerns Susan had raised a second thought.

'George thinks they should have some sort of prenuptial agreement organised so that she could protect her assets.'

'Come off it, Susan, this isn't a Netflix romantic comedy.'

'But what if she changes her will and benefits Elfed's children.'

'Do you really think she'd do that?'

'I don't know... No, of course. But I'm worried, Ian, can't you see that?'

'I just think you're worrying about nothing at the moment.'

'I'm going to see her tomorrow.'

'Does she know you're here?'

Susan shook her head. Drake realised she planned to

arrive unannounced to see their mum in the morning. 'I wanted to talk to you and Annie first. I'm just conflicted about the way I should be acting towards her.'

'What does George think?'

Drake focused on studying her reaction.

She waved a hand in the air. She took another slurp of her wine. Something wasn't right between them. Drake thought about Vanessa Grant and her husband. And he needed to satisfy himself about what was going on in the Grant household. Now he applied the same forensic analysis to his sister and her family. He scolded himself for being too much of a policeman. Perhaps there was nothing wrong at all.

'He's very busy. Frantic at work.'

So Susan doesn't see him that much.

'Have you talked to him about it?'

'Like I've said, Ian, George is very busy. We are like ships in the night.'

There is something wrong then. Drake retreated, judging he was too curious. Being inquisitive was second nature, having been drilled into him as a young detective. He tried to switch off from analysing Susan, but Luned's comments about Sam Chandler played in his thoughts – he was an odious man who refused to give a straight answer about his whereabouts on the night Jason Ackroyd had been killed. The complicated interlocking relationships in the inquiry hadn't been something he'd anticipated might intrude into his family.

Drake glanced in Annie's direction and saw the implied criticism in her eyes. Now he really had to switch off. So he got up and volunteered to organise their evening meal although Annie had done a lot of the preparation so far.

Drake set about preparing the table, laying out place settings and wine glasses and opening a bottle of French Merlot. Annie took charge of Susan, announcing she would show her one of the guest bedrooms. Susan took her small overnight case upstairs and Drake heard both women making up the bed, exchanging small talk.

Annie joined Drake in the kitchen as he finalised the preparation.

Susan started a one-way conversation that sounded as though she were talking with George – her tone flat and disinterested. Then Susan's tone sounded more upbeat and Drake assumed she was chatting to one of her sons. He wondered if anybody really knew what went on in that house, much like the Ackroyd's home.

Susan picked at her food although she complimented Annie who deflected the praise by telling her it was one of her mother's favourite beef stew recipes. The green beans had been grown by her father in the small raised beds in his garden. Susan showed more interest in the wine which meant opening a second bottle – a rarity in the Drake household.

Returning to discuss Mair Drake by the end of the evening, Drake sensed he had to be positive with his sister. He suspected her melancholia hadn't been entirely created by his mum's news.

'You need to be positive with Mum. She's very happy.'

'I'm just worried for her.'

And about your inheritance, Drake wanted to add.

'I think they'll be very happy together. I don't think Dad would have wanted Mum to be lonely. He would have wanted her to be content.'

'I know, but…'

'I want Mum to be happy. And you should too. Elfed makes her happy and he loves her. What more could a person ask? You're overreacting for no reason.'

'Doesn't stop me being worried. It's like never stopping being worried for your kids.'

'She's not a child.'

'Of course not, I didn't mean that.'

'Mum knows what she's doing, and she's faced difficult decisions in her life. I trust her to know her feelings and judge what's best. She loves Elfed and she loves you and me. And our families.'

Drake looked over at his sister as tears filled her eyes.

Chapter 18

Zoe slept fitfully. She checked the clock on her mobile at three a.m. and then at four twenty-three and finally at a little after six when she decided to give up any attempt at a proper sleep. She got up and went downstairs to the kitchen. She wasn't seeing Paul until much later and it felt like an eternity.

Anxiety had dominated her mind so much that she had felt physically sick. It had pulled and tugged at her chest. She fretted her parents suspected something was amiss. The previous evening they'd exchanged glances as though she had been the subject of an earlier conversation.

She made a cup of weak tea, found digestives in a biscuit tin before going back to bed. There she began searching for anything she could find about Jason Ackroyd. Articles in websites linked to local newspapers said so little. The BBC website carried more details about his death and the piece displayed the photograph of the journalist responsible. It took a little longer to find the article written by Mr Oldfield and another bout of anxiety gripped her heart like a vice when she read about the organised crime groups that were infiltrating the villages and towns of North Wales.

She turned to Facebook. She wasted far too much time reading the various posts extending condolences to his family. How many of these people actually knew him? Nothing gave her any solace. Zoe couldn't imagine Vicky Ackroyd's pain and grief.

She was doing an eight-hour shift in the convenience store that day. After a shower she dressed and went downstairs.

'How did you sleep?' her mother asked when Zoe reached the kitchen.

She shrugged.

'Are you going to be home for tea?'

'I'll text you later.'

'But you haven't eaten anything.'

'I'll get something at the shop.'

Zoe dragged the door closed behind her.

It was a short walk to the convenience store where she worked part-time. It would do until she had a better job after leaving college. She and Paul often talked about moving away and working in a city where they could save money. She dreamed of travelling – Europe or South America maybe. She hadn't been able to think of any of these things after the events of the past few days.

She bought a breakfast bar and made a coffee in the tiny kitchen before starting work. After the usual pleasantries with the manager the morning passed uneventfully. She exchanged the occasional text with friends and she messaged Paul who didn't reply for a long time. Even that worried her. Why didn't he reply immediately? He knew how concerned she'd be.

At lunchtime she boiled a kettle and poured water into a pot of instant noodles she'd bought. No perks working here. The manager joined her in the kitchen and the place felt crowded.

'I haven't seen you since the cops have been here,' the manager said.

Zoe's heart wanted to stop.

'They've requisitioned all the CCTV footage from the cameras. Perhaps they can spot Jason Ackroyd being taken away in a car or something.'

Through drying lips Zoe said, 'Did they say if there are any suspects?'

The manager turned to look at her, frowned. 'Don't be stupid. It's too early for that. They might never even find who killed Jas. Did you ever serve him?'

'I don't remember him.' Zoe replied far too quickly.

The manager seemed to pay her no attention. 'Everyone's talking about it. Everyone who has come into the shop the past couple of days has had a visit from police officers doing the house-to-house enquiries. It's like being on a set of Midsomer Murders.'

Zoe recalled her mother occasionally watching the TV series the manager referred to. She hoped and prayed he hadn't thought there was anything untoward about her responses to his questions. Did her voice shake? She said nothing else just in case he suspected something.

Relief washed over her when Paul replied to her messages, explaining he had overslept. How could he sleep at a time like this? The rest of the day they exchanged texts confirming their plans to meet that evening.

She served lots of the regulars during her shift and they all mentioned the ongoing police inquiry into Jason Ackroyd's death and their respective conversations with the team of officers doing house-to-house enquiries. By the end of the afternoon she had decided to scream at the next person who engaged in conversation about Ackroyd's murder.

She cursed when she read Paul's message that he'd forgotten about his plans to see some of their friends at a pub that evening. Socialising was the last thing she wanted to do. So she texted him, insisting that they had to talk.

When he replied suggesting they meet for something to eat she let the relief sink in. Then she messaged her mother, telling her that she wouldn't be home for tea. She didn't offer an explanation.

The rest of the afternoon dragged and she kept checking the time on her mobile. She left at the end of her shift without exchanging further conversation with the manager or with the girls starting the evening shift.

Zoe met Paul in a car park on the outskirts of the village. He left the car, and they embraced. She hadn't realised until she felt his arms around her how much she wanted to be held.

'Let's drive over to Moelfre and go for a walk,' Paul said.

After the journey through the lanes of Anglesey, Paul

parked in the centre of the village. Then they walked down into the village and around the small bay and up over the headland. Once they were clear of the houses and no one was within earshot Zoe turned to Paul.

'I'm really worried. Everyone's talking about the murder.'

'The van that we spotted was in the caravan park today,' Paul murmured.

'What!' Zoe said. 'Did you see who was driving it?'

Paul shook his head. 'I stood around for a while, but I couldn't tell who it belonged to.'

'That's dangerous, Paul. They could have seen you. Those people killed Jason Ackroyd.'

'We don't know that. We can't be certain.'

'Don't be stupid,' Zoe hissed.

'We need to do something. Maybe go to the police with the photograph. Maybe we can remain anonymous.'

'That's mad,' Zoe retorted. 'My mum would never speak to me again. She might even throw me out.'

Paul paused and untwining his hand from Zoe's stared out to sea. He pulled his fingers through his hair. 'I heard on the radio that the police have called for anyone who may have been camping or caravanning or who might have seen Ackroyd riding his motorcycle in the area to come forward.'

'The police must know. Jesus, they know and that means the people who killed Jason Ackroyd might guess we were there. We could be next.'

'I think we should go back to the field. I remember where we pitched the tent. We could search for the condom.'

'The hedge was full of brambles and gorse bushes. We'll never find it. Why the hell did you throw it away?'

'I couldn't think of anything better to do with it.'

'What if the police have found it already?'

'I'll collect you later. It's worth a try.'

Slowly, Zoe nodded her agreement.

Chapter 19

Susan hadn't emerged when Drake woke the following morning. No sound drifted down from the bedroom upstairs and he kept his movements to a minimum to avoid disturbing her. Annie reassured him that she'd make certain Susan ate a good breakfast before leaving.

He sped along the A55 towards headquarters, counting himself lucky that the traffic was light. He put Susan and his mother to a carefully curated corner of his mind. He'd deal with any issues from the conversation between them in good time. In the meantime, he had a murderer to catch.

After parking he took the stairs to the Incident Room. Sara was already at her desk and as soon as he closed the door behind him, he heard Luned and Winder chatting as they walked along the corridor. They called out a greeting in unison as they entered, Luned shrugging a coat off which she draped over the back of a chair as Winder dropped a bag of pastries on his desk.

Drake placed his jacket on a wooden hanger on the coat stand in his room and returned to the Incident Room. He stood by the board. Under the images of the Haddock brothers was a photograph of Owain Hughes.

'Did someone do a PNC check against Owain Hughes?' Drake said looking back at the team.

'Nothing, I checked,' Winder said.

'We've had more details through about the finances of Mr and Mrs Ackroyd,' Sara said. 'They don't have a mortgage. And they own the garage premises. The business uses stocking loans to purchase cars, which is commonplace in the second-hand car world.'

'Any savings?' Drake said.

'A lot. More than I can earn in ten years. And they were mostly in stocks and shares or bonds.'

'That would give somebody one hell of a motive,' Winder said.

'I wonder if Vanessa Grant or Sam Chandler knew about the Ackroyds' money?' Luned said. 'And before you ask, boss, I'm still waiting for details on Sam Chandler's finances.'

'I did some preliminary enquiries into Mr and Mrs Grant. She works in an accountant's office as a tax adviser. She's been working there for a while. That's how Jason Ackroyd got to know her. Mr Grant works in the court service and he volunteers with some sporting clubs on the island. They encourage youngsters to take up boxing and martial arts – that sort of thing.'

'And we know that whoever killed Jason Ackroyd was well built,' Drake said. 'Grant didn't strike me as particularly muscular though.'

'And there's nothing remarkable about their financial position. Mrs Grant owns the house – no mortgage. They have credit cards, everything paid on time and regular income coming in. No kids, although he has been married before.'

'Money is the greatest motivator,' Drake said looking back at the board. 'People will kill for money even if at first glance they don't need it. We keep them all as persons of interest in the inquiry for now. How many employees does the Ackroyd business have?'

His question was met with silence.

Drake nodded at Gareth. 'Get over there with Luned and talk to the staff. A garage must have a salesman or somebody who can tell you if they had any disgruntled customers.'

Winder and Luned scrambled to their feet and headed for the door.

He allocated Sara to reviewing all the house-to-house enquiries. Back at his desk he was determined to get a better understanding of the Haddock brothers and the prosecution they faced. He had skimmed through Tony Parry's report but now he resolved to spend more time on all the details. Both men had the perfect motive for killing Jason Ackroyd.

It made uncomfortable reading. It contained more than a summary of the current prosecution. Everything about the previous inquiries into the alleged criminality of the Haddock brothers suggested clever and devious men who would stop at nothing. Several men and two women had reportedly been badly assaulted by both men, but when pressed to make a complaint none were prepared to proceed. Anyone within their orbit was encouraged to lie, cheat and defraud anybody who might stand in their way.

The evidence in the burglary case involving the O'Rourkes had been clear and persuasive. But with Jason Ackroyd dead that all changed. It would give the defence barrister an opportunity to argue that there wasn't sufficient evidence to convict beyond reasonable doubt.

Drake sympathised with Tony Parry's frustration that the justice system could work in the favour of obviously guilty men. But he knew too that without that system they couldn't do their work properly.

Drake's mind turned to the three persons of interest he'd been discussing with the team earlier. Clearly the Haddock brothers had a motive and a history of physical violence. He couldn't say the same about Sam Chandler, but from Luned's description of him he seemed well built enough and perhaps Vicky Ackroyd had been with him on that clifftop.

Maybe it was Vanessa Grant and her husband. Jealousy could be a powerful emotion. Perhaps Mr Grant had had enough of Jason Ackroyd and decided he had to pay the ultimate price. He might even have persuaded Vanessa to help him. From the body language he certainly seemed to be the dominant personality in their relationship.

Drake had three sets of suspects and until he had the evidence, he would have to keep an open mind. The appeal for eyewitnesses to Ackroyd's motorcycle and the campers had still not produced a response. At some point he would have to consider a televised news conference – it might be the catalyst for someone to come forward.

After finishing Tony Parry's report he typed 'Russian omelette' into the browser of his computer. There was no immediate explanation of where the name came from. The search produced references to recipes for omelettes, and reports in various newspapers about murders perpetrated by men preparing a poisoned omelette for their wives. And there were lots of results for Russian roulette. Drake found a reference to the method Lee Kings had suggested on an American website.

He closed the browser and checked his emails for copies of an updated report from Lee Kings. In his inbox he found the supplementary report prepared by Kings which confirmed what he had been told already. The killer hadn't left to chance the possibility Jason Ackroyd could have survived the fall from the cliff, however remote that might have been. It suggested a cold-bloodedness that made Drake's blood chill. And that pointed to the Haddock brothers.

Sara appeared at his doorway. 'I've just made progress with some of the house-to-house enquiries, boss. The team visited a hotel on the road to the crime scene. A couple of the staff have been interviewed. At least one of them had been working late on the evening that Jason Ackroyd was killed.'

'Excellent. We'll go and see them.'

Drake didn't get a chance to make progress with this decision because his mobile rang. 'DI Drake.'

'Area control, sir. You're needed at the scene of a suspicious death.'

Chapter 20

Winder was unusually quiet that morning as they drove over to visit Jason Ackroyd's second-hand car business. Luned decided against engaging in personal conversation. It never seemed to be productive. Winder wasn't the sort of man to share his feelings. And it had struck Luned recently that Winder seemed less than happy in his role in Inspector Drake's team. Perhaps he might be more suited to life as a traffic cop – speeding up and down the A55 might give him the adrenaline rush he craved.

'I googled the words 'Russian omelette' after the boss mentioned it the other day,' Luned said.

'I did the same and I got lots of recipes. I never knew there were so many different ways to make an omelette.'

'It makes it sound as though whoever killed Ackroyd is involved with some sort of mafia or organised crime.'

Winder slowed for some roadworks a few miles before he reached the Britannia Bridge. 'A piece by a journalist on the news suggested a link between the death of Jason Ackroyd and organised crime. I wonder if he's got hold of the information about the Russian omelette?' Winder said.

'I wouldn't trust journalists. I wouldn't put it past them to just make things up to create a good story.'

Winder mumbled his agreement. They made good time after crossing the Britannia Bridge and a few minutes later they reached the forecourt of the second-hand car showroom on an industrial estate on the outskirts of Llangefni. Dozens of cars parked in neat rows covered the sprawling site. A modern single-storey building with floor-to-ceiling windows dominated one side of the lot.

'Looks like business as usual,' Winder said nodding towards the salesman deep in conversation with a couple next to an Audi A4.

They left the car and headed for the showroom. No sign of an orange Range Rover Evoque and, even if Mrs Ackroyd had been present, their conversations with the staff would have excluded her.

The showroom held two small cars, each less than a year old. Luned wondered if the new-car smell had been created by some artificial spray. A tall man with wavy hair and a lumpy suit smiled broadly at them as he stood up from his desk.

His smile quickly disappeared when he stared at both their warrant cards. 'You've come about Jason Ackroyd haven't you?'

'We would like to speak to all members of staff,' Winder said.

'Mrs Ackroyd isn't here.' It was said as though it ended any prospect of Luned and Winder interviewing anyone.

Winder ignored him. 'Is there a staff room we could use?'

He let his mouth droop open before stammering a reply. 'I... I suppose so.'

It surprised Luned that the rooms out of sight of customers were equally as clean and fresh-smelling as the showroom she had seen. The salesman introduced himself as Glenn Jones, once he'd shown them to the staff room at the rear of the building.

'Sit down,' Winder said.

Glenn gave Winder and Luned a frightened look as he sat in a hard plastic chair. Before they started, he'd given instructions to all the members of staff that they would be needed in turn.

'How long have you been employed here?' Winder said.

Luned had a notepad at the ready and scribbled down his replies. He had worked for Jason Ackroyd for two years, having previously been with a Ford dealership. He managed all the right platitudes about how he valued team working and that Ackroyd had been a fair and decent employer.

Luned added as the brief interview came to an end, 'Did

you ever suspect anyone had a reason to kill Jason Ackroyd?'

It was the first question to wrongfoot Glenn. He paused, dragged the palm of his hand over his nose and mouth. 'I suppose you know about the Haddock brothers. Jason told me about the court case.'

'It's part of the complete picture we're building of possible persons of interest.' Winder said. His bland reply impressed Luned.

'You should talk to Sparky.'

'Who?' Winder asked.

'The other salesman. He noticed the Haddock boys outside once.'

Glenn let the significance sink in for a moment.

'We'll speak to him next,' Winder said.

When Sparky entered Luned gawped at the salesman's vibrant blonde hair, clearly justifying his nickname. He was a couple of years younger than his colleague – mid-thirties at a guess.

'It's the Haddock brothers, isn't it?' Sparky said before even sitting down. Then he settled into his chair, giving Winder and Luned a world-weary I'm-in-the-know look.

Winder gave him his best professional reply. 'We are pursuing several lines of inquiry. What can you tell us about Simon and Tim Haddock?'

'The boss was giving evidence against them. He didn't say nothing to me of course – wouldn't dream of telling me how he felt.' Then he lowered his voice slightly as though he were sharing an intimacy not to be shared with anyone. 'I saw them Haddock brothers outside. They were parked in a layby nearby, as though they were waiting for him to leave.'

'What did you do?'

'I texted the boss. He was going to call you lot.'

'Did they follow him?' Luned said.

'He didn't say nothing, but they followed him the second time,' Sparky added with a dollop of conviction.

'Second time?' Winder said.

Sparky nodded.

'We need the dates for both these occasions,' Luned said, 'and do you remember the vehicle they were driving?'

She jotted down the dates and the details of the van.

Once they'd finished with Sparky they interviewed two of the girls who booked cars in for the services and generally saw to the smooth running of the garage. Neither had anything significant to add.

Jennifer Thomas was a woman in her mid-fifties that introduced herself as the financial controller. 'I work mostly with Mrs Ackroyd.' Her tone sounded defensive.

'How long have you worked here?'

'Only a few months. My predecessor went off sick.' She added in a whisper, 'Stress.'

'Do you know anybody with a grudge against Jason Ackroyd? Somebody who might want to see him dead?' Luned began seizing the initiative from Winder.

She shook her head.

'No disgruntled employee or former employees or customers?'

Luned stared into the woman's face. She started to blink rapidly and she rubbed the back of her neck, a sure sign that she was nervous.

'Jennifer,' Luned added, using a soft tone, 'this is a murder inquiry and it's very important we get all the facts. Is there something we should know?'

The woman looked startled as though she had been caught unawares.

'I do all the bookkeeping.' Jennifer cleared her throat noisily. 'Although it's none of my business... this is confidential, isn't it?'

'We treat all the information we are given with the utmost seriousness.'

Jennifer seemed content with Luned's response. 'This man... he was called Sam Chandler. I'm not certain if Mrs

Ackroyd was... involved with him but he visited here on a couple of occasions when Mr Ackroyd was away.'

She paused and gazed at the fingers of her hands that were threaded together.

'I'm certain she gave him money. Envelopes full of the stuff.'

'We'll need all the details,' Luned sounded engaged. The morning was proving productive. They thanked Jennifer once they had the dates and times for Sam Chandler's visits, and left the showroom.

'What did you make of that, Gareth?' Luned said.

He didn't have time to respond as a voice behind them diverted their attention. Luned turned and saw Glenn pacing towards them.

'Something else you should know,' Glenn said when he reached them. 'A couple of months ago I clocked Jason arguing with Bill Grant. Jason was...'

'We know about Mr Ackroyd and Vanessa Grant,' Winder said. 'What were they arguing about?'

'Grant told him to leave his wife alone. Then Jason got all mouthy with him and started pushing him around. Grant didn't lift a finger at Jason – even though he deserved it.' Luned's mobile rang and she noticed Sara's number. 'He's got the training to control himself, otherwise....'

Sara's voice sounded urgent when Luned answered the call. 'Boss wants you back at headquarters. There's been another death.'

Chapter 21

Drake accelerated hard into the outside lane of the A55. Soon the speedometer registered eighty miles an hour and cars ahead of him filtered into the inside lane as he sped past them. Sara punched the postcode that had reached her mobile into the satnav.

'It should take us thirty-seven minutes, boss,' Sara said.

'The hell with that.' Drake pressed down on the accelerator. 'And find out the status of the CSI team and the pathologist.'

He listened to Sara's one-sided conversation, noting her confirmation to various bits of information she was being told. Roadworks that seemed to be a perennial feature of the A55 inevitably slowed their progress as he reached Llanfairfechan and then on towards Bangor. Drake glanced at the satnav – it told him the journey would take thirty-two minutes. Damn, he'd only gained five minutes. They could be precious minutes too.

'The victim is a Norma Ellston. One of the neighbours found the body this morning. The CSI team should have arrived before us and the pathologist won't arrive for another hour at least.'

Drake approached the Britannia Bridge and had to slow for traffic, but as he did so the hands-free system of the car came to life with a call. He glanced at the screen and recognised the number of Detective Inspector Tony Parry.

'I can't talk now, Tony, I'm en route to a crime scene.'

'That's why I am ringing. Is the victim a Norma Ellston?'

'That's what I've been told, why?' Drake suspected he already knew the answer. The traffic slowed to a crawl now.

'She's another witness in the case against the Haddock brothers.'

'I've read the summary you sent me but I haven't read all the statements nor the list of prosecution witnesses. Was she important to the case?'

'Of course she fucking was.'

The traffic accelerated single file over the bridge and seconds later Drake was in the outside lane. 'I'll speak to you later.' Drake finished the call.

'It sounds as though the Haddock brothers are on a real killing spree,' Sara said.

'Or somebody's making it look that way. They'd be mad to kill off witnesses in the trial against them. But they've got the history and motivation and, damn...' Drake struck the rim of the steering wheel. 'Who the hell do they think they are?'

After another ten minutes the satnav directed them through the narrow country lanes of Anglesey to a cottage with thick walls, small windows and a gravelled parking area occupied by two scientific support vehicles and a dirty brown van. Drake and Sara hurried towards the property.

A uniformed officer stood outside the rear door and straightened almost to attention when Drake and Sara approached. 'She's in the kitchen, sir.'

Drake nodded and followed the officer's brief instructions as they snapped on latex gloves.

Inside there was a stifling muggy atmosphere. Drake took a step down into a parlour-type room he sensed was below ground level. Neatly cut timber was piled near a log burner.

They passed through a doorway which led to a narrow corridor and at the far end was a modern extension. Drake could hear activity and in particular Mike Foulds' voice.

The kitchen was larger than Drake expected. In one corner was a high-backed armchair and sitting on it was Norma Ellston. The blank look in her eyes and the colourless cheeks made it quite clear she was dead.

Drake turned to Foulds, standing with one of the investigators. Another uniformed officer stood behind him. 'What can you tell me?'

'My guess is she's been dead for some hours – probably overnight. I've done a preliminary examination and it seems very probable she's been strangled.'

'Any sign of a break-in?'

Foulds shook his head. 'You'd better talk to PC Williams here.'

PC Williams volunteered a reply. 'No sign of any forced entry so far as we can see, sir. A neighbour discovered the body. Apparently they were supposed to meet this morning for coffee. They both do car boot sales on a regular basis. When she realised something wasn't right she called 999.'

'Does the neighbour have a key?'

'No, but there is a key safe and she knew the code so we were able to gain access.'

'So, no sign of a break-in suggests she must have invited the killer or killers into the house.'

'Do you need to do anything else here,' Foulds began to sound exasperated. 'I've got another two investigators en route. I need to get this finished today.'

'We'll be out of your hair soon as we can. And we won't contaminate anything.'

Drake took a moment to look around the kitchen. Every spare surface was cluttered with pots and pans and dirty mugs. Different boxes of cereal were lined up on a shelf above a microwave.

'I need a full report, Mike. Her death might be linked to the Jason Ackroyd death.'

'Really?'

'She was a witness in the same case as Ackroyd.'

'Hopefully we'll be finished tonight. You'll have a report in the morning.'

Drake followed Sara out of the kitchen. They paused to peer into a utility room. It had more clutter and shelving units from floor-to-ceiling covered in random order with cardboard boxes and lever arch files.

Back in the room with the log burner, Drake ran a finger along a bookshelf: mostly romance or cosy mysteries although he did spot the first book in the Millennium trilogy by Stieg Larsson.

'Nothing obvious has been pinched,' Sara announced as she opened a display cabinet with tea sets and cut-glass vases.

'Who would want to steal this stuff anyway?'

'It might be valuable.' Sara stared at the contents.

Drake turned to look at the log burner and wondered whether it could ever effectively warm the place. The sofas had collapsed into heaps of material, no vestige of a spring left. He jerked his head at Sara for her to join him in the other rooms.

They passed the small entranceway and the corridor led to the opposite side of the cottage. It led to a room which Norma Ellston must have used as some sort of office-cum-study. There was a computer, as well as more shelving units with lever arch files in cardboard boxes.

Nothing seemed to have been touched, and there was an equal amount of chaos to this room as existed in the kitchen. He made a mental note to make certain that Mike Foulds would coordinate with the civilian support staff to remove the computer as part of their investigation. Retreating from the study they headed to the bottom of the corridor and entered Ellston's bedroom. A quick preliminary search told Drake she lived alone – no sign of a man's clothes at least. And the bedroom smelled – glancing at the bedclothes he guessed they hadn't been changed for weeks.

'Place is disgusting,' Sara said.

'I wouldn't like to be the investigators going through all this.'

Sara grunted her agreement. 'They should ask for extra pay.'

'Let's go and talk to the neighbour who found the body.'

Chapter 22

Norma Ellston's murder troubled Drake, Sara could see that on his face. Her name but not her address would have been disclosed to the solicitors acting on behalf of Simon and Tim Haddock in their defence. It wouldn't have taken the brothers long to establish where she lived.

The death of another witness increased the likelihood of the case against the Haddock brothers collapsing. Drake had shared with her how determined his colleague Detective Inspector Tony Parry had been to prosecute both men.

They left Norma Ellston's cottage and walked over to Drake's car. Sara decided that when they interviewed the woman who had found the body she'd take more of the lead in asking questions. She suspected Drake was impatient to return to headquarters which meant he might be brusque.

He started the engine, then paused for a moment when a text reached his mobile. Once he read the details he turned to Sara. 'I've got a meeting with the super as soon as we've finished. The case against the Haddock brothers is going to be reviewed.'

'How important was Norma Ellston's evidence?'

'I'll find out later this afternoon.'

It was a short journey back to the nearest village where Nancy Toogood lived. She had a small bungalow set back from the main road. Drake reversed up the narrow gravel track, glancing in his mirrors as he did so.

Sara followed Drake up to the front door. Toogood was a duplicate version of her friend. Dishevelled clothes, long silver-grey hair and wrinkled complexion which made it difficult to guess her age.

Drake and Sara held up their warrant cards. Toogood gave them a frightened look.

'I thought you'd call,' her voice shook.

'May we come in?' Drake said.

'Yes, of course.' She opened the door and pointed at a room down the corridor. Inside, it was filled with display cabinets heaving with ornaments and tea sets. Cardboard boxes were stacked against one wall.

'Norma and me did the car boot sales. She loved doing them.'

Drake and Sara sat down uninvited and before Nancy could do the same Drake questioned her. 'I need you to tell me everything you can remember.'

Toogood blinked rapidly. 'Well, I was expecting to visit Norma for coffee this morning. We often do. It's...' Toogood's voice broke.

Sara took the initiative. 'Were you and Norma good friends?'

Toogood nodded.

'How well did you know her?'

'We met at one of the car boot sales a while back and we struck up a friendship.'

Sara had moved to the edge of the sofa and kept her tone soft and low. It seemed to be doing the trick to engage Toogood.

'This must be very distressing for you. And I can't imagine how you felt discovering Norma like that, but it is important that you recall as much as you can.'

Toogood's eye contact was straight and engaging. Sara smiled.

She took a deep breath. 'Normally when I go over to Norma's I just open the front door and shout that it's me. So when I arrived this morning and found the door locked I was a bit surprised. I thought she might have overslept. I knocked on the door and then went around to peer into her bedroom but I could see she was up and about.'

Sara sensed Drake's impatience as he adjusted how he sat on the sofa. So she decided to continue, fearing Drake's rudeness.

'So what did you do after that?'

'I went around to the back where I peered into the kitchen. I saw her there – just sitting there. I thought she might be asleep or sick or...'

Drake cleared his throat noisily. 'Mrs Toogood did you see anybody else? Was there any sign of activity? Something unusual?'

Sara sighed to herself – three questions, staccato style one after the other. Toogood looked frightened before answering. 'There was nobody else. And what do you mean by unusual?'

'Did Norma mention anything that was worrying her?' Sara said a fraction too quickly.

'Nothing, she was always calm. Nothing much affected her. She wanted a simple life.'

'Does she have any family?'

Toogood frowned. 'She mentioned a brother who lives somewhere on the south coast but she never had any kids and her ex died a couple of years ago.'

'Did she have any problems. Money worries?'

'She got a good settlement after her divorce. She didn't need much. Bit like me really that's why we were good friends.'

'Did she mention she was giving evidence in a court case?'

Toogood nodded.

'Was she worried about that?'

'I think she was. Although she quite enjoyed the attention. Do you think this is connected to that case?'

'It's far too early to tell. Was she ever threatened or did she ever feel something unusual had happened? Perhaps somebody had been prowling around her property?'

'No, nothing like that ever.'

'If you think of anything else, Nancy, then please do not hesitate to contact either myself or Detective Sergeant Morgan.' Drake announced, ending their conversation. He produced one of his cards and leaned over in Nancy's direction. Then he got up and nodded at Sara to do the same.

'Thank you for your time, Nancy,' Sara said.

'You will let me know.... about developments. I mean when you catch the person who did this.'

'Of course,' Sara smiled.

Sara and Drake shook her hand warmly before leaving the property. Drake drove down the narrow track and once he was out of the village accelerated hard for the A55. 'I need to return to headquarters. Can you do the post-mortem?'

'Sure thing, sir,' Sara replied, pleased that he had delegated this important role.

A thick muggy atmosphere filled Superintendent Hobbs' office. A window badly needed to be opened to allow some fresh air in. The superintendent sat at the head of the conference table, Andy Thorsen on one side and Detective Inspector Tony Parry on the other. Every square inch was covered in paperwork. Hobbs' secretary followed Drake into the room with a tray of cups and saucers and a full cafetière. The coffee looked dark and intense, just as Drake liked it. He took one of the empty chairs and sat down.

'Detective Inspector Drake, please bring us up to date with the developments at the crime scene.'

Drake was still unaccustomed to Hobbs' overly formal approach. Surely it wouldn't hurt him to have called him Ian, occasionally. Hobbs' secretary poured the coffee and placed a tray of biscuits in the middle of the table on top of some papers before leaving.

'The body of Norma Ellston was found this morning. She was discovered by a friend. They are about the same age and share an interest in car booting. Her friend called 999 but had nothing constructive to tell us. Ellston hadn't been worried about the court case although she had mentioned it and had never complained about anybody lurking around her property.'

'This is very serious, Ian,' Thorsen said. 'Norma

Ellston's evidence was an important part of the case against Simon and Tim Haddock. She saw them flogging items they'd stolen in various burglaries, and they even tried to get her to buy some of the stuff they'd nicked. She had a good knowledge of antiques and spotted stuff she knew had been stolen. Consider them the main persons of interest in your inquiry into her death. Their motive is clear and undisputed.'

Drake couldn't recall seeing Andy Thorsen quite so animated. Even if he hadn't raised his voice, and employed his usual monotone, the intensity of his language and tone couldn't conceal his strength of feeling. Drake took the first sip of his drink. It was an improvement on what Hobbs' predecessor, Superintendent Wyndham Price, used to offer.

Thorsen continued. 'We've decided to instruct a King's Counsel to prosecute the case. I have a meeting with her on Monday to assess all the material.'

Involving a senior barrister meant the Crown Prosecution Service were taking matters seriously.

'And that's why we're reviewing everything today,' Hobbs said.

'I've got a team of detectives talking to every witness in the case against the Haddock brothers. We've told them all to be careful, take extra precautions, make certain the doors are locked at night,' Tony Parry said.

Drake imagined a warning to take extra precautions would frighten most people. 'How many are there?'

Tony Parry sorted through some of the paperwork and found a list. 'There are twenty.'

'The Haddock brothers can't possibly hope to kill all the witnesses in the case against them. So if they are responsible—'

'Of course they did it.'

'Why did they target Norma Ellston?'

Thorsen replied. 'She saw them selling some of the stolen goods from the O'Rourke's home. So she was a crucial link in the evidence chain.'

'The number of people who knew Norma Ellston's address is limited. It wouldn't have been disclosed to the defence,' Hobbs said.

'A Google search would have found the address.'

'It's the Haddock brothers without a doubt,' Tony Parry said.

'We've got to keep an open mind. My team will do a full background search on her and once we have all the evidence from the CSIs and the post-mortem report we'll look at everything *objectively*.'

'And then decide it's the fucking Haddock brothers.'

Tony Parry was far too closely involved in the prosecution. He'd lost his detachment. Emotion had taken charge and that could be a bad thing.

The others around the table had barely touched the cups and saucers so Drake took a refill. He wasn't going to let decent coffee go to waste.

Drake turned to Thorsen. 'What's your take on the case, Andy? Is it doomed to failure without Norma Ellston and Jason Ackroyd?'

Thorsen looked straight at Drake. 'It will be challenging without their evidence. Juries can be fickle. You can imagine yourself what it might look like if the Haddock brothers turn up at court smartly dressed, pretending to be successful businessmen with a razor-sharp barrister. A jury might be persuaded to find them not guilty.' And he added with a depressing tone. 'Very possible indeed.'

Chapter 23

The mortuary assistant looked over Sara's shoulder, clearly expecting Inspector Drake to accompany her. Then he gave her a lecherous scan before wordlessly pushing a health and safety form towards her. She scribbled her signature.

She found her way to the mortuary itself and Lee Kings greeted her warmly.

'On your own?'

'Detective Inspector Drake has an urgent meeting back at headquarters.'

'Let's get on with this then. I don't think it's going to be too complicated.'

Kings removed the white sheet exposing the body of Norma Ellston. Sara had never been able to acclimatise to the impact of seeing a corpse on the table. There was something utterly final about it. It deprived the human being of any dignity. But Norma Ellston was dead – what dignity do the dead expect?

'This is the post-mortem of Norma Ellston. A woman, 53 years of age and in reasonable health from an initial inspection of her body. She appears to be of average weight for a person of her age.' Kings continued dictating a general summary of his preliminary findings.

It was when he turned to the instruments on the adjacent table in the stainless-steel tray that Sara's stomach tightened. It wasn't the same without Inspector Drake present. Without his reassuring presence there was no hiding place for her now. She had to grit her teeth and get on with things.

But Kings didn't start with his usual 'Y' incision. He took a few moments to examine her feet and legs before moving to the fingers of each hand and her forearms. Nothing remarkable, although Kings announced that he would be taking samples from her nails for forensic analysis.

Then he turned to the obvious bruising on Ellston's neck. He moved her head from side to side before glancing over at Sara. 'Have you ever seen a victim of manual strangulation?'

Sara shook her head.

'The evidence of the bruising on her neck suggests she was strangled. It's only once we dig a little deeper that we can get greater clarity and confirm the finding.' Kings stood back for a moment, looking down at Ellston as though he were appreciating the bruising around her neck. 'An exact forensic evaluation is crucial when we're attempting to determine cause of death. Bruising can occur in many examples of non-fatal strangulation and in those sort of cases prosecutors often interrogate me for the minutest detail. Sadly, in this case that will not be necessary.' He looked up at Sara and gave her a weak smile.

Sara nodded but didn't say anything.

Kings continued with his examination before taking close-up photographs of specific locations of Ellston's neck.

'It is the case that the contusions you see are caused by the assailant's grasp. The thumb generates more pressure than the other fingers.'

It was a few minutes later before Kings had finished examining the skin on Ellston's neck. Performing the usual 'Y' incision, he dictated matter-of-factly as he removed the body's vital organs. Sara stood rigid, unable to move, almost, determined that she would stay at the post-mortem to the end.

'I'm going to dissect the neck now,' Kings looked over at Sara as though he was warning her of what was ahead of her. 'It is a rather unusual procedure for a normal post-mortem but, given the degree of injuries on her neck, I think it prudent. I have already had the body scanned.' He gave Sara another reassuring smile.

Sara didn't keep track of time and she stared, willing herself to accept this was just another part of her job description. Once he had finished, Kings stopped and turned to Sara.

'I've got enough evidence to be able to confirm from

the soft tissue injury, including the subcutaneous and intramuscular haemorrhage, that everything suggests she was strangled. The scan indicates that her hyoid bone is fractured which is only found in a minority of fatal strangulations.'

Sara's mouth was parched and she ran her tongue over her lips. 'So your formal conclusion is death by strangulation.'

'That's correct, Detective Sergeant. Was this your first post-mortem flying solo, so to speak?'

Sara nodded.

'Not the easiest experience.'

'Part of the job. It gets easier every time,' she lied.

'And she had this ancient website,' Winder said.

Drake paced over to the Incident Room board once he'd entered, registering the snippet of Winder's conversation. 'Explain please, Gareth.'

'Norma Ellston had this website selling her stock of second-hand trinkets and memorabilia. Must have been put together years ago. Can't imagine anybody buying anything from it.'

'And it has her address, presumably, in the contact details?'

'It wouldn't have been difficult to find out where she lives, boss,' Winder said.

Drake turned to Luned, who must have been engaging with Winder when he'd interrupted them. 'How did you get on at the Ackroyds' garage?'

'Most of the staff seemed upset but the woman who was employed to do the books suggested Mrs Ackroyd had given Sam Chandler envelopes stuffed with cash.'

'Have we had the full details of the financial background on Sam Chandler?'

'That's what I was working on now. He's got financial problems. The mortgage on his house is in arrears and his business loans for the fish and chip shop which he runs are enormous.'

Drake took a moment to allow the implication to sink in. 'So with Jason Ackroyd out of the way it would clear the way for Mrs Ackroyd and Sam Chandler. Did he kill to get his hands on Ackroyd's money?'

'It looks like he's doing that already, boss,' Winder said.

Sara arrived back in the Incident Room holding a mug of coffee that she placed on the desk. Her cheeks didn't have their usual colour and Drake recalled feeling the same after the first post-mortems he'd attended.

'I'll summarise what the CPS think about the Haddock brothers and then we'll hear about the post-mortem,' Drake said, hoping Sara could compose herself given a few minutes.

He gave his team a summary of his discussion with Thorsen, Hobbs and Tony Parry.

'We can't just assume it's the Haddock brothers who killed Ackroyd and Ellston and not consider the possibility others might be involved.' Luned struck a serious tone.

'That's exactly right. I want a full search done against the background of Norma Ellston. She was divorced, no children and we believe that she has a brother who lived somewhere on the south coast. There may be something in her background to point us towards somebody who wanted her dead.'

'Sounds like Simon and Tim Haddock to me.' Winder sounded convinced. 'Open and shut case.'

'We still need evidence. So, Gareth, requisition every CCTV within five miles of her home and coordinate with the house-to-house team. I want every home in the area contacted, every occupier spoken to and identified. Make sure they ask about any unusual activity – vehicles in the area they haven't seen before– you know the score. Whoever was responsible for killing Norma Ellston probably reconnoitred the cottage. They must have parked somewhere and walked. And they would have stood out. So make certain the house-to-house team is fully briefed.'

'Yes, boss.'

'And establish full details of the activity she was doing through the website. Get the usual warrant organised so that we can see exactly what she was doing and how much she was selling.'

'You think the person who killed her might have been a disgruntled customer?' Luned couldn't disguise the incredulity in her voice.

'I'm not going to dismiss anything.' Drake turned back to look at the board. 'Let's get a picture of Norma Ellston pinned up.' He allowed his gaze to drift towards the images of Simon and Tim Haddock. They had the perfect motive for her death. They had a track record of violence. Drake wanted to believe that they were responsible, wanted to arrest both men, get them into the custody suite and extract a confession. But with men like the Haddocks he had to be careful. They had fancy lawyers who knew how to protect their clients.

He moved away from the board and sat at one of the chairs by the desks. 'Have officers been to speak to the Haddocks' neighbours to check out the alibis?' Drake said to Winder.

Winder nodded. 'There's no love lost between Simon Haddock and his neighbours – none of them have anything to do with him. But nobody had seen anything that challenges his wife's alibi.'

'And the same for the other Mrs Haddock?'

Winder nodded.

He looked over at Sara: she was staring at the surface of the cooling drink in her mug.

'How did you get on with Lee Kings?' Drake said to Sara.

She looked up and gathered her thoughts, taking a

moment before replying. 'He thought it was a classic example of manual strangulation. She wasn't exactly a strong woman but even so it would have taken considerable force.'

'We should have the full CSI report later today or first thing in the morning. When we were at the property there didn't seem to be any sign of a burglary. So, Gareth, first thing tomorrow I need you to talk to Sam Chandler.'

'Yes, boss.'

'And Luned – I want you getting those financials completed whilst Sara and I will visit Mr Grant in the morning.'

Drake needed to think. He walked back to his office and sat at his desk, pulled out a pad of paper and started scribbling a mind map. In the middle he started with the name of Jason Ackroyd and underneath it Norma Ellston's. To the right he added 'Haddock brothers' and circled it three times. Then to emphasise their importance he drew an arrow to the names in the middle. They had the motive, but was it that simple?

On the left-hand side he listed the names of Vicky Ackroyd, Sam Chandler and Vanessa and Bill Grant. At the bottom he wrote 'campers', which was the catalyst he needed to find the details of the person who had spotted them.

Once he had the name and contact details, he rang the number. There was nothing better than speaking to a witness himself. He heard the voice of Oliver Davies answer the call, and introduced himself.

'Detective Inspector Drake and I'm in charge of the inquiry into the death of Jason Ackroyd.'

'That was tragic. Have you caught the killer?'

'Not yet. I wanted to ask you about the campers you saw in the field near the cliff the evening before the murder.'

'I live on the road leading to the church and I was walking my dog onto the headland nearby. I do it most evenings. It was an unusual place to camp so it stuck in my mind. And by first thing in the morning they had gone.'

'Can you describe them?'

'Not really…they looked young and the girl had long blond hair. I do recall that as it was pulled into a knot behind her head.'

'Anything you can recall about the man?'

'He looked tall but other than that I can't help. The tent was green with yellow stripes on the zips.'

'Anything else? Did you notice a vehicle or van in the car park near the church?'

'Sorry, Inspector. I can't help.'

After thanking Davies, Drake rang off. He looked again at the sheet on the desk.

Were the campers local or visitors? It was an odd place to camp – not part of an established campsite but that could mean anything. They needed to be found and an appeal for a young pair in a green tent was bound to focus minds, but the last thing he wanted was to risk the killers being aware of possible eyewitnesses. He turned again to his notes and reminded himself that someone had called Jason Ackroyd after he'd returned from his pub crawl. Who had that been? And why had Ackroyd driven off on his motorcycle?

Chapter 24

Finishing early was high on Winder's to-do list that morning. Liverpool football club were hosting Everton, their local rivals, for a three pm kick-off and he had promised to meet a couple of his friends at a pub near his home to watch the game. Interviewing Sam Chandler couldn't possibly take all morning and, if he got back to headquarters promptly, he'd get his paperwork up to date and scoot off. It was Saturday after all.

After joining the traffic on the A55 he tuned into a radio station that featured a summary of all the major football games being played that weekend. There was a piece on Wrexham football club – nothing new, as their Hollywood owners had created intense interest in the North Wales club. Winder had visited their ground, the Racecourse Stadium, a couple of times, but it couldn't match the size and atmosphere of Anfield, the home of Liverpool.

He paid attention as the journalists discussed the latest tactics they thought the Liverpool team manager would employ. As he entered the tunnel between Penmaenmawr and Llanfairfechan, he spotted a coach emblazoned with Liverpool scarves heading in the opposite direction. A pang of jealousy filled his mind – perhaps it was time to give up being a detective and work a regular nine-to-five. Then he'd be able to take up the offer from one of his colleagues to join him for a trip to Anfield that afternoon.

Winder shook off his frustration and accelerated on towards Bangor and Anglesey. He made poor progress once he was off the A55 dual-carriageway and onto the two-lane road skirting the east side of Anglesey.

It was mid-morning when he drew up outside the fish and chip shop Sam Chandler ran. It was a modern building set back off the main road, with large glass windows and two doors: one at one end for entry and one at the other for customers to exit. Three women sat at a wooden picnic table and they each gave Winder a challenging, inquisitive look as he left the car and made his way over towards them.

Behind them, inside the building, the stainless-steel fittings of the fryers glistened in the morning sunshine.

Special offers were pinned to a board hanging to one side of the window near the entrance door. There was nobody inside and Winder wondered if they were waiting for it to open.

Winder had only just reached the table when one of the women announced in a pronounced Scouse accent. 'If you're looking for Sam Chandler, he's done a fucking runner.'

Both her companions nodded vigorously.

'Everyone is looking for him. The man who owns this place,' the same woman continued, jerking her head at the building behind her. 'Including the company that supplied him with potatoes.'

'We're owed a couple of weeks wages,' one of the other women piped up.

'Donna's right. He promised he'd pay us. Said he would look after us. He said he'd solved all his financial worries,' the third woman added.

Winder looked up at the building. 'Do you know where he went?' If he had disappeared it was suspicious and they'd need to track him down.

'Don't be stupid.' The first woman again. 'There'd be a long fucking queue at his door. My husband will be at the front of it ready to dish it out to him.'

'He can't let people down like this,' one of the other women announced. 'And anyway who are you? Are you police?'

'Detective Constable Winder.'

'Good, can you get my money back?'

'Did he live above the fish and chip shop?' Winder looked up at the windows on the first floor.

'No one in their right mind would live in that shit hole.' More of the Scouse accent.

'Don't say that, Pam. You know those two youngsters

overheard the previous day that the detective constable was looking forward to watching the Liverpool derby that afternoon. Drake had never been one to enjoy football. He followed Wales of course, revelled in their success in reaching the World Cup finals and shared in the nation's collective disappointment when they performed badly.

Before he'd left the house, Annie had reminded him he had to see his mother that evening. She wanted him to tell his mother about Susan's visit. Susan could be difficult and obstinate but she was family after all, and families survive difficulties. But Drake didn't see his mother's marriage to Elfed through the same prism as his sister did. Susan's determination to control her mother disappointed him. Why couldn't she realise their mother's happiness was the important thing? He was going to support his mother, even if that meant challenging his sister.

Sara was waiting for him outside Bangor police station at the prearranged time.

'Morning, boss. Lovely fresh morning.'

'Have you been running this morning?'

Drake pulled out into traffic.

'No time. Maybe I'll get 5K done tonight.'

'I don't know how you do it – tramping the streets in all weathers.'

'I live in the middle of nowhere so it's nice and quiet.'

Drake had to be content with threading his way through the city centre traffic at a gentle pace until he reached the entrance for the housing estate where Bill and Vanessa Grant lived. He parked outside the property. They left the car and Drake pressed the doorbell. He noticed that it had a camera recording every visitor's movement. There was no sound from inside the property, no indication of any sign of life and Drake wondered if that Saturday morning Mr and Mrs Grant were out shopping together at one of the local supermarkets.

'Maybe they're shopping.' Drake said, taking a step back and looking up at the bedroom windows. 'I don't think they are the sort to play happy families.'

Drake pressed the doorbell again. He stood defiantly facing the camera, making it abundantly clear to anyone watching on their smartphone that he wasn't leaving. One of Drake's neighbours had recently installed a floodlight with cameras attached as well as a video doorbell and he had shown Drake how exactly he could make the house ultra-secure. Drake imagined that Grant would be keen on the latest surveillance equipment. After all, the footage could be watched on a smartphone anywhere, inside the house, at the local supermarket or on holiday.

He pressed more firmly the second time. And now he heard the sound of movement behind the door and he shared an optimistic glance with Sara. He expected a voice to emerge from the video doorbell but it remained silent. Moments later the front door eased open against a security chain and the sleepy face of Vanessa Grant looked out of them.

'I was asleep. What do you want?'

Drake peered at Vanessa. Her hair was dishevelled, and he caught a glimpse of the tired-looking T-shirt and baggy leggings. The absence of make-up made her face look grey, almost unhealthy. But he couldn't see enough to make a real judgement.

'We need to speak to your husband.' Drake took a step nearer to the door. Vanessa pushed it towards him closing the gap.

'He's not here. He's gone to the community centre where he volunteers.'

'Where is that?'

Vanessa Grant gave them the details before adding, 'Now leave me alone.'

The door closed with a firm thud.

'Something's not right with Vanessa Grant,' Sara said as they reached the vehicle, Sara hesitated for a moment. 'There was no eye contact. Or at least very little. She seemed him again – and that he shouldn't contact her.'

'You could have telephoned him.'

Grant chortled. 'I don't think he's the sort of man I could have spoken to on the phone.'

'The eyewitnesses say that you were shouting, being abusive.

'I agree, Inspector, that I behaved badly.'

His admission created a brief silence, which hung in the air between Drake and Sara and Grant. He hadn't challenged anything they had put to him. Gathering his thoughts, Drake decided on a different tack. 'What do you do here?'

'I got involved with this group a few years ago. We help disadvantaged youngsters. We try and give them a bit more of a purpose in life.'

'And how is Vanessa?' Sara asked.

'She's well, thank you.'

Drake cast a glance around the room; their discussion with Grant was coming to an end. Framed photographs of the various groups in full martial arts regalia hung all over one wall. He spotted Grant in one, posing for a photograph with three youngsters holding a cup that had clearly been won for some activity.

'If there's nothing else then I'd like to get back to finish...'

Drake's mobile rang and he straightened, realising he needed to take Winder's call. 'Thank you, Mr Grant, if we need to speak to you further we will be in touch.' He answered Winder's call and listened as the officer explained about Sam Chandler's disappearance.

Drake was halfway across the main hall by the time Winder had finished.

'You need to get over and speak to Mrs Ackroyd immediately. I'll authorise the usual alert and we'll go and visit her friends.'

Chapter 25

'So it's you again.' Marion Walker's voice made quite clear that Drake and Sara were unwelcome. She stood at the threshold of the front door holding it open barely enough for Drake to see inside. 'I told you everything when we spoke last.' She began to close the door.

'Do you have any idea where Sam Chandler might be?'

Marion Walker guffawed. 'What's wrong with you people? I have no clue where he is. Why would I?'

'Have you spoken with Vicky Ackroyd about his whereabouts?'

'This is absurd. Of course I haven't.'

'It is very important, Mrs Walker, that we speak to Sam Chandler. Your cooperation would be greatly appreciated. Has Vicky Ackroyd ever mentioned family he might have? Or friends?'

Walker shook her head. Her eye contact was direct, which satisfied Drake that she was probably telling the truth. He found a business card in his jacket pocket and thrust it at Marion Walker. 'If you believe you have any information that might be of assistance, please call me.'

Drake marched back to his car, Sara following in his slipstream. 'I don't think she knows anything boss.'

'It's her attitude that narked me.'

Drake accelerated hard out of the estate and had to brake sharply as he reached the junction for the main road. His mobile, which was connected to the hands-free system, rang and he noticed Winder's number, so he took the call.

'No sign of Vicky Ackroyd, boss.' Winder's voice boomed out through the cabin. 'Nobody has seen her today. The car hasn't been here.'

'Get back to headquarters but en route call at the garage. Somebody must know where she is.'

Drake ended the call and accelerated, heading south towards Menai Bridge. He didn't like it when persons of interest couldn't be contacted. And he didn't like jumping to conclusions either, but everybody connected with this case seemed to be deceitful. Nobody was giving him a straight answer. The relationships were interconnected and complicated and he needed to make sense of everything.

The road leading to Ruth Salier's home was less crowded than it had been on his first visit although he had to negotiate around several parked cars at a snail's pace. He pulled into the same parking spot as he had used when he had visited before and jumped out of his BMW. Sara was behind him when he knocked on the door.

A tall man with a carefully manicured beard, wearing an immaculate navy suit, white shirt, no tie answered the door. 'Yes, how can I help?'

'We're looking for Mrs Salier.'

'And who are you?'

Drake and Sara produced their warrant cards.

The man examined them both intensely.

'Why do you want to speak to my wife?'

'Is she available?'

'I'm not in the habit of repeating myself but why do you want to speak to her?'

Drake stared at this man while trawling through his memory, trying to recall exactly what his wife said about her refusal to assist in the inquiry. Drake curbed his annoyance and breathed out slowly. 'We want to speak to a man called Sam Chandler we believe was in a relationship with Mrs Vicky Ackroyd.' Drake kept his eye contact fixed on Mr Salier's eyes – he had unusually dark irises.

'I see.'

'Your wife refused to cooperate with us when we called previously, indicating it had been a decision you had made together. I hope I don't need to remind you about the significance of withholding information or evidence that might assist the Wales Police Service in a murder inquiry.'

Salier gave Drake a tired look as though he had heard it all before.

'We can't help.'

Salier shut the door in Drake's face. He stared at the black painted surface for a moment allowing his mind to control the frustration he felt.

'Nothing we can do, boss,' Sara said.

Drake noticed the worried look on her face. He nodded. 'Bloody annoying though.'

They reached headquarters in good time and Drake bounded up the stairs to the Incident Room on the first floor. Winder was chewing on a pastry, a mug of tea on the desk in front of him.

'How did you get on boss?' Winder said.

'Nobody wants to bloody well cooperate. What is wrong with these people. Both of Vicky Ackroyd's friends basically told us to take a long walk off a short pier.' He walked over to the board and peered at Sam Chandler's face. 'Somebody must know where he is.'

'And where Vicky Ackroyd has gone,' Luned added.

Drake turned to face the rest of the team before sitting in one of the chairs by a spare desk. He glanced at his watch. He needed to leave promptly so that he could speak to his mum. And after seeing her he planned a long walk with Annie before enjoying a meal and a bottle of wine. They might even get to bed early and he smiled to himself at the prospect. Tomorrow he'd take a few precious hours away from the inquiry.

'I called into the garage premises on the way back boss,' Winder said. 'Nobody had seen Vicky Ackroyd today. A couple of the staff looked worried when I told them she wasn't at home nor answering her mobile.'

'Where the hell is she?' Drake said, allowing his frustration to show. 'Her husband has just been killed and she's out of communication.' Drake stood up and before making for his office announced to his team, 'I want to dig up everything you can about her family. Find out if her parents are still alive, whether she has any siblings. And do the same for Sam Chandler. I don't like it when people disappear in the middle of an inquiry.' Then he made for his room, but before reaching the door he stopped and retraced his steps to the board.

'I want the image of Bill Grant up on the board too. He's got the motive and there was something odd about his behaviour when we saw him at his home and at the community centre earlier.'

'He's a classic abusive and controlling male,' Sara said.

'If it's more than that we need to know. Do some digging into that martial arts group and the background of the members. At least get started today. Then we'll finish early. Everyone back first thing Monday.'

Then he walked over to his office and as his computer booted up he adjusted the photographs of his daughters by the phone until they were just as he liked them to be. A trace of dust had collected over his desk and he hoped the weekend cleaners would make certain everything was spotless by the time he arrived on Monday morning. He aimed to spend time gathering his thoughts, making priorities for the investigation. He started by reviewing the results of house-to-house enquiries, with a view to focusing on Vicky Ackroyd and Sam Chandler. There was something odd about her. Was it more than just wanting to hide her relationship with Sam Chandler? It was hardly a secret – everyone knew about it. He found a notepad and began jotting down the threads in the investigation. Drake couldn't ignore the other persons of interest and when he wrote the name of the Haddock brothers at the top of the first page he knew Superintendent Hobbs would be critical if he failed to give them his almost undivided attention.

He read the time from the clock on the monitor and realised he had to leave. He wasn't late, yet. Years ago when the rituals drove his obsessions he would work long into the evening without realising the impact it had on his family. At least now he was a little bit more in control. He turned his computer off, scooped the car keys off the desk and headed out to the Incident Room. Three pleased faces greeted him when they realised they could go.

Drake slowed for the junction to the track leading down to his mum's smallholding. It was a journey he had done a thousand times before. Although he hadn't lived at the property since his university days, it still held a special place in his heart. Driving down towards the house always made him recall his father. He had been a man content in his skin, happy with his lot in life. It had taken Drake a while to come to terms with his father's premature death. He wondered how his mum had fared with his sister. He wondered if Susan's lifestyle was a disappointment to her. And he often wondered whether his broken family had caused his mum regret.

He parked and walked over to the rear door, his feet making a welcoming crunching sound on the gravel. Mair Drake was standing by the kitchen window, and she smiled broadly when she saw Drake approaching. Once the doors opened, he kissed his mum and she scanned his face. 'You've been working today?'

'I finished early to come and talk to you.'

'You're working too hard, Ian. I worry about you and about Annie.'

Drake injected maximum reassurance into his voice. 'I'm fine, seriously. Don't worry. Now, tell me about Susan.'

They sat by the kitchen table. Mair Drake organised a pot of tea and, as she did, chatted about nothing in particular. She told Drake how she and Elfed were looking forward to their cruise. She listed the ports at which the ship was calling, keen for him to learn a little bit about the history of each that she had been researching. Her infectious enthusiasm made the holiday seem like an exciting adventure.

When she had sat down with a china mug in front of her, she began telling him about her discussion with Susan. She had no recrimination for Drake not having told her that Susan had stayed with him the night before she had met her.

'I know what she's like. She could be too intense as a child. I know she's worried about me,' Mair Drake said, reaching out and squeezing Drake's hand on the table by his mug of tea. 'As I'm sure you are. But you know Elfed. We want to spend the rest of the time we have left together.'

Hearing his mother talk like this made Drake uncomfortable. She wasn't going to live forever but did she have to be quite so blunt?

'I told her she needn't worry.'

Drake nodded. He listened to his mum explaining what she had told Susan about Elfed and their relationship. She had explained all about his previous life and the fact that he had lost his wife at a young age. It had taken time to reassure Susan that Elfed's intentions were entirely honourable. It had sounded so old-fashioned when his mum used those terms and he imagined Susan enjoying that sort of convoluted, highbrow language. Drake had assumed the meeting between his mum and Susan would have been fractious, driven by his sister's argumentative streak. Before his mug of tea was cold it became clear to Drake that his mother had been in charge – she and Susan had reverted to the parent–child relationship. Mair Drake knew her daughter better than Susan realised and from what she told Drake it seemed his sister's fears had been assuaged.

'I told her I was expecting to see her at the ceremony,' Mair Drake said.

'Good. I'm pleased that she'll be there. And will—'

'Do you think everything is all right between her and George?'

Chapter 26

Drake chose his newest charcoal grey suit that Monday morning which he paired with a powder blue shirt and a tie with several garish coloured stripes Annie had chosen as a birthday present. Having Sunday off had done Drake the power of good – he sensed his mind was fresher than it had been when he had left the Incident Room on Saturday afternoon. They had spent Sunday morning enjoying a long walk around the beach at Traeth Lligwy before having lunch with Annie's parents at their home in Beaumaris.

He was halfway on his journey towards headquarters when a piece on the Welsh news turned to the journalist who had made contact with him the previous week. Oldfield's self-important tone and his clipped public-school accent sounded odd when most of the broadcasters or journalists on BBC Radio Wales had a distinct Welsh twinge to their accents. As Drake focused on what Oldfield was alleging, he became more and more annoyed. He wanted to banish from his thoughts the prospect that someone had leaked the details of the murder and the method used by the killer. He trusted all of his team but there'd be others at headquarters with access to the information. Unless, of course, Oldfield was making a link to suit his own agenda. It was scaremongering of the worst possible sort. Superintendent Hobbs would be likewise displeased although his former boss Superintendent Wyndham Price would have been on the phone already threatening hell and damnation for the journalist.

Drake reached the tunnel after Penmaenmawr and switched off the radio. He had had quite enough of that reporter for one morning. Running an inquiry was tough without having to contend with a hack who wanted to make a name for himself. Before reaching headquarters Drake took a brief detour to the newsagent he had visited most mornings whilst living in Colwyn Bay. He bought his usual broadsheet and folded it open at the sudoku page. Completing a few squares of the puzzle first thing would always settle his mind for the rest of the day and once he had diced and sliced some of the lines, he laid it on the passenger seat. He would return to it later, maybe lunchtime, maybe with his coffee. Its presence in the meantime would be reassuring.

Once he had parked, he headed over for reception and then up towards the Incident Room. Saturday's jaded, tired looks had been replaced by a fresh-faced enthusiasm and determination. There was a collective 'Good morning, boss' from Luned and Sara as he entered. He nodded and returned the greeting as he walked for his office. He shrugged off the jacket and carefully hung it on a wooden hanger. He sat after checking the bin by his desk – empty just as he liked it. Then he scanned the top of his desk pleased at its dust-free environment.

His computer had barely booted up when he heard chairs being moved and he registered Sara's voice, a little louder than usual – 'Good morning, Superintendent'. Moments later Superintendent Hobbs appeared at his door.

'I want to talk to you about that reporter – he was on the radio this morning.' Hobbs shut the door and sat down on one of the visitor chairs.

'I was listening as I was driving in.'

'What the hell is he playing at? Is there anything to suggest a connection with organised crime?' Hobbs didn't wait for Drake to answer. 'Because if there is we need to get a full intelligence team working with you.'

It struck Drake as a classic case of Hobbs overreacting. He was protecting his back, after all, making certain there could never be any repercussions for his decisions.

'I have nothing at the moment to suggest Jason Ackroyd or Norma Ellston had any involvement with organised crime groups.'

'I spoke to Wyndham Price earlier. Actually, he called me after he heard that piece on the news. It was very useful having a conversation with him. He suggested a news conference might well be beneficial to take the heat out of all this reference to OCGs.'

A discussion between Wyndham Price and Superintendent Hobbs shouldn't come as a surprise. What wrongfooted Drake was the fact Hobbs acknowledged that advice he had been given might be actioned.

Hobbs continued. 'We'll organise a press conference later this afternoon in good time for the evening news. I'll get the PR people to work up the necessary announcements and press releases.'

And with that Hobbs got to his feet and left.

Drake always had misgivings about press conferences. He never felt they achieved as much as senior officers hoped they would.

Drake thought about contacting Wyndham Price. Doing so might seem as though he was checking up on Superintendent Hobbs but his former superior officer didn't have a role in the structure of the Wales Police Service. Before he came to a conclusion the phone on his desk rang. 'DI Drake,' he replied.

'It's Frank Jones. I'm the farmer who owns the land near Porth Padrig.' Drake recalled the name of the farmer because he'd made complaints about the inconvenience it was causing his business having teams of CSI's crawling all over it.

'How can I help?'

Drake was certain that the CSIs had finished. All the fluttering yellow crime scene tape had been removed, the temporary incident rooms hauled away and the lane from the main road had been reopened to the public. If this man wanted to complain any more he could raise it formally with Superintendent Hobbs; let his superior officer earn his salary.

'There was something funny going on last night.'
'What do you mean?'
'There were lights in the field and people wandering

all over near where they threw… you know what I mean near where the murder took place. One of my neighbours saw the lights. It was in the middle of the night for goodness sake. It can't have been your people, can it?'

Drake stood up still holding the handset of the phone. 'It wasn't any of the crime investigators so far as I'm aware. I'll be with you as soon as I can. I want you and your neighbour to be present so you can show me exactly where you saw the lights.'

Then Drake bellowed at Sara. 'We've got to go.'

Chapter 27

The disembodied voice from the satnav sounded almost pleased when Drake had reached his destination a good ten minutes before the one hour and four minutes the system had actually predicted the journey would take. Sara hadn't complained, so he couldn't have been driving dangerously.

'Did the farmer sound angry?'

'Baffled more than anything.'

Drake indicated left to take the narrow lane off the main road that they had negotiated on the first morning of the inquiry. He spotted a dark Land Rover stationary in the car park near the church and as soon as he approached the driver jumped out followed immediately by the passenger.

Frank Jones and his companion walked over towards Drake and Sara and greeted them as they got out of the car. Jones had a broad Welsh accent and, had it not been for Sara, the conversation would have been in Welsh but Drake knew Sara's understanding of the language made it difficult for her to follow what was being said. Jones introduced his companion as Mervyn Evans.

'When we spoke earlier you mentioned seeing lights in the early hours. What time was it?'

Evans was the first to reply. 'It was about one o'clock in the morning. I don't sleep very well. So I thought I'd take the dog for a walk. I use a path across one of the fields. I looked down and over towards the bay. It can be really tranquil at night. Nice and quiet and usually once I've had a bit of a walk I get back inside and sleep like a baby.'

'So tell me what was different about last night?' Drake tried to hide the impatience his voice.

'There were two lights bobbing in the field,' Evans nodded his head to an area behind Drake.

'How far away were you? Could you see if it was more than one person? Or whether it was a man or a woman?'

'It was dark. Pitch black.'

'Mervyn called me,' Jones interjected. 'I came down

straight away. We met by the gate leading to the path down to the cliff.'

Drake nodded his head – he knew where Jones referred to.

'I want you to show me exactly where you saw the lights.'

Both men led Drake and Sara down along the same path they had taken on the first morning of the inquiry. It formed part of the coastal path that circled the island. Hundreds maybe thousands of visitors traipsed the path every year and it led to a stony path down to the beach below.

Evans stopped halfway and peered over the hedge into an adjacent field. 'They were in this field, I'm sure. I saw them walking around for a few minutes.'

'When you say 'they' are you certain there was more than one?' Sara said. 'After all if one person was wearing a head torch he or she could have been holding a torch in the other hand'.

Evans pondered for a moment. Then he shook his head. 'Definitely two people because the lights weren't close to each other.'

'How do we access this field?' Drake said.

'Follow me,' Jones took the lead as he paced down the path before finding a small, rusted gate he heaved open.

The grass brushed Drake's brogues and he judged his steps carefully. Sara was scanning the hedgerows edging the field. Then she looked at a section of the pasture and he guessed she was thinking exactly the same as he was – had the nocturnal visitors been the campers? And why had they returned?

'Who do you think it could be?' Jones said.

'It's impossible to say,' Drake sounded authoritative. He wasn't going to share anything with Jones or Evans. It would have been all around the village of Cemaes within no time.

Sara contributed. 'It could be anybody – probably some

voyeur wanting to see where Jason Ackroyd was killed. You know what people are like these days.'

Jones and Evans nodded sagely as though her comments on modern life made perfect sense.

'Even so,' Drake said, 'I'd like to take a photograph of exactly where you thought these people were walking, just in case.'

It took a few minutes to organise to take photographs on the smartphones from the top of the field, looking down over the cliff top path in the bay and out over the sea.

Drake turned to both farmers and raised his voice. 'You've been very helpful. If we need a more formal statement from you, Mr Evans, an officer will come over to see you but for now this has been very constructive.'

'What's going to happen?' Jones said. 'I'm not going to have more of those investigators tramping over my field, am I? A journalist visited the other day poking his nose in asking questions. He said it was his father who had been responsible for finding the body and that he had been assisting and cooperating with your inquiry.'

'We don't have any journalists helping in the inquiry and it was completely misleading to suggest he was assisting us. Please contact me if he tries to speak to you again. And do you have his name?'

Jones nodded over at the houses at the edge of Cemaes, visible from the fields. 'Oldfield – he lives in one of those grand houses. I don't know what the world is coming to. Nobody local much living here anymore.' He tramped off back towards the gate, Evans keeping him company.

'I'm sure that's where the campers had pitched their tent,' Sara whispered to Drake when she was certain both Jones and Evans were out of earshot.

'Let's get back to the car.'

Sitting in the BMW, Drake looked over at Evans and Jones deep in conversation as he messaged Winder at headquarters, asking him to send him one specific file containing the photographs of exactly where the crime scene investigators believed the tent had been pitched.

'I wonder what they're talking about?' Sara said. Both farmers were a few yards away.

'Got it,' Drake announced as he opened the email from Winder. He scrolled through the contents, clicking open the images he needed. 'Just as I thought. That field is exactly where Mike Foulds and his team found evidence of a tent having been pitched and, more importantly, where they found a used condom in the undergrowth.' He looked over at Sara.

She nodded slowly.

Drake continued. 'If the individuals in the field last night were the campers they were probably looking for the condom. Which means they will probably be witnesses.'

'Who may have important evidence.'

'And that changes everything. We need to find them before the killers do.'

Chapter 28

The Bay View Hotel's decking area stretched out onto a carefully manicured lawn filled with several pieces of garden furniture and play equipment for young children. Drake parked and reminded Sara that being near Cemaes gave then the opportunity to speak to Gideon Pepper, the hotel staff member that hadn't been interviewed by the house-to-house team.

Speaking to Pepper seemed too good an opportunity to miss, despite the urgency to deal with the latest discovery. At least two eyewitnesses had to be traced. These people were at risk, and they must have known they were taking a risk going back to the fields late at night. Sara knew Drake would want to return to headquarters, but he had complained vociferously about Mr Oldfield and his troublesome journalist son after the farmers had mentioned them. Sara resolved to talk him out of visiting Mr Oldfield if he threatened to do so.

Pushing open the main door Drake marched over to the bar. 'Is Gideon Pepper available?'

'I'm not certain if he is working,' a young woman with long blonde hair and a thin face replied.

'Find out, this is a police matter.'

Sara realised the discovery of two potential witnesses would have put Drake on edge. It would have exacerbated his irritability and if she wasn't careful this young member of staff and Gideon Pepper would get the rough edge of his tongue.

The member of staff left the bar area trying to make a face that suggested she wouldn't be too long. Drake turned to scan the inside of the Bay View Hotel. Two elderly ladies were enjoying coffee in one corner and an important looking man in a navy suit, white shirt and designer stubble was conducting a whispered conversation with the pods stuck in his ears. The clatter of pans and cutlery and muffled conversations drifted from the open door of the kitchen behind the bar.

Gideon Pepper looked young enough to still be at school. Angry pimples covered his cheeks and a lost, rather innocent, look filled his eyes. The other member of staff who led him towards Drake and Sara pointed at a door at the end of a corridor. 'You can talk in the staff room if you want. It's not being used now.'

'Thanks,' Drake said jerking a head at Sara and Pepper to follow him.

Gideon Pepper sat on the edge of one of the stiff plastic chairs in the small room. 'Some of the others told me you might call.' He shared an agitated look between Drake and Sara.

'I'm in charge of the investigation into the death of Jason Ackroyd.'

Pepper nodded vigorously.

'I understand you were working on the evening he was killed.'

'Yeah, that's right. I was on night shift. We do some tidying and cleaning mostly and we look after any guests arriving late.'

From the tone of his voice, it was clear Pepper didn't enjoy his work.

'What time did you start?'

'I'd usually arrive by about midnight, but I was a bit earlier that night. I'd rowed with my mother and I couldn't wait to leave the house.'

Pepper averted his gaze towards the fingers of both hands he was threading together.

Drake looked over at Sara, who gave a brief frown.

'Is there something you think might be of assistance? Did you notice anything unusual when you were arriving at work? Or perhaps somebody acting suspiciously?'

'Well, there was…' Pepper looked at Drake. 'I mean I can't be certain, but I noticed a van was parked just off the main road. It had pulled into the junction towards the farm.'

'What can you tell us about this van?'

'It looked a bit battered.'

'And the colour?'

Pepper shook his head. 'It was dark.'

'Try and remember. Any details might be important.'

'Sorry. It wasn't white – I would have noticed that.'

It was Sara's turn to ask the next question. 'Did you see anybody inside?'

Another nod of the head. 'I think there were two people inside. But I couldn't tell if they were a man or a woman.'

'If you think of anything else please contact us immediately.' Drake got to his feet.

Pepper gave Drake a stunned look, as though he had hoped his involvement had finished.

'We'll need your address and contact number.' Drake nodded at Sara. Pepper stammered the details as Sara jotted them down in her notebook.

Sara joined Drake as he paced out of the room and back into the main section of the hotel. He stopped abruptly and stared over towards two men sitting by the window overlooking the decking area. From a distance it was difficult to see exactly what they were doing but from the images on the smartphone one of them was holding they were looking at a video.

'That's Oldfield,' Drake said. 'And his interfering bloody son.'

'I think we should get back to headquarters, boss.'

Drake ignored Sara and paced over towards both men.

'Good morning, Mr Oldfield.'

The older man looked up, recognising Drake.

'And I believe we've spoken on the phone.' Drake turned to the younger Mr Oldfield. 'Detective Inspector Drake.'

The journalist scanned everybody in the room in a brief second. 'What brings you here? Is there somebody you're interviewing as part of your inquiry?'

Sara wanted to drag Drake away from this conversation. She could see nothing but trouble ahead.

'Everything involved in a police investigation is confidential,' Drake said directing his comments at Mr Oldfield junior. 'Anything that impedes a criminal investigation can be a very serious matter. Including passing yourself off as assisting the inquiry to a local farmer.'

'I don't know what the hell you're talking about, Detective Inspector,' Oldfield snapped.

'As a journalist, Mr Oldfield, you must know the dangers of compromising an inquiry or indeed publicising unhelpful material.'

'This is a free country. And there is such thing as a free press.'

'Thank you for your time, gentleman,' Drake said before nodding at Sara to join him as they headed for the door.

As they reached the car Drake turned to Sara. 'That was fun. I've probably ruined their day.'

Sara wasn't so certain.

Chapter 29

Winder pulled into the car park at the Llewelyn Fawr public house. He knew the name referred to a native Prince of Wales but he couldn't remember from which century. The Coach and Horses where he'd spent the final couple of hours of Saturday afternoon and most of the evening was a far more common name for a public house. A mobile incident room was parked against a long wall that skirted the car park. At the far end were single-storey farm buildings converted to different uses.

Winder parked and met a uniformed officer leaving the mobile Incident room.

'The sergeant's in there,' the young constable said.

Winder nodded his understanding and moments later stepped inside.

'You're up bright and early, Detective Constable.'

'Good morning to you too, Terry.'

Winder had known Terry Wilson long enough for the formalities of rank to have evaporated.

'Have you picked up anything interesting?'

Terry sat back in his chair, blew out a mouthful of air. 'Ellston lived out in the middle of nowhere. We've had a full team working on Saturday and they restarted this morning. There were the usual sort of time wasters – people thought they'd spotted her in the pub the night she was killed.'

'Anybody seen her abducted by aliens?'

Terry chuckled before replying. 'Funny you should mention that – we did get one old man who was convinced he saw her being bundled into a van by three men wearing Batman facemasks the previous week.'

Winder groaned.

Terry continued. 'We've got a couple of homeowners it might be worth your while talking to. I'll get you the details. And the landlord of the pub is back today – apparently, he's been away for a few days on holiday. Plays golf in the Algarve – all right for some.'

Terry organised coffees for Winder and himself and they spent a few moments gossiping. Liverpool's success on the football field was always an easy topic for Winder to discuss and most of his colleagues in Northern Division had an interest in the game. Terry was no exception. And he shared his take on the result which had seen Liverpool beat their city rivals Everton easily.

A couple of other junior officers entered, seeking clarification from Terry Wilson about their duties and he sent them on their way soon enough.

'What's the name of the person I need to see?' Winder finished the last of his coffee.

'Richard Harris. I've got his address here somewhere.'

Moments later Winder was leaving the mobile Incident room with the directions to Harris' property. He drove out of the car park and took a few minutes to familiarise himself with the geography surrounding the village. He knew it was something he should have done before leaving headquarters. He made a mental note to organise a map for the Incident room board. Detective Inspector Drake would be certain to ask for one and if he organised it before being told to do so he might get some brownie points.

The map on his satnav was good enough to give him a working knowledge of the local area. He drove in the direction of Norma Ellston's home along the country lanes lined with hedges and narrow ditches. It wasn't the sort of place he had expected a murder to take place. But then again murders can take place in the oddest of places.

All the curtains were drawn in the windows of Ellston's cottage, which had a lonely feel about it. Winder wondered who was going to get the benefit of her estate – would it be the brother on the south coast of England? It didn't sound as though they had much of a relationship. But she might have made a will and promised everything to the local donkey sanctuary. There were no cars parked in the hardstanding near the property. Winder drove on, spotting easily enough the bungalow where Harris lived. There was a large garage with an extensive driveway in front of it. Its door was open and inside Winder could see a joinery workshop.

He drove in and parked.

A high-pitched noise emerged as a circular saw was plunged into wood, the intensity of the grinding oscillating. Winder peered in and saw a figure moving in the workshop area that filled the garage space. Once the sound had stopped he called out a greeting.

'Richard Harris?'

There was no reply and it was only when the man removed his ear defenders that Winder could see why he hadn't responded. He tried again. The man turned sharply and stared over at Winder.

'That's me.' Harris walked towards Winder.

Harris was well into his sixties with deep wrinkles and large well-worn hands. He filled the overalls.

Winder pushed out a hand with his warrant card and Harris' face warmed as he realised what the visit was about. 'Come inside.' Harris jerked his head for Winder to join him as he threaded his way through the tools and equipment. A table saw had pride of place together with lathes and benches with various sized routers waiting for work.

Inside a small kitchen area at the rear Harris didn't need to point to the only spare chair. Winder duly sat down and Harris lit up a cigarette.

'Terrible business that with Norma Ellston.'

'Did you know her well?'

'I wouldn't say so. I replaced a couple of the windows at her place a few years ago and we got chatting. She was quite a character. She was friends with my wife and my sister too. They were really sad about the news.'

'I'm one of the officers on the team investigating her death and the sergeant of the mobile Incident room thought you might be able to add some useful information.'

'Norma liked to visit the car boot sale in the

showground. She was dead keen. She had boxes and boxes of rubbish. But sometimes she would try and sell stuff that was dodgy – do you know what I mean?'

'Stolen?'

He nodded. 'Because she was at the car boot sale so often I think people thought they could get her to sell stuff innocently.'

'How do you know this?'

Harris took a long drag of his cigarette allowing the smoke to permeate deep into his lungs.

'It was Jack at the pub who told me. You should talk to him. Mind you, I've also seen people visiting her place at odd times of the night.'

'Did you go past the place regularly?'

Harris looked away for a moment and give a rather sheepish reply. 'If I drove down to the pub and I've had a couple too many I'll take the lane past her house back home. No chance of the traffic cops catching me there.' He smiled.

Winder didn't smile back, wasn't going to indulge this man. 'Any details? Descriptions or numberplates of cars?'

Harris shook his head.

Winder thanked Harris and after reversing the car out into the road headed down into the village. Was there more to Norma Ellston than they had initially thought? He needed to carefully jot down and write up Harris' comments and he wondered whether the landlord of the Llywelyn Fawr might have something to say.

Winder took time returning to the pub. He tried to pick out any possible CCTV cameras. He had already requisitioned details of all the public camera positions, but this was a small village in the middle of Anglesey and he guessed he would be disappointed with the results. He'd be better focusing on the video doorbells and floodlights with cameras attached. The house-to-house team would have the information he needed.

The only evidence of previous shops were larger

windows and one property had 'Post Office' carved out of the external render above the main door. A development of new houses with solar panels had replaced the old school and even Winder understood the sign 'Yr Hen Ysgol' – the old school – that named the estate.

After parking, he headed for the rear entrance of the pub. The old, slightly dilapidated feel to the outside of the place was not replicated inside. The smell of fresh paint attacked his nostrils instead of the usual smell of stale alcohol. He found Jack Faulkner standing behind the bar. He was at least six feet tall with a domed shaved head almost uniformly russet in colour. A drunken argumentative customer taking one look at his broad shoulders and pumped arms would have second thoughts about challenging Faulkner.

Winder flashed his warrant card.

'I want to talk to you about Norma Ellston.'

'I've only just got back. I was playing golf in the Algarve yesterday and now back to this murder in the village.'

Faulkner made his way from the bar area and sat with Winder at a small table.

'I met Norma a couple of times. She was dead keen on car booting. She could sell ice cubes to Eskimos. And she could prattle on. But everybody liked her.'

Faulkner paused and Winder sensed that he had something else to share.

'I spoke to Richard Harris earlier. He said that he'd seen people leaving her house late at night.'

Faulkner nodded. 'Dick's a bit of a busybody.' Faulkner rested his elbows on the table. 'I'll tell you things about Norma.' Another pause drew out the dramatic effect. He dragged his right hand over his nose and face as though it was helping him compose his next comment. 'As a landlord you hear a lot of things. She had some medical issues a while back and made no secret of the fact that she was a regular cannabis user. I think it got to be more than that. It might have been small-scale but I'm sure that she was dealing.'

'Do you have any names?' Winder said realising that this latest information put a different complexion entirely on Norma Ellston's death.

'I'll ask around. Don't hold your breath.'

Chapter 30

Luned settled down to a morning's work, pleased that Winder wasn't in the Incident Room. It gave her an opportunity to focus on the work in hand. Working with him was always a challenge and, whilst he was more experienced, she couldn't help but think his attitude was a little relaxed, as though he didn't take what they were doing seriously enough. Her aim was to have a comprehensive analysis of Sam Chandler's finances and more details about Norma Ellston's family ready for when Detective Inspector Drake returned later that day. But first she'd look at Bill Grant.

She took a moment to scan the faces on the Incident Room board. Everything pointed to the Haddock brothers being responsible for both deaths. The Haddock brothers had a clear and unambiguous motive and they deserve to be locked up. But was it as simple as that? It pleased her that Detective Inspector Drake had kept an open mind.

Her gaze settled on Jason Ackroyd's photograph before moving to Norma Ellston's. They were victims of a vicious crime and Luned refocused her resolve that it was her job and the others in Drake's team to find their killer or killers.

Establishing the names of the members of the martial arts group took longer than she expected and, once she had a list, she requisitioned a search of the police national computer for any records against the individuals involved. As she waited, she checked her emails and was pleased that a full background check on the finances of Bill Grant had come through.

As she read them, the more her mind focused on absorbing all the details. They knew he had been married before, but they had discovered that he owned a property jointly with his sister, following the recent death of his mother. But it was the scale of his debts to a bank after a failed investment with his sister in a restaurant and bar that grabbed Luned's attention.

As she finished reading the reports the PNC results arrived. Three of the members of the martial arts group had records for violence, mostly minor assaults as young men and one, a Jasper Heath, had a conviction for a more serious assault. She took time to make certain she had all the details and to get everything clear in her mind, knowing that Inspector Drake would want a coherent summary.

Turning back to her monitor she clicked into the documents provided by the various financial institutions where Sam Chandler had accounts. She already knew his mortgage was in arrears and that the building society were contemplating repossession proceedings. There were emails from the institution clarifying the position and indicating they were investigating whether Sam Chandler's original application for a mortgage contained inaccuracies. Luned ignored the comments – any fraud in his mortgage application would have to be dealt with by the economic crime unit.

Trawling through his bank account Luned looked for patterns of payments and receipts. The substantial cash receipts into his personal bank account troubled her. She began to cross-reference some against deposits into the business bank account for the fish and chip shop. There was a pattern for the business account – much as she expected from a business where customers could pay by cash.

The payments into his personal bank account were more erratic. Sometimes twice a week, sometimes no payment at all for a week. And the sums were still not enough to keep the mortgage repayments up to date. By mid-morning she had prepared a spreadsheet with the cash payments he had made into his account over the past three years. The pattern suggested only one thing – he had another source of income. And if the envelopes from Mrs Ackroyd weren't enough it occurred to her to check one other option. She sent an email to an officer in the squad responsible for investigating drug offences.

While she waited for a response she turned her attention to tracking down Norma Ellston's brother. There had been no details in the dead woman's possession to assist them – no address or contact details or mobile phone number. Officers had been able to recover an ancient laptop from Ellston's cottage and she booted it up and waited for the machine to crawl into life.

It surprised her how well organised Ellston had been. She had folders for business and personal matters. Luned tried the folders marked 'Business' first and found at least three dozen folders marked with different titles, including 'Accounts' and 'Bank Statements' and 'Invoices'. She clicked on the 'Customer Orders' folder and found details of the orders placed on the website. There weren't many, which made Luned ponder why she kept a website.

Intrigued by a folder that said 'Solicitors – Claim', Luned read the details of a possible claim against Ellston for having sold an item that had been incorrectly described. It had cost over a thousand pounds and the customers must have been particularly litigious to have instructed lawyers. In any event Ellston had refunded them without delay.

Revived by a coffee mid-morning she continued with her work on the laptop, but when another hour spent trawling through the folders in the business section hadn't produced anything of substance, she turned her attention to the personal folders.

She didn't have a name for Ellston's brother. Nancy Toogood had never met him and Norma had never discussed him with her. They may as well have been strangers. Nothing in any of the paperwork suggested her brother had the same surname. Luned assumed that Ellston had been her married name.

The folder had a Christmas card list and for a moment Luned's hopes were raised, but none of the men's names had addresses on the south coast. Most of the recipients had been local to Ellston in North Wales. Luned called Nancy

Toogood on the off-chance Ellston may have discussed family with her in the past. Nancy sounded vague. She hadn't been able to help and she kept asking if they had discovered who had killed her friend.

'Do you think there's any possibility Norma's brother might have moved away from the south coast?'

'I can't say.'

Luned spent another few minutes going round in circles with Nancy Toogood until she drew the conversation to a close.

Luned called the civilian in charge of processing the possessions the administration support team had removed from the cottage. The woman promised to send someone to the Incident Room with a box they recovered. She had time to make herself another coffee before a civilian from the admin team carrying a box file pushed open the door to the Incident Room. 'Detective Constable Thomas?'

Luned nodded and pointed at the desk by her side. Luned began rifling through the box. Trawling through someone's life when there was no immediate next of kin who cared for the deceased was always a sad part of her job. Ellston's life had been a lonely existence, although from what Toogood had told Luned and shared with Inspector Drake she had enjoyed her lifestyle.

Ellston had a modest amount in her current account, a little more in a savings account and a business account related to the website. Some books and a shoebox with Christmas cards caught Luned's attention. She flicked through each one hoping to find a card from Ellston's brother. She found half a dozen cards from couples and put those to one side, hoping they might give her the details she needed. The rest she discarded back into the box. The final item she removed from the box that joined the other things littering her desk was an old address book.

Luned focused more sharply now. It was divided by the letters of the alphabet. By the time she reached the letter 'P', her attention and hope of discovering a name and an address had waned. She ploughed on and under the section 'S' she discovered a Richard Stanford with an address in Sittingbourne, Kent but alongside it was another address in Portsmouth that had been deleted.

She stared at the details. Was Stanford Ellston's brother?

She did an immediate search against the name hoping for a number, but none was listed. It meant she had to go through the usual protocols to establish if there was an ex-directory number. She didn't have to wait too long for the information she needed.

She punched the number into the phone on her desk and waited. She allowed the phone to ring for far longer than she would have normally. She had to hope someone would be home. She was about to finish the call when a breathless voice sounded.

'Hello.'

'I'd like to speak to Mr Stanford please.'

'He's at work. Who is this?'

'My name is Detective Constable Luned Thomas of the Wales Police Service. It's a family matter we'd like to discuss with him.'

'What do you mean "family"?'

'When will I be able to speak to Mr Stanford?'

'I... don't know. Look, give me your number and I'll ask him to call you.'

Luned dictated the contact number for reception at Northern Division, making certain she also gave the woman her full name and rank.

If he wasn't Ellston's brother she had very likely caused considerable commotion in the Stanford household. She carried on looking through the address book content. There was no other person with any address, past or current living in the south coast of England.

She had almost completed returning all of Ellston's

property to the box when the phone rang and reception announced that Mr Stanford wanted to speak to her.

'Richard Stanford here, what's this about?'

'I'm trying to locate the brother of Norma Ellston. We found your name and details in her address book.'

'That's correct. I haven't heard from Norma for years. What's this about anyway?'

'I'm afraid I have bad news. Your sister was murdered last week. I'm one of the detectives on the team conducting the inquiry.'

'What! I can't believe it. Why, I mean how?'

Luned gave Stanford a summary of what had happened. He listened silently.

'When did you last see your sister?'

'It must have been four years ago. We never had much in common and we argued bitterly when I came to stay with her. She accused me of stealing from our parents. She got extremely irate and I just told her never to contact me again.'

Luned could see that this was going to be a dead end for any useful information. But she persevered. 'Did you meet any of her friends at that time? Was there anything about your sister's behaviour you thought unusual?'

'It's a long time ago, but I was a bit uncomfortable when a couple of young lads called at the house quite late one evening. They came back the following night. Norma was very secretive.'

'Did you know what they were doing?'

'No, I didn't ask. I couldn't help but feel she was mixed up in something unsavoury.'

Stanford couldn't elaborate any further, but Luned felt pleased she had been able to establish the basics about Ellston's life. And it gave them another thread to follow. After the call, Luned checked her emails, pleased when she saw a reply. It had an intelligence briefing attached which made very interesting reading.

Chapter 31

Drake's conversation with Sara on the journey back to headquarters was dominated by the prospect that eyewitnesses existed. And the fact that they hadn't come forward troubled Drake. There was no escaping the conclusion they were frightened, even terrified, about being identified.

His final comments to Frank Jones and Mervyn Evans before leaving them had been to warn them about not sharing what they had seen the previous evening with anyone. If they began to gossip about what they had witnessed, then there was a possibility the killer or killers might get to hear of it. Cemaes, Amlwch and North Anglesey were small communities, and the recent killings were the subject of rumours and half-truths, of that Drake could be certain.

'I think you should call Jones and Evans again,' Drake said to Sara as they neared the Britannia Bridge. 'Warn them again not to talk to anybody about what they saw the other night.'

'I think you were clear enough, sir. And if we labour the point it might encourage them to share the details. Less is more and all that. After all, we have no idea who they might have spoken to before calling you.'

Drake mumbled an acknowledgement as he slowed the car to negotiate the single file of vehicles over the bridge. Once he was on the mainland, he accelerated hard in the outside lane and headed back for headquarters.

He was cutting it fine for his meeting with Superintendent Hobbs. The PR department would want to make certain any press conference was in good time for the evening news, but the latest development had to be discussed. He called Superintendent Hobbs' office, warning his secretary that new information was to hand. Then he called the PR department and spoke to the manager.

'I'm on my way back to headquarters. There's

something I need to discuss with you and Superintendent Hobbs as soon as I arrive.'

'But I'm in the middle of something.'

'It'll have to bloody well wait. I'll see you in ten minutes.'

Drake finished the call and nudged the car to over ninety miles an hour in the outside lane.

He parked in a slot reserved for visitors by the main entrance and took the stairs up to reception two at a time, Sara behind him. An idea had been formulating in his mind. He needed to discuss it with the PR department and he wanted Hobbs' approval.

Drake pushed open the door to the senior management suite and nodded at Hobbs' secretary. She acknowledged his presence and moments later Peter Charleston, the public relations manager Drake had spoken to earlier, arrived.

'What's this about, Ian?'

'There's a press conference this afternoon.'

'Yes, I know, everything is prepared. The press release was emailed to you earlier.'

'I've only just got in so I haven't seen the damned thing. And anyway, things have changed.'

Hobbs' secretary announced he would see them, and Drake took the initiative leading Sara and Charleston into the superintendent's office.

'What is this latest development?' Hobbs asked as soon as everyone was seated around his conference table.

'We've just spoken to the farmer who owns the land abutting the footpath near the cliff and the beach where Jason Ackroyd's body was found. The farmer and another householder nearby saw two people in the early hours of this morning with what looked like head torches. And we know there were campers in that field the evening before Ackroyd's murder. They were in the exact location where the CSIs discovered evidence of a tent recently being pitched and where they found a used condom in the hedge round the field.'

'How does this change things?' Charleston said.

Drake ignored him and continued. 'The people seen in the early hours must have been camping at around the time the killers were present.'

'It could have been somebody completely different.' Charleston again.

'Continue, Inspector,' Hobbs said formally. 'I want to hear exactly where you're going with this.'

'I suggest that in the press conference I make a personal address to the cameras asking for any eyewitnesses to come forward and making reference to visitors to the area, people who may have been walking the coastal path, people in camper vans or others who may have been camping or just visiting for the day.'

'So you think they may be witnesses?' Charleston said.

'It needs to be worded carefully, but if it is sufficiently bland but at the same time contains a specific reference to camping it may be possible to appeal to those witnesses without tipping off the killers.' Drake looked over at Hobbs, wondering how his superior officer would react.

'But there has already been one appeal,' Hobbs said. 'How is another going to help? And what could possibly be the explanation for those two people in the field in the middle of the night?'

Drake glanced at Sara. He wasn't sure whether it was a question addressed to him or simply rhetorical.

'Maybe they were youngsters – teenagers, messing around,' Charleston said.

Drake struck a serious tone. 'Our eyewitnesses were very clear. The individuals they saw were scouring one corner of the field.'

'Can they be certain of that?'

'What we can be certain of is that a man's body was found on the nearby beach.' Hobbs used his most authoritative voice. 'And until we know who these people were and what they were doing there we assume they can help us with our inquiry.' He glanced at his watch. 'We have less than an hour until the agreed time for the press conference. I suggest you both get on and agree the wording of a statement for Detective Inspector Drake to read.'

'Yes, sir,' Drake said.

Hobbs turned to Charleston. 'And I suggest you make certain the TV crews know that Detective Inspector Drake will be reading a prepared statement.'

'But they may think that's unusual.'

'Get it done.' Hobbs' voice verged on irritated. 'Back in good time for me to approve everything.'

Drake nodded at Charleston, signalling that they were leaving.

Silently Drake led Charleston through the corridors of Northern Division headquarters, although he sensed the PR manager wanted to say something, raise a complaint, make an issue of things. Drake barged into the Incident Room where Winder and Luned looked up but he ignored them and made for his office, Charleston in his slipstream.

Sitting at his desk he pointed at one of the visitor chairs as Sara stood leaning against a cupboard. Winder and Luned appeared at the threshold to his office. Drake sprinted through a summary of the events that morning and when Winder and Luned offered to share their progress Drake raised a hand. 'Everything can wait until after the press conference.'

Once his computer had booted up Drake downloaded the draft press release Charleston's department had already prepared. With a couple of clicks he enlarged the text to fill the monitor and, as he did so, sent a copy to his printer for Sara to read. He read it carefully, conscious Sara was doing the same, and he sensed Charleston's gaze.

'This will be fine for Superintendent Hobbs to read. We need to draft something more personal I can read directly to the camera.'

'We don't have an autocue or anything like that remember, Ian,' Charleston said.

'It doesn't matter. I'm only suggesting a few sentences that hopefully those two individuals will hear. My guess is they are local, otherwise it's likely they would not have returned. So hopefully they'll be watching the TV news, or at least see a clip of this on social media.'

Drake reached into the drawer of his desk and pulled out an A4 pad.

Then he got out a ballpoint and started to write an initial draft.

'Excellent,' Hobbs announced.

Drake had been convinced that, as his superior officer had taken far too long to read the three paragraphs, he was going to make substantial changes. He and Charleston had drafted and redrafted the brief text. They were fast approaching the deadline for the press conference to catch the early evening news.

Hobbs looked up from his desk. 'Is everything ready?'

'Yes, Superintendent,' Charleston said.

Hobbs stood up, pushed the chair away from his desk and pulled on the jacket of his uniform. 'Let's get this done.'

Charleston led the way to the conference and training suite that doubled as a room where press conferences were held. Drake's reservations about press conferences crowded into his mind as soon as he saw the table set out with microphones and name badges in front of chairs filling up with journalists and, behind them, camera crews.

Were they ever successful? He had always doubted their effectiveness in contributing meaningfully to apprehending suspects. But today was different.

'None of the journalists will think there was anything unusual about you reading a statement,' Charleston whispered to Drake as they stood at one end of the room.

'Good.'

'We need to get started. And S4C want you to do an interview afterwards.'

Drake had often been called upon to contribute an interview for the Welsh-language television channel. 'The important ones are the TV journalists and their editors will be screaming at them to get the right footage.'

Charleston didn't wait for a reply. He nodded at Superintendent Hobbs and Drake followed his superior officer down to the table at the front.

The PR manager took the opportunity of explaining to the assembled audience that Superintendent Hobbs would be making a statement before Detective Inspector Drake – as the senior investigating officer – would make a more detailed statement about current progress.

Drake scanned the faces in front of him. He recognised a number from their appearances on the nightly TV news. He listened to Superintendent Hobbs outlining the basis of their investigation. He finished far too quickly for Drake's liking.

'Detective Inspector Drake?' Charleston said leaning forward and looking over at Drake.

Drake cleared his throat. Then he looked over at his audience. He wasn't really talking to them, he was talking to the two individuals that in the early hours had been seen scouring the fields near where Jason Ackroyd's body had been discovered.

'As the senior investigating officer, I would urge any member of the public who has any information that might be of assistance to come forward. Jason Ackroyd's body was found on the beach known as Porth Padrig near Cemaes on the north coast of Anglesey. It is a popular tourist destination.

'The coastal path goes through the village and passes very close to where Jason Ackroyd's body was discovered. It may be the case you were visiting the area, perhaps walking along the coastal path or visiting St Padrig's church nearby.

If you were and if you can recall anything you think might be important, please contact us. And local residents may be able to contribute valuable evidence that could assist with identifying the perpetrators of this terrible crime.'

Drake looked up the cameras and reporters. 'Caravanning is a popular pastime and we are aware that the car park at the church is used by people visiting the area. There is a nearby campsite too and campers in the local fields may have something vital to contribute. We would urge anyone with information they think is important to contact us.'

Chapter 32

Zoe's message to Paul was simple – *I need to see you – usual place. X*

She sat in the lounge of the house, unable to move. She had become utterly convinced, having watched the BBC Welsh news, that the police knew about her and Paul. It had been a stupid decision to go back to the fields to search for the condom. God, she was so annoyed with Paul. One of her girlfriends had said he was immature and needy but throwing it away like that… what was he thinking?

The image of that police officer referring to walkers and campers filled her with trepidation. The only conclusion she could draw was that they had been seen – why else would he refer to campers? Who could have seen them? And who else might have been told? That worried Zoe more than anything. She knew what Cemaes was like – rumours spread so quickly.

Her father came in and sat by her side. 'Did you see that stuff about the police press conference regarding Jason's death?'

Zoe didn't reply. She was convinced her lips were so dry they were incapable of forming words.

'I heard Jason was involved with some gangs from up the coast.'

Typical, thought Zoe. Rumours, just petty rumours.

Her father continued. 'And nobody has seen Vicky Ackroyd for a couple of days. Apparently, she's done a runner to Spain. Somebody reckons they have a villa in Majorca.'

'I'm going out.' Zoe squeezed out the words after running her tongue over her lips.

'Oh… What's wrong with you?'

'Nothing, I'm fine. I'm going to Ffion's.'

She caught the bus with seconds to spare and as it left the village she texted Paul again. *On my way. Don't be late.*

She wanted to leave this place, find somewhere nobody

would recognise her, where nobody would be searching for her. After their camping trip had turned into such a disaster, she wasn't at all certain she wanted to have Paul around. The journey dragged, even though it was only a few miles, and eventually she saw Paul's car parked in a layby. She got off and ran over to Paul.

'How are you?' Zoe asked.

Paul gave her a lost look as though he didn't know how to respond. Then he shrugged. 'Let's go to the pub.'

Zoe used the rear entrance while Paul organised drinks. She was annoyed that two other customers were sitting at one of the other tables. Paul came in with their drinks, giving the other couple a wary glance. Zoe took a mouthful of her drink, Paul downed a generous glug of his pint of beer. They talked about nothing in particular hoping for their unwelcome companions to leave. And when eventually the landlord came through announcing that a taxi had arrived for the other couple Zoe and Paul relaxed.

'I thought they'd never leave,' Paul said.

'Did you see the news?'

Paul nodded. 'That was when I got your message.'

'That policeman who spoke at the end was… It was as though he was talking to us. Talking to me directly. He knows we were there.'

'We are not going to the police. That other woman has been killed by the same people. It has to be them.'

'We can't do nothing.'

'What do you suggest, Zoe? Go to the police and tell them that we were there when Ackroyd was killed. And that I've got photographs of the van they used and shots of the two men involved. You know what people are like. Before you know it everyone in Cemaes and Anglesey will know, including the people who killed Ackroyd and the other woman.'

'They can protect us. It's the right thing to do. If my parents find out they'll be mad.'

'A friend of mine works in the Bay View Hotel. The police called the other day to talk to one of the members of staff who told them about a van he had seen. So it's only a matter of time until they find the culprits. We don't have to do anything.'

'Have the police been back to the caravan park? You said they'd spoken to someone.'

Paul didn't reply. Another customer stepped into the room casting a glance around, looking for somebody. He gave a brief nod and headed for the main bar area.

'I haven't seen the police back at the premises. So I can't tell you.'

'I'm frightened Paul, really scared.'

'There's nothing we can do.'

'Of course there is. That's just nonsense. We could go to the police. We should go to the police. Tell them what we know.'

Paul finished his pint, placed the glass on the table and pushed it away in disgust. 'And what? Just wait to get killed? And then your parents would know. Don't be stupid, Zoe.'

Zoe turned down Paul's invitation for another drink. 'I should be getting home.'

'Do you want to get a pizza or something?' Paul said without much enthusiasm. 'Let's go to the King's Arms for a game of pool.'

'I'm not in the mood.' Zoe got up. 'Drop me off near the house.'

'What about tomorrow night?'

Zoe didn't reply for a few seconds and then shook her head. Her chat with Paul had done nothing to help. It wasn't going to help her get a decent night's sleep. Ever since their stupid camping escapade she hadn't slept throughout the night. Nightmares had occasionally kept her awake and at other times she had simply lain in bed staring at the ceiling.

Things had to change.

Chapter 33

Drake arrived early at headquarters the following morning. He had made satisfactory progress with the sudoku puzzle in the newspaper, and it lay folded on top of a cupboard in Drake's office. While the computer booted up, he adjusted the photographs of his daughters on the desk near the phone. They were supposed to be staying with him the forthcoming weekend and he tried to put to one corner of his mind the possibility that the demands of the inquiry would make it impossible. Annie had already made tentative plans and she had persuaded Drake that he needed to take them both to visit his mother, who wanted to share with her granddaughters the details about her marriage.

He had barely sat down when a civilian from the administration department rapped his knuckles on the door to his office. Drake waved him in. The man had a big head on a long thin neck and hair parted in the middle, which gave him a rather incongruous appearance.

'We've had dozens of people contact us after the appeal for witnesses that you made last evening.'

'Good,' Drake replied.

'When I mean dozens, I think there were over 200.'

'That many.'

'And we simply don't have the resources to be able to manage those sorts of calls. Your team will have to take over fielding any responses.'

'No chance,' Drake said, sensing his temper rising. 'The officers on my team will do the detective work. If you need more resources to manage the work then talk to Superintendent Hobbs.' Drake stared at the man willing him to defy him. Then he added. 'Did the call handlers find anything of value? Any useful intelligence?'

'A woman who claimed to be a medium offered her help, believing she had already received a message from Jason Ackroyd. And there was the usual collection of crackpots and lunatics who thought they'd seen people leaving the scene with bloody knives and axes.'

'Some people watch too much television.'

'Not the sort of television I watch. One of the call handlers took a call from the same mobile on two occasions. But nobody spoke. Reminds me of a case a few years ago of a pervert who called. He'd make certain of speaking to a woman call handler and begin making lewd comments and heavy breathing.' It brought a grin to the civilian's face.

'Send me the details that you've got. But it doesn't sound as though there's anything valuable for us to work on.'

'I'll let you decide.'

Once the civilian had left, Drake sat back and wondered if the two nocturnal visitors to the field near Porth Padrig had seen the news broadcast and his direct appeal to the camera. They'd keep the phone line open of course and he took a moment to compose an email to Superintendent Hobbs. It congratulated his superior officer on the introduction of the dedicated helpline and that preliminary feedback had been positive from the press conference.

Hobbs would have difficulty resisting a request for more resources. It occurred to Drake that it might even be an option to organise a second press conference to announce that an unknown caller had left vital information, but it was incomplete. The caller would be invited to make contact again.

Once Sara and the rest of the team had arrived in the Incident Room, Drake joined them keen to get on with reviewing progress. He stood by the board, staring at his team.

'I've already had the preliminary feedback from the admin team about the response from the public to our appeal for assistance. Identify anybody who lives in the Cemaes area or anywhere near to Norma Ellston. And don't waste time on any of the usual nutters who called in.'

He nodded at Luned. 'Did you make any progress with

Grant and Norma Ellston's families?'

The young detective straightened in her chair, cleared her throat and announced in the measured, thoughtful tone typical of her, 'Bill Grant has massive financial problems arising from a failed business venture with his sister. And they've inherited a house on Anglesey after the passing of their mother. It's on the market.'

'That puts a new light on Bill Grant,' Drake said.

'And a few of the martial arts group have minor convictions – from their teenage years mostly – although a Jasper Heath has convictions for more serious assaults. And he's ex-military.'

'Really? Get more background on him. And Norma's family?'

'I was able to eventually track down her brother. He doesn't live on the south coast any longer. He moved to Sittingbourne in Kent. He's a project manager for a building company, and he last saw his sister about four years ago. They fell out over an inheritance.'

'Typical bloody families,' Winder added.

Luned ignored him and continued. 'When he was staying with her, he said she had visitors late at night. Young men calling at the house – he found the whole thing rather odd.'

Winder piped up. 'It matches what I was told by a resident of the village near where Ellston lived and also by the landlord of the pub. Everybody knew her and he thought something wasn't right with her.'

'I think I know what that might be boss,' Luned announced. 'I had this email from a sergeant I know in the squad investigating drug offences. Sam Chandler is definitely known to them, and Norma Ellston is associated with him. A couple of the officers in the team have been attending the car boot sale where she was a regular.'

'Get him to send us a briefing memorandum on Chandler and Ellston. We need to get to the bottom of any connection to drugs,' Drake said. 'And still no sign of Sam Chandler?'

'Nothing yet, sir,' Sara said. 'The West Mercia police had a sighting, but it came to nothing and a man meeting his description was taken off the Fishguard ferry this morning. It wasn't Chandler and the man was furious.'

Drake turned back to the board and looked over at the image of the Haddock brothers and then at Chandler and Mrs Ackroyd. Bill Grant was the last to get his attention. 'I want full triangulation searches done on the mobile numbers we have for all our main persons of interest. Whoever was responsible may have been using a burner but there's a good chance they slipped up and used their own mobile.'

Sara's mobile rang but Drake continued. 'And we have an eyewitness who saw two people in the van parked near the junction down to the car park by the church. Check out all the ANPR.'

'Yes, boss,' Luned said.

'You won't believe this, sir. Mrs Ackroyd is on her way here.'

'What! Where the hell has she been? And why the hell has she turned up now?'

'Reception didn't say.'

Vicky Ackroyd's aromatic perfume filled the small conference room next to reception. Drake smelled citrus and lime. Her hair had recently been styled and nothing of her demeanour or the look in her eyes suggested she was a grieving widow.

Her teeth sparkled as she smiled. Drake sat down; Sara did the same, opening a notebook in front of her on the desk.

'We've been trying to contact you,' Drake said, his eyes hard.

'What's the big fuss about?'

Drake thought about counting to five to curb his anger but in the end didn't bother. 'I'll tell you what's the matter.

We are in the middle of a murder inquiry. A murder inquiry into your late husband's death. Where the hell have you been? We've been trying to reach you for days.'

'I've been away.'

'Is Mr Sam Chandler with you?'

'No of course he isn't.'

'Where have you been?'

'Well, if you must know I was with some girlfriends on a spa weekend. It had been booked months ago and it was very expensive.'

Sara and Drake exchanged a look of desperation. This woman had recently lost her husband and now she had spent a weekend away with friends.

'But your husband was only murdered last week.' Drake couldn't hide his astonishment.

Vicky Ackroyd looked bewildered.

'How would you describe your relationship with Mr Sam Chandler?'

'Am I under arrest? Do I need a lawyer?'

'You are not under arrest.' Drake was sorely tempted to add 'yet'. 'Please answer my question.'

Now Vicky Ackroyd squirmed slightly in her chair, beginning to look uncomfortable.

'I suppose there's no secret to it. I've been seeing Sam for a while.'

She threaded the fingers of both hands together tightly.

'And have you been giving him money?'

Ackroyd's eyes opened wide. 'Who told you? I mean yes, I've given him some cash. It was to help with his business.'

'The business is closed,' Sara said. 'An officer visited and spoke to some of his staff who were pretty disgruntled by all accounts. And his house is empty.'

Ackroyd frowned. 'We don't live in each other's pockets.'

'What were your long-term plans for your relationship

with Mr Chandler?' Drake said.

'I don't know...' Ackroyd stumbled. 'I don't know that we had any long-term plans.'

'Are you aware of the extent of his financial problems?'

A sick, worried look crept over Ackroyd's face. 'We were just having a fling. There is nothing serious about it. He said he'd pay me back the money. Jason was seeing someone else too. He bragged about it all over the place.' She spat out the final sentence. 'So it wasn't just me.'

'On the night of your husband's murder I need you to tell me exactly where you were.'

'I've told you. I've got nothing to hide. I was with my friends. I didn't kill Jason if that's what you're trying to suggest.'

'It's my job to investigate, Mrs Ackroyd. You're making it difficult. I can continue this conversation with you formally in the area custody suite, as failing to cooperate would certainly justify arresting you here and now. The duty solicitor would be called and,' Drake glanced at his watch theatrically, 'you'd probably be lucky to be out of a police cell before midnight.'

Ackroyd pouted. 'I didn't kill Jason.' She paused again. 'After I left the restaurant, I met with Sam. I was at his place all night and I didn't leave until the morning.'

'Did you leave his house at all?'

'No.' She looked away.

'Did Sam leave the house?'

'I don't know... I mean no, of course.'

'What do you mean you don't know?'

'That's not what I said.'

'Yes, it was.'

'No, I meant that I was asleep after... you know... and in the morning he was still in bed.'

'So, it's possible he could have left in the middle of the night?'

'No... no it's not possible. I'm a light sleeper, and I

would have heard him.'

'Do you use drugs Mrs Ackroyd?'

Her shock looked genuine enough. 'I don't know how you could suggest such a thing. I hate drugs.'

'Does Sam use drugs?'

She didn't reply.

'I'm not investigating drug offences and recreational use isn't something we'd be looking to prosecute. But someone who supplies and sells drugs is another matter.'

'Sam wouldn't do that.' Vicky swallowed nervously and averted her gaze again.

'Do you have a mobile number other than the one we tried over the weekend?'

She shook her head.

'And does Sam have other mobiles.'

Now her head shaking was more intense and nervous.

'With Jason out of the way do you think you'll get together with Sam?'

Shock and despair and surprise rippled over her face. She got up. 'I think I need to speak to my solicitor before I answer any more questions.'

Drake and Sara watched her leave headquarters.

'She was right about one thing,' Sara said. 'She needs a solicitor.'

'We need a full triangulation search done on her mobile and any number we know for Chandler. It's possible he got up in the middle of the night to dispose of Ackroyd. It gives him an easy run at Vicky's money.'

'He's probably got a burner phone.'

Drake nodded. Everything now justified a search warrant of Chandler's home.

Superintendent Hobbs read and reread the latest update from Inspector Drake, his mind convinced that his junior officer wasn't paying enough attention to the Haddock brothers. They had the perfect motive and there was even evidence that one of their vehicles had been in the village where Ackroyd lived on the night he was killed. The evidence from the employee who suggested he had been driving was challengeable and any decent barrister would tear the witness to pieces. But was it enough, knowing what the Haddock brothers were like? Hobbs needed to reinforce to Inspector Drake that he had to prioritise them as suspects. And tracing the campers was the best way to achieve that.

He was going to be properly prepared before the meeting with Drake, Tony Parry and Andy Thorsen. He liked to be able to share details that others couldn't possibly be aware of. It gave him a feeling of dominance. After all, he was the superintendent, and the case was high profile enough to justify regular attention. Andy Thorsen had already sent him a full memorandum with a summary of the advice from the King's Counsel. It didn't make for positive reading. It pleased Hobbs that the update from Tony Parry had used the template he had devised for senior officers to use when reporting. Drake could veer away from using the right format occasionally, which irked Hobbs.

He knew what all the others would say in the meeting, which gave him a superiority he thrived on. He finished in good time but reread the summaries once again. He lived for policing. Lived for the buzz his status gave him. And outside headquarters his life was limited to the occasional meal out with his wife and some close friends. He would never admit to himself that he had become distant from his family and utterly absorbed with his job and the legacy he hoped to leave.

Thorsen was the first to arrive and he sat down at the conference table.

'I take it you've read the memorandum and the advice from the Kings Counsel?'

'Yes,' Hobbs said. 'Her advice and comments were most articulate.'

'She is very well thought of and she's probably going to

be lined up for a judgeship in the next few years.'

Hobbs' secretary entered and announced that Drake and Parry had arrived.

Both officers entered and after the usual exchange of courtesies sat down.

'I'll let Andy summarise the advice from the KC.'

Thorsen ran through the advice for both officers. Parry got more and more agitated as Thorsen continued to outline that the case against the Haddock brothers would likely fail. 'We cannot simply give in. Throw in the towel,' Parry said.

'Please don't interrupt, Tony,' Thorsen scolded him.

It took another few minutes before he finished.

'So she's basically saying we haven't got a snowball's chance in hell.' Parry had slumped back in his chair, his voice filled with gloom.

'Is it really that bad?' Drake said. 'Juries can be fickle.'

Thorsen nodded. 'It barely scrapes over the threshold to justify a prosecution so… is it in the public interest?'

'Of course it fucking is.' Parry sounded angry.

'We shall proceed with the case against both men and we'll let the jury decide.' Thorsen turned to Drake. 'Have you been making progress on the Ackroyd case?'

Drake nodded. 'We are still trying to trace the campers seen in the field the day before the murder. The news outlets have run an appeal asking for anyone camping in that area to come forward and uniformed officers will be doing enquiries in the village about the green tent and two young campers.'

Drake's mobile in front of him bleeped with a message and he read the text from Mike Foulds. *DNA from condom has a familial trace to a man in Barrow in Furness.*

'Anything else you'd like to share Inspector Drake?' Hobbs said.

'There's a link to someone in Barrow in Furness.'

'Who the bloody hell lives up there?' Parry said.

Chapter 34

After paying for two coffees and a Danish pastry for himself and a bacon sandwich for Sara, Drake sat at a table by a window of the café at the motorway services. The satnav had told them the journey to Barrow in Furness would take three hours and eighteen minutes. Drake had an address and a name – John Seddon. He had read the report from the DNA result the previous evening several times reminding himself of the confident clear terms used. The 'probability of parentage' was 99.99% that John Seddon was the father of the man whose semen had been found in the condom. DNA hadn't been recovered from outside the condom.

'What was the result of the case review with the superintendent yesterday afternoon?' Sara said.

Drake guessed she had waited to ask, knowing he wouldn't have been talkative while driving.

'The advice from the King's Counsel is very negative. She reckons the case against the Haddock brothers barely gets over the threshold to justify a prosecution.'

Sara was chewing on the first mouthful of her sandwich, nodding as she did so. She would know the prosecution would want any case to have a reasonable chance of success to justify proceeding. And when the case had initially been assembled there was more than enough to ensure a reasonable chance of both brothers being convicted and receiving substantial custodial sentences. Now things weren't that clear.

Drake continued. 'Jason Ackroyd and Norma Ellston's evidence formed an important part of the prosecution case. Tony Parry is furious.'

'Nothing he can do about it,' Sara said reaching for her coffee.

Drake took a mouthful of his coffee. It was stronger and cleaner than he expected. The pastry was stodgy and sweet but it had the desired effect of invigorating him. It would probably be another hour until they reached Barrow in

Furness and most of the journey would be away from the motorway. It had never been a part of the world that Drake had visited, and a brief Google search the evening before told him that Barrow was famous for its shipbuilding expertise. He wondered about John Seddon. All he had so far was a name. He needed to build a complete picture of the man, find out exactly what he knew about his son – the man who might well have crucial evidence to assist the inquiry.

'We should get going,' Drake said, finishing the last of his coffee.

They returned to the car and Drake headed north, taking the junction off the motorway as directed by the satnav. The signs were clear enough and Drake's journey slowed as he took the road through the southern part of the Lake District. His parents had stayed a couple of times in the prettier parts near the touristy spots but he doubted they had ventured south towards Barrow.

Nearing the town, he saw the enormous, enclosed steel structure of the shipbuilding company dominating the skyline above the town. Leading down towards the centre were rows and rows of terraced properties.

Planned improvements by the local authority leading down into the middle of the town had clearly not caught up with the satnav system. Drake took a wrong turn on several occasions, finding himself at dead ends the satnav believed would be through roads. Eventually the voice directed Drake to take a left turn and although his patience was running out, he noticed the sign for Beachcroft Avenue screwed to the boundary wall of the property. The houses were a collection of semi-detached and detached homes that looked to be smarter than the terraces crowded together near the middle of the town.

Drake parked outside number five. 'Let's go and introduce ourselves to Mr Seddon, if he's at home.'

Three shallow steps led up to the main door and Drake pressed the doorbell, noticing the video camera attached to it. He heard music from inside – radio probably, Drake thought. Then he heard movement and the door was opened by a tall, thin woman. She had a mop of thick curly greying hair. It was difficult to tell her age: mid-forties, at a guess.

'We'd like to see Mr Seddon,' Drake said.

The woman frowned. 'I'm his wife – who are you?'

'It's a personal matter. Is Mr Seddon home?'

'He's at work. Who are you?'

The apprehension in Mrs Seddon's voice left Drake with no alternative. He found his warrant card in his pocket. 'My name is Detective Inspector Drake and this is my colleague Detective Sergeant Sara Morgan of the Wales Police Service. Your husband is not in any trouble at all but we'd like to speak to him about an ongoing inquiry we have. Again, Mrs Seddon, I want to reassure you your husband is not in any trouble.'

Drake wasn't certain from the look on her face whether he had succeeded in putting her mind at ease. She shared a look between Drake and Sara as though she were struggling to compute what Drake had just said.

'He's at work,' she repeated, as though she could think of nothing else to say.

'We'll need the address, Mrs Seddon,' Drake said more firmly.

Sara took the initiative. 'Mrs Seddon, it is really important we speak to your husband. Can you let us know where he works?'

Mrs Seddon stared at Sara for a moment and then shared with them the name of the company and the address where her husband worked. Drake turned to leave but Mrs Seddon added, 'You won't find your way there easily. I'll come with you.'

Following her convoluted directions Drake realised the satnav would never have found the premises in good time.

The sign above the door said 'Maskell and Maskell Engineering Excellence'. Drake pushed open the door and headed for reception, following the signs. He didn't expect the modern plush minimalist feel to the offices, judging by the external appearance of the building. The atrium had several expensive, well-fed pot plants and leather sofas. A woman sitting behind the reception desk gave them a professional smile.

'I'd like to speak to Mr John Seddon.'

'And your name?'

Drake flashed his warrant card. 'Detective Inspector Ian Drake of the Wales Police Service.' The formality of his rank and title did the trick she scooped up the phone, tracked down John Seddon and announced. 'He'll be with you shortly.'

Drake and Sara stood by reception having encouraged Mrs Seddon to sit on one of the swanky sofas. John Seddon emerged from a door in reception and marched over towards Drake and Sara. 'What the hell is this about?'

Then he noticed his wife sitting. He raised an arm towards her and started walking in her direction away from Drake and Sara. Drake intervened. 'We need a few moments of your time. It's a matter of some importance. We've told Mrs Seddon to wait.' Drake turned to the receptionist. 'Can you organise some coffee or tea?' Drake smiled.

She nodded briskly.

Seddon led them through to a small, windowless conference room filled with a table and some wooden chairs.

'I'm the senior investigating officer in the murder of Jason Ackroyd.'

'Wow! Murder? I can't believe this is happening.'

'Calm down, Mr Seddon. As I made clear to your wife you're not involved in any way.'

'So, what the hell are you doing here?'

'We have recovered a fragment of DNA in the inquiry that is linked to you.'

'Don't be mad, this is crazy.'

'A used condom was recovered near to the scene of the

murder. The semen provided a DNA sample we have compared against the national DNA database. As you were convicted of a common assault twenty years ago your DNA is on the database and the sample we recovered has a high probability of a link to you.'

Drake could see incredulity in Seddon's eyes.

'It's a mistake,' Seddon chuckled.

'In our experience these DNA results are extremely reliable. And there is a 99.99% chance that the man who used the condom is your son, Mr Seddon.'

Astonishment made Seddon's mouth fall open, then his eyes opened wide. He began to gasp like a grounded fish.

'Do you have any connection at all with Anglesey or North Wales?'

'None, none,' then he paused. 'I... I... worked at the nuclear power plant years ago. I mean it's twenty plus years. I'm an electrical engineer and the company I was with at the time had a contract for repair and maintenance there.'

'How long were you there?'

Seddon placed his head on hands steepled on the table in front of him.

'Six months. There was this girl...'

'Did you have a relationship?'

Seddon nodded.

'What was her name?'

Seddon looked up at Drake. 'Bev.'

'And a surname?'

Now he shook his head. 'I can't remember. Can't even remember what she looks like.'

'Was she local?' Sara said. 'I mean did she have any family in the local area.'

Seddon frowned again. 'It's over twenty years ago. She didn't tell me anything about being pregnant. Jesus, what will I tell my wife?'

The truth, Drake thought.

Sara opened her notebook. 'We'll need all the details

you can remember. Friends and addresses of anybody at the time that you can recall. We urgently need to trace Bev and her son.'

Seddon's memory was sketchy. His face looked pained at the effort to recall the details of this encounter. The company had rented a bungalow, but he couldn't remember the name of the village or the address. Drinking in the local pubs had been the highlight of their social life and that was where he had met Bev. He couldn't even remember whether she had sounded Welsh. There was another engineer whose name he could remember who had shared the bungalow with him but he'd died in a motorcycle accident a few years ago.

'All I can remember is the name of one guy who worked at the plant. He was a larger-than-life character. He smoked these small cigars. He seemed to have a permanent tan'.

'What was his name?'

'We called him Spanish Dave.'

Chapter 35

Luned had most of the day to trawl through the results of the triangulation on the mobiles of the various persons of interest. Criminals had a habit of believing they were above the law, somehow insulated from the normal day-to-day disciplines the rest of the world takes for granted. The clever crooks never used traceable mobiles. They relied on burner phones, which they'd change regularly.

She started with the mobile numbers of the Haddock brothers. She had read the case summary prepared by the detective inspector leading the team prosecuting both men. There was no question in her mind that both men should be locked up for a long time. And it was her job as part of Detective Inspector Drake's team to find the evidence. Both Haddock brothers had the perfect motive and were capable of murder.

The triangulation system could be imperfect, but it was the best they had and with Anglesey being so flat there weren't any mountains, or even hills, to confuse the system.

She checked and rechecked the reports, but she found no evidence that either of the Haddock brothers had been in the Cemaes area on the day Jason Ackroyd was killed. She began to build a spreadsheet of where both men had been and it was a confusing picture. She guessed most of the activity was work-related. They would be moving from one building site to another or visiting prospective jobs. But more than anything, she knew both men could have been using an untraceable burner phone.

The search results for the area around Norma Ellston's home was more fruitful. Both Haddock brothers' mobiles were regular visitors to the nearby village and the surrounding area. Having a scaffolding company offered the perfect cover, Luned concluded. They could easily explain a visit to any area as associated with their business – on the way to see a job or returning from visiting a prospective customer. Luned began preparing a memorandum for

Inspector Drake. At least he could use it as the basis of a further interview. Their best hope would be to unearth some direct evidence to link the Haddock brothers to Jason Ackroyd's and Norma Ellston's murders.

She sat back in her chair and looked over at Gareth Winder who was staring at his monitor. 'Any luck with identifying that van the witness at the hotel noticed?'

Winder blew out a mouthful of air and announced in an exasperated tone. 'I can't see any van approaching on the main road for two hours before the time of Ackroyd's death. But there are so many side roads and junctions. It makes me think the driver was local and that he knew how to get to that location avoiding CCTV cameras.'

'And afterwards?'

'Same. It is like looking for a needle in a haystack.'

'Have you had the ANPR results for Mrs Ackroyd's Range Rover Evoque?'

Winder tipped his head at the monitor. 'Next on my list.'

Luned got back to work. She glanced over at the board and decided to focus on Bill Grant. His wife had been having an affair with Jason Ackroyd, but from the summary of the interviews with Grant he had forgiven her, and the relationship had ended. But could jealousy really be extinguished? She gazed at his face wondering if she was looking at the face of the killer. He had an important role in the court service and no history of any violence or anything to suggest his involvement in such a crime. Luned knew Inspector Drake would want to make certain every person of interest was thoroughly investigated.

Nothing in the triangulation results suggested Bill Grant visited the village of Cemaes or any of the other towns and villages on the northern side of Anglesey. It did surprise her when his mobile was recorded as being in the vicinity of Norma Ellston's home. There were two occasions, one midweek and the other at a weekend, and Luned pondered for a moment if there might be some legitimate explanation. Somebody would have to ask him.

The triangulation reports on Sam Chandler and Vicky Ackroyd's mobiles were much easier to interpret. Her mobile had been switched off early in the evening of Jason Ackroyd's death, as had Sam Chandler's. And on the day Norma Ellston was killed both numbers were at their respective owners' homes. No movement – they'd stayed put.

Winder organised drinks mid-morning and Luned walked through into the kitchen with him, pleased for the opportunity to stretch her legs. Coffee and tea made, they returned to the Incident Room.

It was nearly lunchtime when Winder raised his voice and waved a hand at Luned. 'Come here – you need to see this.'

She left her desk and dragged her chair to sit alongside him.

'What have you found, Gareth?'

'The ANPR cameras picked up Mrs Ackroyd driving into the middle of Llangefni at about one o'clock in the morning. A set of ANPR cameras monitoring traffic for the bridge picked her up when she crossed over to the mainland half an hour later.'

'What was she doing in the middle of the night?'

'Someone has to ask her.'

After spending six hours in the car, Drake pulled into the car park of Northern Division headquarters. He got out of the car and stretched his aching back. He regretted not taking Sara up on her offer to share the driving.

Sara had spoken to Winder on their return journey, warning him and Luned to wait until they returned. He shook off his jaded feeling and picked up the pace as he walked over towards reception. Winder and Luned looked up from their desks as he entered the Incident Room, followed by

Sara.

Drake walked straight to the Incident Room board. He had had quite enough of sitting down for one day, so he stood before pointing at the photograph of the field adjacent to the coastal footpath at Porth Padrig.

'We've spoken with John Seddon this morning. He had a brief relationship with a woman called Bev about twenty years ago when he was working as an engineer at the Wylfa power plant. He was shocked when we told him his son was responsible for the semen in the condom discovered in the hedge. So we'll need to identify and find this Bev woman.'

'Is that all, boss?' Winder said.

A troubled look dominated Luned's face.

Winder continued. 'There must be dozens of Beverleys, it's a very common name.'

'We cannot take the risk that they do *not* have valuable evidence.'

Winder and Luned nodded. Sara had heard the arguments rehearsed during the journey back from Barrow in Furness.

'And John Seddon gave us the name of a man called Spanish Dave.'

'Spanish Dave, the hell does that mean?' Winder said. 'Is he Spanish?'

'That was his nickname,' Drake said firmly. 'We've got no more information. Tomorrow morning, I want both of you in the Cemaes area. I want enquiries made with pubs, shops and cafés about this man and we've got a photograph of John Seddon from twenty years ago – get that circulated. I'll organise for a team of uniformed officers to help you. We need to find this Beverley.'

Sara turned to Winder and Luned. 'How did you get on today?'

Luned was the first to reply. 'Not much on the triangulation reports results. We can place the Haddock brothers near Norma Ellston's home regularly. And Bill

Grant visited the area at least twice recently too.'

'Good, send me the details.'

'And we need to pay more attention to Mrs Ackroyd,' Winder announced. 'I've managed to pick her up on ANPR cameras. On the night of Ellston's murder she was caught travelling through Llangefni and then on to Bangor between one and two in the morning.'

'That could be from the direction of Ellston's property,' Drake said.

The team in front of him collectively nodded, realising that there was more work to do on this tomorrow. The mobile in Drake's jacket pocket rang and he fished it out.

'Detective Inspector Drake?'

'Yes, who is this?'

'It's the Dover Harbour Police here. We have arrested a Sam Chandler. I understand that you have an interest in him.'

Chapter 36

It was after eight pm when Drake parked in the driveway of his home. It had been a long day. At least the final leg of his journey was brief compared to the hours he had already spent in the car.

'You look tired,' Annie said after he kissed her. They stood for a moment in the hallway, and he pulled her close, pleased to be home. 'Do you have another early start tomorrow?'

He shook his head. 'I'll be on Anglesey tomorrow. All local, none of this motorway driving.'

'Was it worth the trip?'

Annie would never ask for details; she knew how difficult it was for him to share anything about an investigation. But she was supportive and always willing to be sympathetic when he wanted to complain when things weren't going well. They made their way upstairs to the sitting room-cum-kitchen on the first floor.

Drake pulled a bottle of beer from the fridge and cracked it open. He sat by the kitchen table as Annie reheated the chicken stew and mashed potatoes she had prepared earlier. They had this understanding that Drake could never be relied on to be home at a given time, so Annie frequently ate alone. She was never one to harbour resentment and accepted that his work as a detective made unreasonable demands on family life.

'Your mother called this afternoon. She wants to discuss the final arrangements for the ceremony.'

Drake took a long mouthful. The cold lager felt refreshing against his parched mouth and he sensed the alcohol working its magic on his senses.

'Have you reminded the superintendent that you're not going to be available a week on Saturday?'

'No, not yet. But he has had a formal memo from me after my conversation with him.'

'Is that going to be enough for him to remember? And

you need to warn Sara.'

Drake nodded; it was another thing he'd forgotten to do. It had slipped his mind, as family things so often did in the middle of an inquiry.

'I'll remind you again in the morning.' Annie smiled, aware that by not answering he had admitted his failure to warn his sergeant.

By the time he had finished his meal and quenched his thirst with a second bottle of lager he began to feel the waves of tiredness sweeping over him. He sat in front of the television watching the ten o'clock news but when he felt an elbow in his side he realised he had to get to bed.

The last thing he thought of as his head hit the pillow was Spanish Dave.

Drake pulled into the parking slot marked 'Reserved Visitors' outside the main administration building for the Wylfa nuclear power station. Signs on the way in made quite clear the plant was under the supervision and responsibility of the decommissioning body. Electricity generation had ceased several years ago but there were people still employed there and Drake hoped there would be somebody associated with the previous management who could assist.

He jumped out of the car, Sara following, and he checked there was a signal on his mobile. He had already messaged Winder, reminding him that if he found anything to establish Spanish Dave's identity he had to text him immediately.

Interviewing Bill Grant and executing the search warrant of Chandler's property would have to wait until later in the day. Officers were en route to collect Sam Chandler from Dover. He would be interviewed later. It was going to be another busy day.

Entering reception, Drake scanned the noticeboards covered with statistics about progress with the decommissioning. Older-looking information displays had a summary of the history of the power plant. It had been built in the 1960s and had operated beyond its anticipated lifespan. There had been controversy about a possible replacement and various companies – Drake recalled from the television news – had hoped to build a new plant to take advantage of the existing site and workforce. So far nothing had come of it and Drake wondered if any of the original employees were still around.

A woman sat behind a desk at the far end of the entrance lobby answering the phone with a standard bilingual welcome message. She finished the call and turned to Drake.

'*Bore da*, good morning, how can I help?'

Drake produced his warrant card. She studied it carefully.

'I'd like to speak to somebody in HR. Is there a personnel manager? I'm looking for a man who may have worked here years ago.'

The woman frowned. 'Give me a moment.'

She dialled a number on the phone, and asked if a man called Mark was available. Then she enquired after an Abbie before finally having a constructive conversation with an unnamed individual. 'I'll tell him you'll be five minutes.'

She turned to look at Drake. 'You're lucky Mr Agnew is here; he worked once in the actual nuclear power plant. He might be able to help you.'

Drake sat down on a hard plastic visitor chair with Sara alongside him. He texted Winder – the reply was instantaneous – *no luck so far*. Sara messaged Luned, who was with another team of uniformed officers. She looked up and shook her head at Drake.

After a few moments, a man entered reception and looked over at Drake. He paced over. Drake couldn't make out the name from the lanyard hanging from his neck. He stretched out a hand.

'Tom Agnew.' Agnew had striking red hair and one eye

that looked slightly out of balance with the other, which made anyone meeting him uncertain which eye to look into.

'I'm Detective Inspector Drake and this is my colleague Detective Sergeant Sara Morgan. We are leading the team investigating the murder of a Jason Ackroyd.'

'I've heard about it, of course. How can I help?'

'We need information about former employees of the power plant.'

Agnew raised his eyebrows. 'That might be tricky. You'd better come to my office.' Drake got straight to the point once he'd sat down, asking directly about Seddon and the contracting company he had worked for.

Agnew looked blank eventually suggesting, 'One of the managers at the time did move to one of the other nuclear reactor plants in England. She is called Gwen Watkins. She might be able to recall other members of staff who might help you. She might even remember someone called Spanish Dave, but there were hundreds of people employed at the time.'

'Thank you, if you could give me the number of where I can contact Gwen Watkins that will be very helpful.' Years of policing and instinct had told Drake that establishing the identity of the condom user was crucial. He had camped with his girlfriend and then left very early. It was an isolated location – not a regular campsite, which meant they were probably locals. Drake was convinced they had valuable evidence.

Sara jotted down the contact number for the plant at which Gwen Watkins worked.

As they stood up to leave Agnew added, 'There is one person you might talk to. He was a bit of a fixer. He knew how to get things done in the department where John Seddon would have worked.'

'What was his name?'

'Colin Chant.' Agnew clicked into his computer. 'He might still be on the system.'

Moments later he smiled at Drake and Sara. 'You're in luck.' He dictated a number Sara jotted into her pocketbook.

'Unless there's anything else, Detective Inspector.'

'No, thank you, you've been very helpful and if someone does happen to know who Spanish Dave is, please contact me.'

Chapter 37

By mid-morning Winder had visited all the shops in Cemaes, with uniformed officers, clutching a photograph of John Seddon which he had pushed under the nose of every assistant and owner. Without exception there had been shakes of the head and incredulity when he had asked about Spanish Dave.

It had been twenty years since John Seddon had worked at the power plant and they were asking if anyone could remember him, even though he had only been working there for a few months. Winder recognised that, although Seddon was the father of the man who had been camping in the field near the cliff, it was going to be difficult jogging memories. And Inspector Drake would have to make a public appeal for Spanish Dave to come forward. After all he wasn't a suspect but Winder realised the killer or killers might well know Spanish Dave's identity. And if, as he suspected, the Haddock brothers were responsible, they'd do anything to stop the witness helping the inquiry. And that would be the last thing Inspector Drake would want.

So Winder persevered, sending some of the uniformed officers with him to the pub over the bridge and then on towards a dental practice and a doctor's surgery. Patient confidentiality meant records couldn't be disclosed, but there might be reception staff who had been there for years, people embedded in the community, who might have heard of Spanish Dave.

Winder turned his attention to the other pubs in the village. A regular sitting at a stool near the bar, with flaccid leathery skin and tired eyes and sporting a long beard, looked over at Winder. Winder joined him and, as he waited for the landlord to appear, he engaged the man. He was about the right age after all.

'Have you ever heard of a man called Spanish Dave?'

The man looked up at Winder. 'Are you the police?'

'I'm part of the team investigating the Jason Ackroyd

killing.'

The man shook his head slowly.

Winder produced the image of John Seddon and passed it along the bar. 'Do you remember this man?'

He gave it a long stare. 'What's he done?'

'Nothing, but twenty years ago he worked at Wylfa with a man called Spanish Dave.'

A shaking hand reached out for the pint glass and he took a mouthful. 'Have you tried the pubs in Amlwch?'

Winder nodded. A man with a tight-fitting shirt straining at the size of his paunch appeared behind the bar. He frowned at Winder. 'You all right, mate?'

Now Winder fished out his warrant card and pushed it in the direction of the landlord. Then he pushed over John Seddon's photograph. 'This man is called John Seddon and he was working at Wylfa over twenty years ago. Any chance you remember him?'

'I've only been running this place for the last five years.' The landlord chuckled. 'I wouldn't have a clue.'

'And have you heard of a man called Spanish Dave? Before you ask, he's not Spanish.'

For a brief second a glimmer of recognition passed over the man's face. 'Is he in any trouble?'

'No, we just want to speak to him. Do you know him?'

'I can't say I do, but the name sort of rings a bell. I'll ask around.'

'And have you heard of anyone camping around the fields locally. Maybe they came in for a meal, you know, or somewhere to keep warm.'

'There have been uniformed officers asking the same and I told them the same. I have had no campers in here.'

Winder left him a card with his mobile number and repeated that Spanish Dave wasn't in any trouble.

Buoyed up by the possibility the landlord of the pub recognised the name they were looking for encouraged Winder to believe he could be found. Inspector Drake might well be vindicated, Winder concluded. He stood on the main street of the village, contemplating whether he could treat himself to a pastry at the bakery he'd visited early in the inquiry, when a message reached his mobile.

The inspector wanted to meet. Then he noticed the second message from Inspector Drake and realised he was needed urgently. Winder jogged back to his car and headed for the police station in Amlwch.

Drake had requisitioned one of the small spare offices in the police station. It had been built in the last century, pre-Second World War at a guess, and it was probably only a matter of time before it closed. There was even a closed magistrate's court building attached to it.

Luned had arrived promptly, and Drake barely contained his irritation at the fact Winder still hadn't turned up despite his requests by two texts. Sara had been able to track down the Colin Chant who had previously been employed at the power plant but, as yet, hadn't been able to speak to Gwen Watkins, despite her mobile being pinned to her ear for the last ten minutes.

A car drew up outside and seconds later Winder burst into the room. 'Sorry, boss, I only just got your messages. I was talking with a publican.'

'Bit early isn't it, Gareth?' Sara smirked.

'He was helpful, he thought he might have heard of Spanish Dave.'

Drake turned to Luned. 'Let's have a summary of what you've done this morning.'

Luned opened her notebook and cleared her throat. 'I haven't spoken to anyone who remembers John Seddon.'

Drake nodded. 'That was always a long shot. He was only here for a few months.'

'And nobody had heard of anybody called Spanish Dave. I've left all the contact details with cafés and shops and uniform lads are going round all the pubs and some of the bed-and-breakfast places. I don't think it's very hopeful.'

Drake didn't want to sense any degree of criticism in her last comments. But tracking down Spanish Dave was going to be difficult.

'We're going to go back to headquarters and en route we're going to speak to Colin Chant. Sara and I will do the interview with Sam Chandler once he's back from Dover and I've got a couple of uniformed officers going to invite Vicky Ackroyd in for an interview too. There's no way she could have got hold of Sam Chandler once he was arrested in Dover. There must be other caravan parks, camping sites and pubs outside the towns and villages you can speak to. Get some of the local constables to tell you the best locations to try.'

'Yes, boss,' three voices said, almost in unison.

Drake clenched a fist and banged it on the table. 'We need to find this man.'

Half an hour later Drake indicated into the drive of an arts and crafts home from the 1920s. Sara had just finished on her mobile, disappointed that she had still not been able to track down Gwen Watkins. Drake had become utterly single-minded about tracking down Spanish Dave. Sara had tried to dispel from her mind the possibility it had distracted him. But he had already announced they would visit Bill Grant and supervise the execution of the search warrant at Chandler's property. She hoped by then Chandler would have reached headquarters after his journey from Dover.

It meant any interview wouldn't be started until quite late. She abandoned any hope of a run before bed.

A deeply patterned, vibrantly-coloured cravat clung around Chant's neck, which made him look like an extra from some period drama. His corduroy trousers and heavy suede brogues complemented the appearance.

'Good afternoon,' Chant announced, his voice booming, his accent cultured and very English. 'And to what do I owe the pleasure of two police officers from His Majesty's constabulary paying me a visit.'

Chant waved a hand at Drake and Sara's warrant cards and gestured them inside.

Chant called the room into which he ushered them the morning room. It was filled with furniture and decorated to match the style of the property. Sara guessed Chant had deep pockets.

Drake explained the reason for calling before they had even sat down, a clear sign he was impatient. 'I'm the senior investigating officer in charge of the inquiry into the murder of Jason Ackroyd and Norma Ellston. We need to establish the identity and speak to a man known as Spanish Dave. We believe he was employed at the Wylfa nuclear power plant.'

'How long ago was this?'

'Over twenty years.'

Chant gave Drake a questioning look.

'We've just been to the plant, and it was suggested you might be able to assist with identifying him.'

'Why do you want to talk to him?'

'All I can tell you is that it's part of the inquiry.'

'Spanish Dave,' Chant said as though repeating the name was going to jog his memory. 'I don't recall anybody with that nickname. There were hundreds of employees at one time.'

Drake didn't waste time exchanging small talk and got to his feet. 'Thank you, Mr Chant.'

Sara joined Drake as he headed out to the car and then down the drive for the main road.

'We've got to find the man who'd been camping,' Drake said, clutching the steering wheel. 'He and his girlfriend must have seen something. I'm convinced of that and they could be in danger.'

'I'll try and contact Gwen Watkins again.'

Drake nodded as he pressed the accelerator.

Chapter 38

A dark cloud was shifting ever closer to the forefront of Drake's mind as he journeyed south along the east coast of Anglesey. He wanted to dismiss the possibility the campers and possible eyewitnesses were in danger. He couldn't shake off his detective's instincts that told him he had to identify them. The obsessions that so often drove his behaviour could also make him determined and he squashed a grain of doubt developing in his thoughts.

The nocturnal visitors to the field must be local. Tourists would simply not have bothered returning to search the field in the following days. And even if he was right, why had they revisited the scene? Whenever he posed this question the answer was always the same – they were worried, concerned about something and it had to be the used condom. It even occurred to him to double check with Mike Foulds that the CSI team had done a complete search of the field and the possibility of cutting back all the hedgerows even played in his mind. Superintendent Hobbs wouldn't contemplate that expenditure, Drake decided.

A sense of impending disaster threatened to develop in his stomach at the prospect of finding two more people killed for no apparent reason. The families then interviewed on television explaining they had been camping near the cliff edge above the beach where Jason Ackroyd's body had been found. And everyone pointing the finger of blame at the police. He wasn't going to allow that to happen. He was going to find these two individuals.

He had been paying little attention to the one-sided phone conversation taking place in the car as he focused on driving. Sara appeared to be making progress with tracking down Gwen Watkins as she scribbled various names and numbers in her notebook.

'Gwen Watkins was very helpful,' Sara said, once she finished the call.

Drake indicated off the main road and followed the

satnav instructions for Sam Chandler's home.

'She thought we might be able to trace the staff of the department where John Seddon worked. She gave me some contact details for the records department for the nuclear power company who ran the plant.'

'Good, at least that's something, I suppose.'

A marked police vehicle stood stationary outside Sam Chandler's property and Drake spotted another tucked into a hardstanding area in the field opposite. He parked and a uniform sergeant emerged from the side of the cottage. He was a regular search team supervisor Drake knew.

'You keep trying to track down the identity of Spanish Dave. I'll tell the team to get on with things.'

Sara nodded. Drake left the car and joined the officer who was now in a huddle with three other uniformed constables.

'Good morning, Inspector,' the sergeant said.

'Don't delay,' Drake said. 'I need to be back in headquarters as soon as.'

The sergeant nodded at one of the junior officers clutching a red mini battering ram quaintly called 'the big red key'. They walked around the side of the property and over towards the rear door. Seconds later there was a loud thud and the crash of the splintering wood as the door caved in.

Walking around the property of a person of interest in the inquiry was entirely different from inspecting the home of a murder victim. In that case Drake always felt a sadness at a life cut short, a family left to grieve, friends nursing their loss. Trawling through the inside of Sam Chandler's home was different.

The officers began working in the bedrooms of the old cottage and Drake heard their methodical approach as they opened drawers, examined cupboards and rifled through wardrobes. He walked through into the kitchen. A composting bin sat on the worktop near the sink, its top flipped open, the contents filling the air with the noxious smell of decomposition. Discarded pizza boxes were piled in one corner as though they were being readied for recycling. But from the state of the place Drake concluded making the planet green wasn't high on Sam Chandler's priority list.

In a sitting room dominated by an enormous television and expensive-looking sound system Drake stood for a moment, the smell of second-hand cannabis playing in his nostrils. Recreational use wasn't something that troubled the Wales Police Service, but from everything they knew about Sam Chandler his involvement with drugs was more than simply personal use. Drake spent a few minutes inspecting the contents of cupboards and drawers. Then he drew a finger along the shelf of the bookcase and turned his nose up at the dust collected. The search team would open every book, examine every ornament, and even rummage through bins.

Later he'd have the opportunity of speaking to Sam Chandler. Before then he hoped the search team would turn up something of significance he could use as part of the interview. When the sergeant yelled, Drake retraced his steps to one of the bedrooms that doubled as storage-cum-office.

The sergeant dipped his head at a box he'd placed on a desk. Its Formica surface was badly chipped and Drake caught a glimpse of the mould growing inside a mug sitting at one corner. 'We found this tucked at the back of a cupboard.'

Drake snapped on a pair of latex gloves. He looked down and spotted three small mobile handsets.

'How many people have three mobiles?' the sergeant said.

'Anything else?' Drake reached a hand into the box knowing the CSI team would get to grips with examining each in due course. It suggested Sam Chandler had more than a recreational interest in drugs.

'One of the search team thinks he found drug residue on

one of the bedside tables.'

'I want everything of interest boxed up and brought back to headquarters.'

The sergeant nodded.

'Sarge, you're needed outside.' The shout came from one of the search team constables. Drake followed the sergeant out and saw another officer by the door of a shed. They walked over and Drake noticed the industrial pliers propped by the door, a padlock broken and useless on the paving slabs nearby.

'Something you should see, Sarge, Inspector,' the young officer said.

Drake didn't expect such order and neatness. For a fraction of a second it impressed him that Chandler had been so organised. Garden implements hung from a wooden rail specially designed for the purpose. A cupboard had fertilisers and plant food carefully labelled. And what impressed Drake most was the dust-free floor despite the lawnmower pushed into one corner. The young officer pointed at bags he had placed on a workbench that sat under a window. A detailed examination wasn't necessary, each bag was filled with several smaller bags filled with white dust.

'Now I wonder what Sam Chandler will have to say about these,' Drake said.

Drake still hadn't been told about progress the team were making returning Sam Chandler to Northern Division. All the officers escorting him had to do was call headquarters, for goodness sake, Drake thought, as he drove away from Chandler's home. He didn't want to start interviewing Chandler late in the evening. Some smart-arse solicitor would only complain his client needed a decent night's sleep before being interviewed.

'How did you get on with tracing Spanish Dave?' Drake

turned to Sara who was scribbling furiously in her notebook.

'No luck so far, sir. I've been chasing people who worked for the company. I've tried the central admin department. Someone even told me they thought the records might have been destroyed.'

'Damn, that's no good. Why the hell would they do that? Isn't everything digital these days?'

'Apparently not. It might take days for them to dig out the records we need. I have told them it's a matter of urgency.'

Drake thumped the steering wheel with an open palm. 'These people could be at risk. What the hell are we supposed to do?'

'I don't know that we can do any more.'

Drake nodded, conscious he was sounding desperate. 'I need to get back to headquarters so let's not take too much time talking to Bill Grant.'

Drake reached the junction for the main road skirting Anglesey and indicated left. He had to wait for traffic and found his irritation building until eventually a slot emerged and he powered the vehicle ahead.

During the journey to Bangor, Drake listened to Sara's conversations. Occasionally she sounded pleading, other times more demanding, but the conclusion was still the same – frustration at getting any information that might lead them to Spanish Dave. Drake was beginning to contemplate the only realistic option was to make a public appeal and he began drafting in his mind the form of words for a memorandum to Superintendent Hobbs.

As though he were driving on autopilot Drake took the junction of the A55 and followed the road through the outskirts of Bangor until he reached the estate where Bill Grant lived. Luckily his flexible working allowed him to work from home, which meant Drake didn't have to trouble him at his place of work.

Drake parked. Sara announced, 'Still no luck.'

Drake looked over the house. 'We haven't got much time. Let's keep this short with Grant.'

Grant opened the door and gestured for Drake and Sara to enter. They sat in the same room that they had done on the first occasion, although Mrs Grant wasn't present. And her husband didn't offer any explanation for her absence.

'You said you wanted to speak to me,'

'I'm the senior investigating officer in relation to the murder of Norma Ellston. I'm sure you've seen the reference to the tragic circumstances of her death in the news.'

Grant nodded, rather formally. 'And why on earth would you want to speak to me about her death?'

'Did you know her?'

'No.'

'Do you know where she lives?'

'No, how can I possibly know where she lives?'

'As part of our normal enquiries we've established your mobile was traced to the village and area surrounding Mrs Ellston's home.' Drake glanced at the clock on the mantelpiece – time was at a premium.

'Where is that exactly?'

Drake shared details of the village where Ellston lived.

Grant nodded as a brief flicker of recognition crossed his face. 'That's near the Llywelyn Fawr pub. The voluntary group with which I'm connected visits the community centre at the rear. We ran some sessions there. If you give me the times and dates, I can probably confirm exactly when I was there. And Jasper Heath who works with me in the group would vouch for me, I'm certain.'

Drake nodded at Sara who had the dates available. Then Grant consulted his own smartphone and with a professional ease confirmed that on the dates referred to he had been present at the centre. 'It's all extremely valuable for the local community and for some of the more disadvantaged members of society.'

Drake's mobile pinged with a message before he had an

opportunity to reply. *Sam Chandler has arrived back at headquarters – please report progress.*

Drake stood up and thanked Bill Grant.

As they left Grant's home he said to Sara, 'Chandler's arrived.'

Chapter 39

Drake peered at the sandwich Sara had organised from the canteen at the area custody suite. He poked it with a finger – the bread was stodgy, but he had to eat. So he took a mouthful and the contents were as disappointing as he had expected. There was an odd, metallic taste to the tuna filling.

'It was the only thing they had, sir,' Sara said.

Drake mumbled a reply. He ate one half of the round and turned to the chocolate bar on the desk in front of him. Then he drank coffee. At least Sara had made certain sufficient instant powder had been added to the plastic mug to satisfy his usual caffeine hit.

Then he texted Annie – *I don't know when I'll be home. Sitting in area custody. Interview next x*

She replied seconds later. *Make sure you are drinking enough and have something to eat. See you later x*

He gave the second round of the sandwich a glance, wondering what Annie would make of it.

He had taken a few moments whilst Sara was organising something to eat to gather his thoughts. He had been told that Mrs Ackroyd was sitting in one of the rooms off reception, waiting for Sam Chandler, who must have called her after his arrest in Dover. The processing of Chandler into the custody suite had been completed and a duty solicitor had been called. Drake had spoken briefly with Winder and Luned both of whom had reported on their progress that afternoon. It wasn't good news – nobody recognised John Seddon or knew anybody called Spanish Dave.

At least they had recovered enough class A drugs from Chandler's home to formally arrest him on suspicion of possession with intent to supply. A technician at the CSI department had been dismissive when Drake demanded an update on their work with the mobile handsets removed from Sam Chandler's property. His team could make progress tonight with a triangulation search for the numbers in each handset. One of the numbers might be traced to Cemaes on the evening Jason Ackroyd was killed or to the area near Norma Ellston's home.

A preliminary interview with Sam Chandler that evening would give him the opportunity of cogitating overnight. And that was exactly what Drake wanted.

Once he had finished his coffee he nodded at Sara. 'Let's go and see what Sam Chandler has to say for himself.'

Drake punched his security code into the pad allowing him entrance to the custody suite. It was manned twenty-four hours of every day, each day of the year. There'd be a sergeant in charge and other officers, together with civilians. An air conditioning unit hummed in the background – no windows to let fresh air permeate.

The custody sergeant had long curly hair drawn into a knot behind her head. Spectacles perched on her nose and her pale complexion seemed to reflect the lack of sunlight that working in the suite entailed.

'Detective Inspector Drake. Good to see you,' Sergeant Ellis said.

'Manon,' Drake replied, simply using her first name.

'Mr Chandler is in one of the interview rooms with his solicitor.'

'We want to get an interview started as soon as possible.'

Sergeant Ellis didn't have time to respond as a man in a sharp suit, white shirt and dark navy tie walked up to her desk. 'This is Detective Inspector Drake. He'll be conducting the interview this evening with your client.' Ellis turned to Drake. 'Have you met Huw Probert?'

Drake reached out a hand. Probert gave it a tentative shake. 'If you're intending to interview Sam Chandler this evening then I'm going to object in the most vigorous terms. He's spent all day being escorted back up to North Wales. He needs to see a doctor and have a decent night's sleep. Apparently, he complained vociferously to the officers at the

Dover harbour police but they refused to seek medical attention.'

'We need to speak to him tonight – there are matters we need to put to him.'

'I can't make myself any clearer, Detective Inspector – it's not going to happen. You know what the guidelines say about interviewing suspects at this time of night. It's not in their interest or yours.' Probert looked up at Ellis. 'Do I really have to quote chapter and verse sergeant about your responsibilities as the officer in charge of the custody suite. I would remind you that you have a duty for the care and welfare of my client.'

Ellis narrowed her eyes slightly at Probert. Then she looked at Drake. 'Inspector Drake what do you have to say?'

Probert was right of course, and it was clever suggesting he needed to see a medic. There was no way Drake could object.

'What's wrong with Mr Chandler?'

'It's a matter for the doctor to decide, Detective Inspector,' Probert spat out Drake's title.

Probert was making it difficult for Ellis to decide other than to call a medic and postpone any interview until the morning. A preliminary interrogation was always important but overnight they might get more details on Chandler's mobile and the full results of the search.

So he said nothing further. Ellis stared at the solicitor, the frustration on her face evident. She must have heard a suspect's request for a medic dozens of times before and often it was a ruse to buy more time.

'I'll call the doctor. And we'll postpone any interview until tomorrow. Eight am, Mr Probert?'

A self-satisfied grin played over Probert's face. He nodded.

'That was a waste of time, boss,' Sara said as they left the custody suite.

'The doctor will give him a couple of aspirin and in the morning, he'll be magically restored to full health,' Drake said. 'Let's go and talk to Mrs Ackroyd.'

Sara was pleased their interview with Sam Chandler had been postponed.

She was tired, Drake was tired and giving the suspect a decent night's sleep meant he couldn't complain about being unfairly disadvantaged. Sara didn't believe anything would be lost by the delay in speaking to Chandler. She was more interested in hearing what Mrs Ackroyd had to say for herself.

Drake barged into the room where Mrs Ackroyd was sitting, scrolling through a mobile. Everyone did the same these days, Sara observed. She'd be checking emails, looking at Facebook, but the absence of any ear pods suggest she wasn't listening to podcasts or music. Vicky Ackroyd didn't strike Sara as the sort of person who enjoyed a decent audiobook.

She sprang to her feet. 'Why the hell have I been kept here all afternoon?'

Drake gave her one of his professional smiles.

'Do sit down, Mrs Ackroyd,' Drake said as he and Sara did so.

'You haven't answered my question.'

'Please forgive me, Mrs Ackroyd. We are investigating your late husband's murder, in case you've forgotten.'

It had the desired effect of puncturing Vicky Ackroyd's bravado. She sat back into the chair and pouted at Drake.

'I want to ask you about Sam Chandler. We have reason to believe Mr Chandler was involved with the supply of drugs. That's a serious matter and if he were to be convicted it would mean a substantial custodial sentence. Were you aware of his activities?'

'Don't be absurd – of course I wasn't.'

'Did you ever see Mr Chandler with more than one mobile phone?'

Ackroyd looked away briefly before returning her gaze to Drake. 'No, I didn't. He's got one of these ancient handsets. I keep telling him to get a new one.'

'I'd like to remind you that when we spoke to you initially regarding your movements on the evening that your husband was murdered you were quite vague. I have to say, Mrs Ackroyd, that your reluctance to cooperate and provide a full explanation of your whereabouts was troubling. We discovered during our investigation that you stayed with Sam Chandler.'

Sara couldn't see anything in Vicky Ackroyd's face suggesting she had any inkling where Detective Inspector Drake was heading with his questions. She kept scanning Ackroyd's face for any glimmer, anything to suggest she wasn't being truthful. Sara had been unhappy with the interview with Bill Grant. It was as though something had been left unasked or unanswered. Drake had been in too much of a hurry to get back to headquarters. It had been a frantic day. She resolved to review all her notes once she was back at headquarters.

'Did Sam Chandler ever mention a Norma Ellston?'

Ackroyd shook her head.

'I'm also the senior investigating officer in charge of the inquiry into the death of Norma Ellston.'

'I know that.'

'Apparently they were known to each other.' Drake produced an image of Ellston that he pushed over the table towards Vicky Ackroyd. 'Do you recognise her?'

Another shake of the head.

'We believe Mrs Ellston may have been dealing in drugs on a small scale and that Mr Chandler was her supplier.'

'Let me look at the picture again.' Ackroyd scanned the image searching her memory. 'I think I may have seen her at the house. I think she called a couple of times. I was arriving once when she was there, and she called one evening.'

'Did you ask Mr Chandler for an explanation?'

'No, why should I?'

Sara piped up. 'A middle-aged woman calling to see your boyfriend and you're not intrigued as to why she might be there?'

'I don't like the word 'boyfriend' – he was... '

'You were having an intimate relationship with him – surely you would have been interested to know who she was and why she was there?'

Vicky Ackroyd shrugged. 'Why would I? She might have been involved in his business.'

'And as you were supporting him financially that must have been of interest to you.'

'I have no idea what you are driving at, Inspector.'

'I'd like you to tell me how much you knew about Sam Chandler's activities. Were you aware that he was dealing in drugs?'

'You've asked me this before,' Ackroyd sounded bored. 'And the answer is the same as before.'

'Norma Ellston was killed a few days after your late husband was murdered. We are treating both inquiries as connected.'

'Good, excellent. She was involved in giving evidence against the Haddock brothers. Surely they were responsible.'

'Have you heard of automatic number plate recognition cameras, Mrs Ackroyd?'

'Yes, I've seen them on TV.'

'They are an important tool that we use as part of any inquiry and on the evening that Mrs Ellston was killed your vehicle was seen in the Llangefni area and then crossing the bridge in the small hours of the morning. Would you like to explain your movements?'

'If you think I'm going to stay here and listen to any more of these ridiculous accusations against either Sam or myself then you have another think coming.' She stood up and stormed out.

'What did you make of that, boss?' Sara said.

'Once we've spoken to Sam Chandler and got some forensics from his mobiles and hopefully something more constructive from the search of his property, I think we invite Mrs Ackroyd in for a formal chat under caution.'

'There's something she's not telling us. I can sense it.'

'Let's go back to headquarters. We need to prepare for tomorrow morning's interview.' They strode out of the area custody suite and as they reached Drake's car his mobile rang. Sara got in and waited for him to finish the call.

He got in and gripped the rim of the steering wheel. 'That was Andy Thorsen. The prosecution has an application tomorrow before the judge to allow Jason Ackroyd's and Norma Ellston's statements to be used in the trial.'

Chapter 40

Drake slept fitfully and woke early the following morning. He pulled back the duvet slowly and slipped out of bed. He showered and dressed as quietly as he could, hoping he wouldn't disturb Annie. He leaned over and kissed her on the cheek, but she barely stirred. Their plans for that weekend had already been changed. As Drake was working tomorrow morning, Saturday, and probably all of Sunday, Helen and Megan, his daughters, would visit in the afternoon and evening of Saturday. On Sunday he would return them to Sian, who lived not far from Northern Division headquarters. The conversation he had had with her hadn't been easy. She blamed any inconvenience to her childcare arrangements on the demands his work made on his time.

She had never appreciated that being a police detective didn't involve regular hours. Whenever he had to rearrange his time with his daughters, he always felt the weight of guilt. He was trying to make it up to them, take extra time off, make certain he could take them on special outings and events. It wasn't always that easy.

And with the prosecution of the Haddock brothers coming before the courts that afternoon there was every possibility Superintendent Hobbs would be demanding action and results over the weekend. Drake drank a glass of water before leaving the house, foregoing his usual coffee. He didn't have time.

He joined the traffic on the A55 heading east and accelerated into the outside lane, keeping to the speed limit, just. He called Sara, who sounded out of breath from her early morning run but she confirmed she'd be at headquarters promptly. He spoke to Winder and Luned, who both assured him they were en route to the Incident Room.

Drake arrived at headquarters and parked his BMW in a convenient slot nearer than usual to the main entrance. There was an early morning feel to the building once he entered. He nodded at one of the reception staff, but the place was quiet and he headed for the stairs to the Incident Room. He was the first to arrive and, after flicking on the light switch, walked over to the board. Once the place was fully illuminated, he scanned the map of northern Anglesey where a red pin had been placed on the beach where Ackroyd's body had been found. Another told the detectives where Norma Ellston's home was located.

It was easy connecting the deaths together. The testimony of both murder victims against the Haddock brothers saw to that. But the complicated private lives of Jason Ackroyd and Norma Ellston had coloured everything. And without direct evidence implicating Simon and Tim Haddock, Drake began to contemplate the real possibility they weren't the killers.

It wouldn't be easy trying to persuade Superintendent Hobbs that that was the case. He had already arranged a review meeting with his superior officer that morning. And top of the list was for a public appeal to trace Spanish Dave.

Drake was convinced that the two nocturnal visitors to the field above the cliff were crucial. Leaving early the morning after the murder suggested they must have known what had happened. And why did they return with torches? They must have realised or been frightened the condom would implicate them. They'd be scared and Drake had to find them.

The call handlers from the dedicated helpline had made reference to a caller that had rung twice without leaving any message. Was it one of the possible eyewitnesses? Time wasters had a habit of drawing attention to themselves. They would have wanted someone to listen to their version of events. So why call a helpline and not leave a message?

Sara was the first to arrive and after shrugging off her jacket and dropping her bag on the floor she joined Drake by the board. 'We haven't got much time before the interview.'

Drake read the time on his watch: it was just after seven-fifteen. Winder and Luned were late but as he was composing a reprimand, they entered the Incident Room.

'Sara and I haven't got long. I want an update now.'

Luned was the first to respond. 'We haven't been successful, sir, in tracking down anybody who knows John Seddon or this man called Spanish Dave. It's such a long time ago.'

'Did you visit all the caravan and campsites?' Drake turned to the board, pointing a finger at all the locations highlighted in yellow.

'Just as you wanted, boss,' Winder said. 'And we discovered caravan parks and some smaller campsites. We drew a blank everywhere. Have you thought about doing a public appeal for Spanish Dave?'

'Yes, of course I have, Gareth. What I don't want to do is put his life at risk if the killer or killers knows who he is. He's our best shot at identifying the man in the field who is very likely to be an eye witness with his girlfriend.'

'That's a long shot,' Sara said.

Drake nodded. 'I know, I know. I'm talking to the super later this morning once we've interviewed Sam Chandler.'

'We did get hold of more CCTV footage from the middle of Amlwch on the night Ackroyd was killed. I am going to work through that today.'

'Good, excellent, get on with it. And Luned plough through the house-to-house enquiries again. There might be something we've missed.'

Drake nodded at Sara and they left for the area custody suite.

A different custody sergeant was in charge and he smiled a greeting at Drake but said little. He treated Huw Probert with a degree of professionalism and disdain when the solicitor enquired about the medical treatment Sam Chandler had received.

'Fit as a flea as far as I can see,' the sergeant replied, his voice devoid of emotion although Drake knew exactly what he'd be thinking. He clicked into the computer system and scanned the record made by the sergeant on night duty. 'It looks as though he's slept for at least nine hours. So he's good to go for your interview.' He pushed over the tapes Drake would need. 'Take your pick of the interview rooms. We haven't got any customers in this early, apart from Mr Chandler of course.'

Drake motioned for Sara to follow him to one of the free rooms while Probert and one of the custody suite staff organised to escort Chandler. Drake nodded at him when he sat down on the rigid plastic chair across from the table screwed to the floor and wall. The slots for the tapes in the machine were open, waiting. Drake wasn't going to prevaricate – he had a busy day. He dropped the tapes into the machine and after Probert had nodded his agreement pressed play. He ran through the standard wording, warning Chandler that anything he said could be taken down and used in evidence against him.

He looked at Chandler. 'Did you kill Jason Ackroyd?'

'Of course I bloody didn't.'

'Then why did you abscond from the area without notice?'

'I didn't *abscond* as you say. I don't have to account to you or anybody else for my movements.'

'Why did you travel to Dover?'

'None of your business.'

Drake sat back and paused for a moment. At least he was answering the questions even if the answers were unhelpful.

'Where were you on the night Jason Ackroyd was killed?'

'I was at home.'

'When we asked you previously you were unhelpful and deliberately evasive. For the purpose of this taped interview can you please confirm who was with you?'

'All right, I was with Vicky Ackroyd. She came to my

place after she'd been out with some friends.'

'Did you or Vicky go out during the night?'

'Of course I didn't.'

'So if Vicky had left in the middle of the night, you might not have heard anything.'

Chandler frowned. He made no reply.

Probert butted in. 'Are you treating Mrs Ackroyd as a suspect in your investigation?'

'I'd like Mr Chandler to answer my questions.'

'Vicky was with me all night.'

'Can you be certain?'

''Course I can. She was there in bed with me. She left first thing in the morning.'

'You know a Norma Ellston?'

'Who the hell is she?' Chandler replied, a fraction too quickly.

Instinct had made him lie from the get-go. Now he had to maintain the lie with more lies which was always difficult. it would take a cleverer man than Chandler to do that.

'Mrs Ellston was murdered in her home a few days after Jason Ackroyd was killed.'

'And she was involved with the Haddock brothers' case I suppose?'

Chandler wasn't clever enough to guess that. Somebody had told him, somebody who knew all about the details. 'Who told you that?'

Chandler fumbled a reply. 'I think Vicky mentioned it.'

Drake pushed over a photograph of Ellston. 'So you've never seen this person before?'

Chandler hardly bothered looking at the image before pushing it away.

'Take a good look, Sam.'

Chandler pulled it back towards him and in a show of bravado stared at the image. 'Nope, never seen this woman.'

'We have an eyewitness who says that Norma Ellston visited you on various occasions. And before you answer, I should tell you that we executed a search warrant at your premises yesterday.'

'No fucking way. You can't do that.'

'A large quantity of pre-packed class A drugs were recovered as well as several mobile handsets which look like burner phones typically used by drug dealers.'

'Pay-as-you-go telephones are very common, Detective Inspector,' Probert added.

'And some of your clothing has also been removed and is currently being forensically examined. Now if there's any risk of us finding DNA to link you to the death of Jason Ackroyd or the brutal murder of Norma Ellston now is your opportunity to tell us. Cooperating at this stage is only going to be helpful.'

'This is a fucking stitch up. I'm not going to tell you anything.'

'I'd like you to tell me if you've ever been to Norma Ellston's cottage? It's in an isolated location.'

Chandler gave his solicitor a bewildered look, as though he were looking for direction before replying.

'I'd like you to tell me where you were on the night Norma Ellston was murdered?' Drake added the day and date.

'I was at home; where do you think I was.'

'And was Vicky Ackroyd with you?'

Now Chandler looked confused. 'What do you mean?'

'Simple enough question. Was Vicky Ackroyd with you?'

'Of course not. It was a Friday night. After I closed the business I went to the pub. I play pool on a Friday night.'

'What time did you get home then?'

'I don't know. I can't remember. I was fucking shit-faced.'

Chapter 41

It was mid-morning when Drake returned to the Incident Room at headquarters. He needed a strong coffee so he made for the kitchen, flicked on the kettle and went through his regular routine of measuring ground beans and timing the brewing process. It gave him time to think. And Sam Chandler's replies dominated his thoughts. They had enough to charge Chandler for possession with intent to supply and until they had completed all their enquiries in relation to the three mobile handsets they had discovered, Chandler wasn't going anywhere.

It also meant they had to speak to Mrs Ackroyd again. He was convinced now she was hiding something. That the ANPR cameras had recorded her car in the early hours of the morning following Norma Ellston's death had to be explained. Once the coffee had been prepared, he headed for the Incident Room and nodded a greeting at Winder and Luned, who raised their gaze from their monitor screens.

Finding one of Superintendent Hobbs' standard memorandum templates, he began composing the details of the latest update. Grudgingly, he acknowledged that adopting a pro forma did have some merit. His former boss, Wyndham Price, hadn't been one for management-speak but had been more of a seat-of-his-pants police officer. Drake had been so accustomed to working with Price he was only now finding his feet with Hobbs.

He scanned the previous memoranda he had composed – he'd want to follow up any outstanding threads. But more than anything he needed to get Superintendent Hobbs to agree for a press release to be issued inviting members of the public to come forward if they knew of anybody called Spanish Dave from twenty years ago. Instead of compiling a detailed memorandum Drake drafted a press release. It was urgent and required Hobbs' immediate attention.

He read the first draft.

As part of the ongoing enquiries into the murder of

Jason Ackroyd, Wales Police Service urgently wish to trace a man using the nickname Spanish Dave who lived in the north Anglesey area twenty years ago.

It all sounded so simple. Somebody must know who he is. All they had to do was pick up the phone and call.

But he knew it would alert the killers and it meant there was a risk they were putting the life of this man in peril. He kept adding sentences then deleting them from the press release. He moved the clauses around, hoping to make them sound punchier.

Then he looked at the draft of the memorandum. It was incomplete and he decided Superintendent Hobbs would simply have to wait to get the template in the format he liked. The printer purred into life as he sent it a copy. Then he left his office after dragging on his jacket. He had chosen one of his dark grey suits that morning, knowing he'd be in court later. Appearing before a judge – even if it wasn't his case – always justified a clean shirt, a newly dry-cleaned suit and a perfectly knotted tie.

Hobbs had expected Inspector Drake to provide an up-to-date memorandum of progress in the inquiry well in advance of the meeting Drake had requested. Its absence from his inbox suggested Drake was behind with his record keeping and it made Hobbs feel uneasy. The detective inspector would have known that getting the paperwork prepared in good time was essential.

Since his appointment to Northern Division as Drake's superior officer Hobbs had begun to appreciate his junior officer was dedicated and thorough. Superintendent Wyndham Price, his predecessor, had a reputation for being a little impetuous, too quick to make rash decisions without thinking through the implications. And it had taken some time for Drake to realise things had to change.

When his secretary announced the detective inspector had arrived he told her to show him in. Drake walked in, clutching the single sheet of A4. He sat in one of the visitor chairs in front of Hobbs' desk.

'Have you sent me your latest memorandum?'

'You should have that later this morning, sir. There is an urgent matter I need to speak to you about.'

Hobbs sat back. 'I see.'

It was one of those neutral statements Hobbs imbued with criticism and an edge of disapproval.

'The DNA from the discarded condom found by the CSI team near the cliff top path led us to a man called John Seddon.'

Hobbs nodded.

'Detective Sergeant Sara Morgan and myself interviewed John Seddon on Wednesday. He was employed by a company that worked at the Wylfa nuclear power plant some twenty years ago. He lived in the area for a few months and had a brief relationship with a woman called Beverley. The DNA results are very clear: John Seddon is the father of the man responsible for the used condom. And just to remind you, sir, two people were seen in the field late at night at the beginning of this week. They must have been the people who were camping in the field. And they're probably terrified the CSI team would have found the condom.'

'They have no way of knowing we've been able to connect the semen sample with this John Seddon. You've only been able to do so because he has a criminal record.'

Drake paused for a moment, gathering his thoughts. 'I know, sir, but maybe they were just frightened and frightened people are just that – frightened. Why did they go back there? They must have thought it was worth the effort in the middle of the night. Perhaps they've left something else the CSI team haven't found.'

'What are you proposing?'

'John Seddon referred to a man with a nickname Spanish Dave. I'd like to issue a press release inviting anybody who knows of this man to come forward.'

Drake reached over and placed the draft press release on Hobbs' desk.

'I think we need to keep it very simple. We need to trace this particular individual. John Seddon can only remember the name Beverley as the woman he had a relationship with. No second name and a description of her was non-existent.'

'And there would be dozens of Beverleys in Anglesey, it's a common name.' Hobbs studied the text Drake had prepared. 'What are the alternatives?' Hobbs said.

'Both the detective constables on my team visited several pubs and cafés in the north Anglesey area with uniformed officers yesterday. We've spoken to former members of staff who worked at the Wylfa power plant but so far we've drawn a blank.'

'And you believe this Spanish Dave can lead us to the woman Beverley who is the mother of the man responsible for the semen sample.'

Drake nodded.

Hobbs continued. 'And possibly they might be able to provide first-hand evidence that Simon and Tim Haddock killed Jason Ackroyd.'

'Well, I wouldn't go as far as that yet, sir.'

'I'll sign off on this press statement – get organised with the public relations department. Let's see what happens.'

Drake stood up and reached the door as Hobbs said, 'I think it's important you're in court this afternoon.'

'It's in my diary.'

'And remind me again which weekend is your mother getting married?'

'Next weekend, sir.'

'Well, you had better warn Detective Sergeant Morgan and if things really get out of hand we'll need you to be present, of course.' Hobbs returned to examining the papers on his desk before adding, 'And don't forget to complete the usual memorandum.'

A massive canopy hung over the paved area leading to the entrance to the Mold Crown Court building. It was part of the civic centre built on a sprawling site outside the town. Drake doubted the vast expanse of windows on the front elevation would be copied these days. After parking he walked over, noticing the press gathering. Two reporters from the television news glanced over at him wondering, presumably, whether he was somebody they needed to film or tackle for a quote. They returned to their conversations, ignoring him.

Inside, Drake found one of the court ushers who directed him to rooms used by the police and the Crown Prosecution Service. Andy Thorsen sat by a table nursing a can of soft drink. Superintendent Hobbs, dressed in his full uniform, cap on the table in front of him sat at Thorsen's side. Inspector Tony Parry paced around the room while gnawing at a fingernail.

'We're just waiting for Myra Harrison to arrive,' Thorsen said referring to the King's Counsel representing the Crown Prosecution Service at the hearing.

'There is some coffee over there.' Parry tipped his head towards an urn and some heavy cups and saucers sitting on a table in one corner.

'Thanks.' Drake walked over and helped himself, regretting doing so after a couple of sips as the coffee tasted at least three days old. 'Who's the judge this afternoon?'

'It's Kevin 'Hang 'em High' Hughes,' Thorsen replied, without any humour. 'So that should work in our favour. You know what he's like with serial criminals. And it's likely the Haddock brothers have been in his court in the past.'

'We'll see,' Hobbs said. 'I came across Kevin Hughes when he was a barrister years ago. I always thought he was pro defence.'

Drake took another sip of the coffee. As he was about to

sit down, a short woman with shoulder length hair and thick black spectacles swept into the room, with a tall, thin man twenty years her junior following in her slipstream. From their dark clothes and court gowns there was no mistaking this was Myra Harrison and her junior barrister. Kings Counsel always had to be supported by another junior member of her profession.

She dumped a pile of papers on the desk and looked over at the coffee urn. She turned to her junior. 'Please organise coffee.' She sat down, cleared her throat and placed an arm on the papers in front of her. 'We have an application today under the hearsay exception rule. Two of our witnesses have been murdered. We need to get the judge to admit the written statements they provided as part of your inquiry.' She fluttered a hand in the direction of Tony Parry. 'Judges are notoriously disinclined to apply the hearsay exception.'

Her colleague appeared at the table with a coffee, and she took a long gulp.

'I've spoken with the Haddock brothers' barrister.' She took another mouthful of coffee. 'He's made it quite clear if the judge finds against them he will appeal. He cited all sorts of precedents, making absolutely clear in his view that applying the hearsay exception would be wholly wrong in this case.'

'And does that mean we have to abandon the case?' Hobbs asked.

Harrison finished her coffee. 'Not at all. But it will make it very difficult.' Then she stood up and nodded for her junior to follow her.

Thorsen got to his feet before Hobbs, Parry and finally Drake joined the procession out for court. Barristers were milling around at the reception, discussing the outcome of the court case that had just concluded. The application by the Haddock brothers was the last item on the list that afternoon. As the courtroom emptied of the participants in the previous case, Drake watched as both men were escorted into the dock at the rear.

They were both immaculately dressed, clean-shaven, recent haircuts and they gave him a long piercing sneer before sitting down. If their lawyers had been as positive as Harrison had been negative Drake guessed they must have been feeling pretty buoyant.

Drake joined Hobbs and Parry in seating reserved for the police and prosecution staff. Being a lawyer, Thorsen sat behind the barristers. It wasn't long until the court clerk announced the case would begin and with a collective shuffle everyone rose as the judge entered.

His Honour Judge Kevin Hughes had earned the nickname Hang 'em Hughes with his robust comments and tough sentencing. Thorsen had commented before that it was commonplace amongst recently appointed judges for them to be overly severe. He had called it early-judge-itis. But Kevin Hughes had been a judge for a long time.

The judge scanned everyone in the court for a few seconds before inviting Myra Harrison to address him. She got to her feet. 'Good afternoon, Mrs Harrison.'

Drake had become so attuned to the likelihood of failure he read into the judge's greeting an advanced warning that her application was going to fail.

'Good afternoon, Your Honour, this is my application for you to apply the hearsay exception rule in relation to the statements of two witnesses who have sadly died.'

Harrison was eloquent and articulate in evincing the prosecution's claim that it was in the public interest for both statements to be included as evidence for the jury when the case came before them. Judge Hughes nodded occasionally, interrupting when he required clarification but there was nothing that suggested he was favouring Myra Harrison. Once she had finished she sat down.

Judge Hughes turned to the King's Counsel representing Simon and Tim Haddock. There was a confident, upbeat tone to his voice as though the arguments he was advancing were unimpeachable. Drake glanced over at the Haddock brothers smirking broadly. A knot of tension tightened over his chest as he contemplated the possibility that Judge Hughes would find in their favour.

Once the Haddock brothers' lawyer had finished, the judge wasted no time.

'This is an application for me to rule on the hearsay exception rule. I am not persuaded by the application and in the circumstances the statements of Jason Ackroyd and Norma Ellston will not form part of the prosecution case.'

Now broad smiles had crossed the faces of the Haddock brothers.

Drake felt sick. Everyone in the court stood up as the judge left.

Tony Parry scrambled to his feet and went over to Thorsen. 'Fucking useless judge.'

Chapter 42

The message that reached his mobile from Gareth Winder was clear – *Something you should see, boss.*

It was late in the afternoon, and he was pleased the team was still at the Incident Room. He jogged down the stairs at the Crown Court building and made for his car. The simple words uttered by the judge dismissing the application made by Myra Harrison kept replaying themselves in his mind as he drove over from Mold to Northern Division headquarters.

He called Annie on the hands-free. 'We've just finished at the Crown Court. It wasn't a good outcome.'

'I'm sorry to hear that. When will you be home, Ian?'

'I've got to call at headquarters first. I'll let you know once I've left.'

'You must be tired. It's been a long day.'

And Drake had a sense that Gareth Winder was about to ruin most of his weekend. 'I'm okay. I'll be glad when this inquiry is over.'

After the call ended, Superintendent Hobbs' comments at their meeting earlier about his presence being required on the weekend his mother was getting married stubbornly refused to leave his thoughts. What was he going to do if Hobbs demanded he be present to interview a suspect? Or interview possible witnesses? Or make an arrest? Sara could do all of that. He resolved that he wasn't going to miss his mother's special day.

Her announcement of her intending nuptials had forced Drake into thinking about his own relationship with Annie. They had talked about marriage, and he had made a point of telling her he loved her more often than he had ever done with Sian. She loved the children, and he didn't want to think he was avoiding discussing their future. There never seemed to be the time. Work and family life getting in the way was a casual excuse. Once this inquiry was all over he'd sit down with Annie.

Drake got on well with her parents and he had assumed

they were pleased she was in a long-term, stable relationship. There must have been a nagging hope in the back of their minds that she'd get married, even have a family of her own. Step-grandchildren were never quite the same as a grandchild of your own.

The car park at Northern Division headquarters was emptying as the normal working day came to an end. He parked and briskly walked over towards reception and then up to the Incident Room.

Sara was the first to speak. 'How did you get on this afternoon?'

Drake sat down on a spare chair by an empty desk. 'It wasn't good. The judge ruled against us. The statements from Ackroyd and Ellston will not be admissible against the Haddock brothers.'

Sara nodded her head. 'I suppose it's only to be expected.'

Winder now. 'What the hell is the judge thinking?'

'You must have heard of the rule of law?' Luned said.

Winder seemed immune to her sarcasm. 'They've both been brutally murdered. They made the statements in good faith. Is it appealable?'

Drake raised a hand telling Winder not to continue. 'So has there been a new development?'

'Sure thing, boss.' Winder dragged his chair back towards his desk and clicked into his computer. 'You should see this.'

Drake pulled his own chair around and sat next to Winder.

'I was able to get some new CCTV footage from cafés and pubs in the Amlwch area on the night Jason Ackroyd was killed. And when I was there yesterday, I found some more cameras fitted onto some commercial properties. I was going through the new footage. I spotted Tim Haddock in one of the pubs.'

Tim Haddock's grinning face as he left the dock at

Mold Crown Court instantly came back to Drake's thoughts. 'Are you sure it's him?'

Winder nodded. He ran the footage and Drake watched the familiar face of Tim Haddock, talking with friends, passing the time of day as though he were a regular. 'We need a detailed witness statement from the landlord of the pub and perhaps we can identify everyone else in this footage.'

'I'm going there later,' Winder said. 'The landlord got quite excited at the prospect we might want to interview him.'

'Great, good, Gareth, well done.' Drake moved back from Winder's workstation. 'So we can place Tim Haddock in Amlwch on the night Jason Ackroyd was killed. It directly contradicts the alibi he gave us and we've got that flatbed truck owned by the scaffolding business.'

'Luned's made progress too,' Sara sounded pleased.

Drake turned and nodded at the other detective constable on his team.

'I've been trawling through all the house-to-house enquiry results. Most of the statements don't help. It was late at night and most people were inside and the crime scene is an isolated spot at the best of times. I found a statement from a woman who lives in a farmhouse a few miles outside of Cemaes. It was one of the last houses the team visited.'

Luned stood up and walked towards the Incident Room board and stood with a pointer fixing a spot a few miles east of Cemaes.

'This is where the farm is located. She visited her mother who lives in a bungalow in Cemaes earlier that evening. She stayed with her mother longer than normal and her return journey home took her along this road.' Luned use the pointer to illuminate the route the woman had taken. 'And on her way home she only narrowly missed a collision with a van.'

'A van?' Drake said encouraged by the news.

'I've spoken with the witness who confirms she remembers the first two letters of the number plate – MA. I requisitioned a DVLA search for vans registered with those two letters. We should have the results in the morning.'

'Excellent, Luned.'

'And the witness thinks she saw a woman in the van.'

'Anything else?'

Luned shook her head.

Drake stood up and marched over towards the board. He stared at the image of Simon and Tim Haddock. He imagined both men celebrating that evening, pleased with their victory in the Crown Court.

'Let's ruin their weekend. We'll arrest both men first thing tomorrow morning.'

Chapter 43

Drake met up with Luned and two uniformed officers a little before seven am the following morning at the prearranged rendezvous. It was close to Simon Haddock's home. Sara and Winder were at a similar location near to Tim Haddock's home. The arrest of both men had been timed for seven am with the sergeant in the custody suite being warned to expect both men for interview.

Winder called Sara. 'All ready, everyone in place?'

'Yes, sir. Uniformed lads have just arrived.'

'Good, let's get this done – see you back at the Incident Room.' Drake nodded to Luned and the two officers standing by his side. He didn't need to say anything. They got into their cars and followed him. It was a short journey to Simon Haddock's home. It was an enlarged bungalow on an ageing estate by the dilapidated look of most of the properties. Three old vehicles occupied a concreted section of the old garden. They all looked to be beyond economical repair.

The two uniformed officers made their way to a rear access, making certain that if Simon Haddock decided to take his chances and escape they would be there to greet him. Paint peeled from the surface of the wooden door and the weak panels shook when Drake fisted it.

There was no response, so he persisted, eventually calling out, 'Police.'

A few moments later a bleary-eyed Simon Haddock opened the door, the stale alcohol fumes on his breath enough to strip paint.

'Simon Haddock, I'm arresting you on suspicion of the murder of Jason Ackroyd.'

'Fuck off. What the hell is this about?' Simon spluttered.

Drake concluded the standard warning before telling Simon to get dressed. Drake followed him inside making certain he spoke to no one and called no one. A bewildered

Mrs Haddock had just sat up in bed, her eyes looked like maps of the world and Drake was convinced she'd be sick any moment. But he was spared that indignity and he pushed Simon out of the bedroom, through the hallway and then out to the waiting police car.

Once the two officers had driven out of the estate Drake made contact with Sara.

'Simon Haddock is on his way to the area custody suite. He must have been celebrating last night. He smelled like a brewery.'

'Same here. We'll let both Haddock brothers sit in a cell until later this morning.'

An hour later Drake was sitting at a desk in the Incident Room, drinking coffee made to his exact requirements and eating one of the bacon sandwiches Winder had organised from the canteen for everyone on the team. The meat was fatty and the bread the spongy sliced variety but still it tasted damned good, especially with tomato ketchup, but when it dripped over his fingers he grabbed a tissue from a box, methodically wiping away the excess.

Drake returned to his office after making certain Winder would chase the CSIs for any updates on the mobile handsets recovered from Sam Chandler's home. Luned was already chasing the DVLA for the results of her search for vans with the right first two letters. He motioned for Sara to join him.

Drake sat down and started to outline an interview plan with Tim Haddock. Initially they would challenge him about being in Amlwch on the night Jason Ackroyd was killed. Interviews like this were always a preliminary skirmish that led to a more detailed forensic analysis. And with the search team going through Tim Haddock's home, Drake felt confident they'd find some piece of clothing to link him to Jason Ackroyd.

The merest fibre would be enough.

And if they could begin questioning Haddock it would only be a matter of time before he'd confess and they'd link him to the murder of Norma Elston.

'He probably thinks he's got away with it,' Drake said.

'We don't know that he is guilty yet, boss,' Sara said. 'Let's wait and see what he says in an interview.'

As Drake was finishing his interview preparation, Luned appeared at the threshold to his office. He waved her inside. 'There were half a dozen vans with the first two letters MA. And guess what, one of them is registered to Tim Haddock. I'll establish if there is any link to any of the other owners.'

'Thanks, Luned.'

Now they had the footage of Tim in the pub in Amlwch and the link to his van in the country lanes near where Ackroyd was killed. The net was closing in on the Haddock brothers. Drake decided against finalising a memorandum for Superintendent Hobbs although his senior officer would be pleased with the developments.

Drake took time to conclude his preparation before Sara joined him and they drove to the area custody suite. Manon, the custody sergeant he had seen previously, smiled when he arrived at her desk. 'Well, I'm glad to see a detective working on a Saturday.'

'Spare me the wisecracks. We have to see Simon and Tim Haddock.'

'And which of these prize specimens do you want to see first? Their solicitors have complained like mad that neither man is sober enough to be interviewed. We've given them the usual test for drink drivers and I'm satisfied they are under the legal limit, so you can proceed.'

'We'll start with Tim Haddock.'

Manon nodded. 'He's with his solicitor in one of the interview rooms.'

Drake took the tapes he needed to record the interview and pushed the door open for the interview room. Richard Redfern was a regular duty solicitor and Drake knew him well. He had a reputation for being fair-minded, as well as enjoying the good life his income as a successful lawyer allowed. 'Good morning, Ian.'

'Richard,' Drake said formally, 'this is Detective Sergeant Sara Morgan.'

Sara exchanged a greeting with the solicitor and sat down alongside Drake.

Once Drake had concluded the preliminary formalities he looked straight over at Tim Haddock. He still looked hung-over, bleary-eyed.

'I'd like you to confirm exactly where you were on the evening Jason Ackroyd was killed. When we initially spoke to you about your whereabouts that evening, you told us that you had been at home with your wife.'

'Yeah, that was right.'

'So, you were at home all night?'

'Just told you. You deaf or something?'

'Do you remember what you watched on television?'

'Same old crap.'

'Did you leave the house at any time? Maybe go for takeaway?'

Tim Haddock gave him a tired, condescending look. 'I. Was. Home. All night.' He said as though Drake were hard of hearing.' The missus can vouch for me.'

Drake read out the brief statement Tim's wife had provided previously. It was no more than a few lines but it confirmed her husband had been with her all night.

'Yeah. See, I told you.'

Drake turned to Sara who flipped open the laptop on the desk in front of her.

'I'd like you to watch this footage we recovered from CCTV cameras at a public house in the Amlwch area.'

Tim Haddock looked at him blankly. The standard lawyerly worry played over Redfern's face.

Sara turned the screen of the laptop so that Redfern and his client could view it. She hit play and the image of Tim Haddock sharing a joke with friends at the bar of the pub filled the screen. It wasn't a long piece of footage and Haddock hadn't realised the camera was even there, judging by Winder's description of its location.

'This is you in this footage, isn't it?'

Tim Haddock said nothing. He blinked furiously in frustration and then anger creased his face. The celebrations the previous evening had been short-lived and were now a thing of the past, which pleased Drake enormously.

'This is clear evidence you were not at home that night.'

Tim Haddock didn't reply.

'And your wife has provided a statement purporting to be an alibi, which is of course a lie. And that could be an offence known as perverting the course of justice. That's quite a serious matter and could well result in a prison sentence.'

Redfern leaned over and whispered something in Tim Haddock's ear. Still he said nothing.

'You and your brother have the perfect motive for the murder of Jason Ackroyd. He was going to give evidence against you in the forthcoming trial.'

'Well he can't fucking do that any longer.'

'Nor can Mrs Norma Ellston. Can you confirm where you were on the night she was murdered?' Drake read out the date and her address.

'I don't know anything about that.'

'But she was going to give evidence against you as well. And with two witnesses in your case having been conveniently murdered there is every possibility you believe you might be acquitted.'

Tim Haddock crossed his arms and pulled them close to his chest. 'No chance of us being found guilty any longer, Detective Inspector. You were in court yesterday. The judge almost threw out the whole case.'

Drake flipped open the folder on the table in front of him and found the record from the DVLA confirming Tim Haddock's ownership of a Ford transit van, its registration number beginning MA. He pushed it over at Haddock. 'Can you confirm this record from the DVLA accurately reflects your ownership of a Ford transit van.'

Tim Haddock nodded briskly after scanning the document.

'We have an eyewitness placing a van with the initial registration letters and in the Cemaes area on the night Jason Ackroyd was killed. Can you explain that?'

'Fuck off.'

'Crime scene investigators will be examining your vehicle in detail over the course of the next few days. And we have removed a lot of your clothes and personal possessions from your home. Now would be a perfect opportunity for you to share with us your involvement with the murder of Jason Ackroyd and Norma Ellston. Because, Tim, if there is evidence, we'll find it. And we will prosecute.'

It was early afternoon by the time Drake had finished his interview with Simon Haddock and returned to the Incident Room. Haddock replied 'No comment' to most of Drake's questions and his supercilious tone which he paired with a condescending look riled Drake. He counted to ten in his mind several times resisting the temptation to raise his voice.

He summarised both interviews for Winder and Luned who listened intently.

'I want everyone back first thing in the morning. We might have some progress from the tech guys on the various items of clothing that we recovered.'

The three officers in front of him gave him serious, intense nods.

Chapter 44

The swirling demands of the inquiry kept bouncing around Drake's mind as he left headquarters. As if on autopilot he took the journey to his ex-wife's home to collect the children. Feeling guilty that he hadn't been able to spend all day with them he would make a fuss of them that evening. They would have been staying with him that evening, of course, and taking them back to Sian early the following morning hadn't pleased her. Even though they had spoken on the phone about the new arrangements, he sensed the moderate death stare on her face directed at him.

Helen and Megan were waiting for him when he knocked on the door. They jogged down to the car throwing their bags into the rear, iPads at the ready.

'I hope all this is worth it,' Sian said. 'After all, they're only going to be with you for a few hours.'

'I'm sure Mam will value any time with them. As I do.'

Sian give him an exasperated look, raising an eyebrow in disbelief at his replies.

'I'll message you when I'm on my way tomorrow morning.'

Drake had barely finished by the time Sian had closed the door.

On the journey along the north-west coast Drake did his best to talk to his daughters. Competing with their social media profiles and the entertainment on their iPads was futile, he concluded. He settled into simply being with them in the car, together. After leaving headquarters, his mind had been able to refocus on talking with his mother and enjoying the evening with his family.

He detoured briefly to collect Annie.

'Have you had a good day?' Annie asked after kissing him. 'Did you make progress?'

They were simple questions with simple replies. He couldn't imagine sharing with her the details of the mechanics of an interview in the area custody suite. Or how the place smelled. The heavy tang of dirty clothes mixed with the bleach and cleaning fluids sloshed around the place could stick in his nostrils for hours. 'Two difficult interviews.'

Annie nodded as though she understood exactly what he meant. But he valued more than anything that she understood he couldn't talk about his work.

He threaded his way through the town of Caernarfon and once he was out in the countryside he took the narrow country road up towards his mother's home. He slowed as he always did to take the junction down to the smallholding. Angry black streaks lined the bottom of the storm clouds billowing in from Caernarfon Bay. His father would have pointed out sagely that a storm was brewing, had he seen the weather.

Mair Drake opened the rear door and smiled as she saw her granddaughters. Helen and Megan beamed in return and gave her a hug each going into the house. Drake and Annie followed suit.

'I want to tell you all about the arrangements for next weekend,' Mair Drake said, ushering Helen and Megan through into the parlour. An enormous fruitcake had pride of place in the centre of the table with plates and cups and saucers ready for teas and coffees.

The words 'next weekend' made Drake think immediately about the comments Superintendent Hobbs had made at the last meeting: that he expected Drake to be available. He looked over at Annie, dreading she might somehow be able to read on his face what he was thinking. But she was fussing over organising tea for Helen and Megan. He'd need to warn Sara in good time that she had to be available. But what would he do if Superintendent Hobbs demanded he be on duty? He couldn't defy his superior officer. Things didn't work that way. Superintendent Wyndham Price would have acted quite differently. He knew Drake's commitment to his work was absolute but if there was an urgent need to interview suspects or make an arrest in the afternoon his mother was due to get married could he really expect to have time off? He was the senior investigating officer after all. He shovelled his worries into the darkest possible recess of his mind.

'Are you going to have a piece of cake, Ian,' his mother said.

'Of course,' Drake said.

They sat around the table listening to Mair Drake sharing with them the details of the arrangements for the following Saturday. She found her iPad and opened it, displaying the page for the wedding venue at the Portmeirion Hotel. Helen and Megan quickly found the details on their smartphones, firing one question after another at the grandmother.

Mair Drake smiled at both girls, enjoying the attention.

'And after the ceremony we're going to have a lovely meal in the restaurant which overlooks the sea.'

'How many people will be there?' Annie said.

'We've invited twenty-two guests. Some are friends and others are Elfed's family.'

'Are we going to be staying in the hotel?' Megan said, her eyes filled with anticipation.

'Of course,' Mair Drake said. 'Everything's been organised.'

'Will I have a room of my own?' Megan glanced at her sister.

'Not this time, *cariad*,' Mair Drake replied. 'But the bedrooms are very big.'

'Will there be speeches afterwards?' It was Helen's turn to interrogate her grandmother.

'There are only twenty-two guests going to be present, Helen. So we won't be having any formalities like speeches. It'll be lovely having you both there.'

'Have you sorted out the seating plan?' Drake said.

'It was one of the things I wanted to discuss with you

today.' Mair Drake left the table, returning moments later with two sheets of A4 paper – she gave one to Annie and another to Drake.

Drake read the names of the guests. They included a cousin he knew vaguely. He asked about some of the names he didn't recognise and his mother explained they were Elfed's family. Annie's parents were to sit on a table with Huw, his brother. Drake had taken time to share with Mr and Mrs Jenkins his family history, warts and all. He often felt disloyal to his father's memory sharing the details of his arguments with his own parents when he had been a young man that had led to him leaving home and fathering a child very young, too young. It had led to a period of estrangement between his father and Drake's grandparents that must have been painful. It had been an enduring regret for Drake that he hadn't been able to speak to his father about it. He'd only become aware of his brother's existence after his father's death.

The Jenkinses would take making small talk in their stride, Drake concluded. And the other guests on the table would pitch in too.

'I thought you might say a few words,' Mair Drake said to her son.

'I thought you didn't want any speeches?'

'Not a speech. Just a few words. It was Susan who suggested you might do that.'

It surprised Drake his sister had engaged with his mother about the arrangements. He glanced at Annie who gave him a smile of encouragement.

'Of course, Mam. I'm sure I can find a few things to say.'

Mair Drake smiled, clearly pleased.

Once the teas and coffees had been drunk and thick slices of cake eaten, Drake stood up at the sound of another vehicle parking outside. Mair went to the door and welcomed Elfed. Drake could never get over the odd sensation he felt knowing that a man, other than his father, would be living at the property. And odder still knowing he'd be sharing a bed with his mother. The prospect unsettled Susan, but Drake was determined he was going to welcome Elfed into their family.

Chapter 45

Zoe didn't sleep much the previous night. She stared into the mirror in the bathroom – dark bags were beginning to develop under her eyes. She was seeing Paul later for a barbecue on a beach with some friends. The convenience store where she worked had offered her a shift that afternoon, but she had declined. She was in no condition to serve customers.

She hadn't got back from a friend's home until well after midnight. God, how she had enjoyed speaking to her friend Amy. It had been long overdue. She had sworn her friend to secrecy, and she knew that she could trust her. Unless she told somebody what had happened, she thought she was going to burst. But the relief she had felt after telling Amy didn't last. That morning a wretchedness had returned. She sensed she was in danger. And no matter how often she told herself that she was being silly and foolish it persisted.

Once she was showered and dressed she headed downstairs. She made herself a tea and a couple of slices of toast before sitting by the table in the kitchen.

'You look pretty this morning,' Zoe's mother said. 'Are you going out later?'

'Amy has organised a barbeque on the beach.'

'And how was Amy last night?'

Zoe shrugged. Her mother had to ask all these inane questions. Amy was the same.

'And who's going to be at the barbecue?'

'Usual I suppose.' What her mother wanted to know was whether Paul would be there.

'Did you hear the news yesterday. The police want to trace a man called Spanish Dave.'

Zoe hadn't seen the news. She took a moment to compose her mind, not wanting her mother to think she was desperate to know the latest snippet of information. 'Spanish Dave? That's an odd name.'

'That's all they said. Apparently, he worked at Wylfa

twenty years ago before it was decommissioned. But there were hundreds of people working there at the time.'

Zoe's mind raced. Who was Spanish Dave? Why did the police want to speak to him?

Now Zoe's heart began to race. She wanted to leave Cemaes and Anglesey. She was fed up with the place. She was angry with Paul, and with herself for having agreed to go camping with him. What was she thinking?

She had some savings that she and Paul could use to get away from the place. Maybe she could get a job in a hotel somewhere waitressing. They could get a small flat. And just live quietly. She made for her bedroom just as a text reached her mobile from Amy. *I still can't believe what you told me yesterday. What are you going to do?*

Zoe texted back. *I still can't decide. And promise me you won't tell anyone.*

Zoe stared at the reply for a long time. *See you later at the barbecue?*

Amy hadn't replied about not telling anyone else and that only added to the anxiety pounding in her head.

She took the long way round to the beach for the barbecue. She wasn't in the mood and it wasn't the middle of the summer so the weather didn't suit a barbecue. Paul's car was already parked and she recognised others belonging to their friends. A narrow path led over the dunes down onto the beach.

A few yards away she saw Paul and then heard his voice bellowing for someone to bring him more firewood. A plume of grey smoke drifted off into the distance from the barbecue he had set up amongst the rocks on the beach.

She walked over and joined him. He sipped from a can of cheap lager. 'Do you want a drink, Zoe?' He tipped his head at a cool bag by his feet.

She grabbed a can of soft drink.

Three of their friends returned, carrying some driftwood that they piled onto the fire he was nurturing. They looked pleased to see Zoe but the inane small talk – who had fallen out with who and whose parents had been particularly obnoxious left her uninterested. She just wanted to speak to Paul and get a decision about leaving.

She sat on a shallow bank of sand looking out over the beach, wondering how she'd got herself into this position. Amy sat down by her side and whispered, 'Got something to tell you.'

Zoe looked over at Paul who was deep in conversation with one of his friends. The barbecue nearby was hotting up nicely. Soon he'd be able to get the burgers and sausages and kebabs started. She began to relax realising that sitting outdoors enjoying the barbecue in the sunshine, such as it was, with Paul and her friends was the right thing to do.

She turned to Amy. 'Sorry, what did you say?'

'I've got something to tell you. I spoke to Darren.'

Zoe looked puzzled.

'My brother, you know – Darren. I told him about you and Paul.'

'You did what! Jesus, Amy, I told you not to tell anyone. It was a secret.'

'But Darren can help. He's been training with a martial arts group. He could protect you.'

Zoe heard her name being called and looked over at Paul. 'Can you fetch the burger baps and the rolls for the sausages from the car?'

Zoe nodded. She scrambled to her feet and Amy joined her as they walked to the car.

'You've got to look after yourself,' Amy said.

'I could go to the police,' Zoe said. 'I should have spoken to them at the beginning.'

'They won't be able to protect you.'

'They have witness protection schemes. You see them on the TV all the time.'

Amy gave her an incredulous look. 'Don't be stupid.'

Bags of rolls and baps in hand, Zoe and Amy returned

to the barbecue. Paul looked pleased to see them. Zoe helped Paul organise the cooking and their friends gathered around, complementing Paul on his barbecuing skills. Zoe had always been gregarious, enjoying parties and gatherings like this but she just couldn't get her mind into being sociable.

Eventually she dragged Paul away from the barbecue and their friends once all the food had been eaten. They scrambled up onto rocks above the beach and sat down.

'I've got something to tell you, Paul.' Zoe paused. 'I've spoken to Amy.'

'Not about the camping business. For God's sake.'

'I had to tell someone. I was going to explode otherwise.'

'And has it made you feel any better?'

Zoe wasn't certain how to reply. It certainly had last night but today here on the beach with Amy and Paul in the harsh light of day she wasn't so certain.

'She told her brother too.'

'Great. Everyone will know soon.'

'Paul, let's leave this place.'

'What do you mean?'

'We need to leave. Tomorrow. I'll pack a bag and we can just drive somewhere.'

'Where exactly?'

'Scunthorpe. There are lots of hotels looking for people to work.'

'Scunthorpe? Why the hell would I want to go there?'

Zoe threaded the fingers of both hands together and pulled them tightly. It mirrored the tension grasping her chest. She looked down at the beach and saw some of her friends improvising a game of football, others gossiping and finishing the last of the drinks.

'I'm frightened and I don't want to stay around here.'

Chapter 46

Drake had to adjust the photographs of his daughters on his desk when he arrived that Sunday morning, so they were just so. He stared at their faces and smiled remembering how they had enjoyed their afternoon with his mother, their *nain*. They had eaten too much of the fruitcake, which had suppressed their appetite for the meal that evening at the pub which they loved visiting.

Despite Sian's protestations that his time with the girls had been curtailed, he valued every moment – even sharing breakfast with them over the kitchen table. He had tried engaging with them, but their answers had been monosyllabic. A suggestion they might have an early morning walk had been met with an incredulous look and a sullen shaking of their heads. So, he had made pancakes instead which had been liberally covered with maple syrup.

The sugar hit seemed to have done the trick. They got to be more engaged and even began talking about what they might have for breakfast at the Portmeirion Hotel. Hearing activity from the Incident Room drifting into his office jolted him into the reality of work. Sara was the first to put her head around the door. 'Good morning, boss.'

Drake smiled an acknowledgement back.

He reached into a drawer and found a sheet of A4. He was well overdue a mind map session.

In a box just over halfway up the page he jotted down – Jason Ackroyd. To its left he added the name Mrs Vicky Ackroyd and drew an arrow towards the box with her husband's name. Underneath her name he added another box with the name Sam Chandler. And with Chandler connected to Vicky Ackroyd all he had to do was draw another short line between her name and her lover.

Before adding the names of any of the other persons of interest he drew another box below Ackroyd's and added the name Norma Ellston. The only people with a clear motive for her death were the Haddock brothers, so on the left-hand side of the sheet of paper he added both their names with three exclamation marks. He found a red ballpoint and drew a line between Simon and Tim Haddock's names into firstly the box with Ackroyd's name in it and then the other box with Ellston's name in it.

Allowing his mind to develop the various threads in the case he jotted down 'campers' at the bottom left-hand side of the page. Then alongside it the word 'motorcycle'. He still hadn't been able to explain satisfactorily why Jason Ackroyd would leave the house, having just returned from a pub crawl. Vicky Ackroyd had called him and he had sounded drunk but in good spirits when she spoke to him. There had been another two calls to his mobile from anonymous untraceable numbers. One or other must have been enough to justify Jason Ackroyd leaving the house. Drake wanted to know why.

Then 'van' was added alongside 'motorcycle'. It made him call the technical team at the CSI department to enquire about progress on Tim Haddock's vehicle. 'You must be joking,' Mike Foulds said. 'You'll be lucky to get anything constructive before the middle of next week.'

It wasn't the answer Drake wanted to hear.

'Have you been able to make any progress with the clothes and personal possessions we removed from the Haddock brothers' homes?'

Drake heard Foulds sigh deeply. 'We are doing our best, Ian. I'll let you know as soon as we have anything we can share.'

Once the call was finished Drake returned to the mind map on his desk and scribbled the name Bill Grant underneath Chandler's. Then he added his wife's name: Vanessa. He dragged to the forefront of his mind his initial meeting with Mr and Mrs Grant. They didn't have a particularly healthy relationship and there was something unexpected about Bill Grant's response when they'd interviewed him alone. It was as though he were expecting to be questioned. There was no expression of surprise or shock or indignation.

'I've got the details of another van that is local,' Luned said standing in his doorway.

Drake looked up at her, encouraging her to continue.

'It belongs to a Jasper Heath. I did a quick check and he's employed at one of the local leisure centres as a fitness trainer. From social media pictures of him he spends a lot of time in the gym pumping iron. And he boasts about being ex- military.'

'Send me the details.'

Drake waited as Luned got back to her desk and sent him the links she had found. He focused afresh on the name of the Haddock brothers at the top right of the sheet in front of him. He scribbled Detective Inspector Tony Parry underneath their names, hoping it would help him draw together some of the outstanding threads. It now looked as though Tony Parry's prosecution of the Haddock brothers was doomed to failure. They had the perfect motive for the murder of Jason Ackroyd and Norma Ellston, and Superintendent Hobbs was convinced of their guilt. Detective Inspector Tony Parry would cheerfully lock them up and throw away the key.

But they needed evidence to do that.

And it seemed the only first-hand possible eyewitness evidence they had were the two campers. He used his red ballpoint again to circle the word 'campers' at the bottom right-hand corner. It prompted him to call the manager of the dedicated helpline in the hope somebody might have called who could identify Spanish Dave. And finding this mystery woman Beverley justified adding her name underneath Spanish Dave's itself below 'campers' at the bottom of the page.

His mind map was getting full.

He scanned it again thinking there was something he hadn't addressed fully. Something he had missed, something he hadn't been happy with. He sat back for a moment pondering everything. The call which reached his mobile didn't allow him the luxury of time and he answered it, still staring at the sheet on the desk.

'Colin Chant here, Detective Inspector.' Chant's accent was unmistakable. 'The name Spanish Dave you mentioned to me when you visited has been niggling me. There was something in the back of my mind and I made a few calls. I think I've found the man you want.'

Drake stood up with a jolt. 'Where? I'll need all the details.'

He pushed his mind map to one side and jotted down a name and an address. Then he yelled, 'Sara, we've got to go.'

Chapter 47

'I've just spoken with Colin Chant. He's given me the name and address of the man he believes is Spanish Dave.' Drake was out of breath by the time he reached the bottom of the stairs out of reception.

'That's brilliant, boss.'

Drake pointed the key at his car and it bleeped open.

He dictated the details for Sara. Chant didn't have a postcode but by the time Drake had accelerated into the outside lane of the A55 the satnav announced it would take forty-seven minutes to reach Holyhead.

'Chant said that he lives somewhere up on Holyhead Mountain. You'd better double check the location.'

It was on journeys like this that Drake would have favoured a vehicle with all the usual lights and sirens. The blues and twos, as they were called, would have cleared the roads in no time. But he got Sara to warn the traffic department that he wasn't going to keep to the speed limits, and he flashed cars and blasted the horn of his BMW as he sped along.

He had to slow for the Britannia Bridge but, as it was a Sunday, the traffic was light and soon he was on Anglesey, accelerating hard in the outside lane.

'I've found the address,' Sara announced as she looked up from the screen of her mobile. 'It means we have to travel through the town and then out to the north of Holy Island before taking what looks like a track up the side of Holyhead Mountain.'

It was just under forty minutes by the time Drake pulled to a halt at the lights by the bridge crossing the railway tracks leading into the station at Holyhead. Three articulated lorries lined up alongside him, waiting for the lights to change to allow them to stream over the bridge and into the port. He drummed his fingers on the rim of the steering wheel, waiting for a green light. He sped off when allowed to do so and followed the directions of the satnav through the town, up past the school and then on towards the mountain.

A few minutes later he parked on a hardstanding alongside a Land Rover Discovery, it's wheel arches scratched, mud caked over most of the paintwork.

'Is that the property?' Drake said peering out of the windscreen.

'It matches the details we were given.'

He didn't waste more time and jumped out. The house overlooked the town and the port and the sea beyond. The flat landscape of Anglesey opened out and in the distance he could see the peaks of Snowdonia jutting out of the clouds. He found the front door, leading out directly onto the road they had just used. If the occupants wanted a quiet Sunday morning they were going to be rudely interrupted.

There was no response and Drake's heart beat a little faster at the prospect that no one was home. He hammered on the door again. Sara peered into the property and turned to Drake, shaking her head. 'I can't see anyone.' She stepped back into the road and glanced up at the bedroom windows.

Now Drake fisted the door. The sound reverberated along the street.

'Where the hell is he?'

'Maybe he's in Spain?' Sara said.

'That's not bloody helpful.' Drake didn't hide the anger in his voice.

Drake sensed movement behind him and saw a man emerging from an overgrown footpath being pulled by a dog on a leash.

'We're looking for a man called Spanish Dave who lives here.' Drake said raising his voice.

'Yeah, I know Dave. I don't think he's here though. He'll be at Mandy's place, in town.'

Pleased that Spanish Dave wasn't in Spain but locally in Holyhead meant they still might be able to find Beverley. 'Do you know where she lives?'

'Yeah, of course. She's my cousin.'

Drake ran up the concrete drive towards the front door of the semi-detached bungalow. An ancient Ford Fiesta was parked by an up-and-over garage door jammed open by a piece of timber.

He hammered on the door, Sara by his side. The door was opened by a woman in her late fifties, a cigarette hanging from her lips, her skin dulled by years of a nicotine habit.

'Is Dave with you?' Drake was dispensing with formalities by now, but as an afterthought he stuck his warrant card towards her.

'It's Mandy, isn't it?' Sara added, when she realised Drake's brusque approach wasn't working. 'We've spoken with your cousin on the mountain. He told us Dave might be with you.'

'What do you want?'

'It's urgent we speak with him.'

Mandy didn't move but shouted over her shoulder. 'Dave. Someone for you.'

The man who emerged into the hallway behind Mandy adjusted the ponytail. For a man in his fifties he kept himself trim, the drainpipe jeans and T-shirt didn't seem out of place.

Before he reached Mandy, Drake raised his voice. 'Are you Spanish Dave?'

'Yeah, that's right,' Dave chuckled. 'I've not been called that in a while.'

The swarthy looks and the rugged features must have been responsible for his nickname.

'We need to speak to you.' Drake stepped inside pushing Mandy out of the way.

It took her by surprise and eventually she led them into the kitchen at the rear of the property. There was no invitation to sit down and Drake wouldn't have bothered anyway. He got straight to the point.

'We've spoken with a John Seddon who was working for a contractor at Wylfa some twenty years ago.' No response on Spanish Dave's face so far. 'He had a relationship with a woman called Beverley. It's urgent that we speak to her and he remembered your nickname from that time.'

Dave lent against the worktop. 'I was employed at Wylfa for over thirty-five years. I've got a fantastic pension and friends for life. It was a good place to work and—'

'Do you remember John Seddon?'

'It does ring a bell.'

'Apparently the company he worked for rented a bungalow for their engineers.'

Dave nodded. 'Now I remember. There were some great parties there.'

Sara butted in. 'And is there any chance you recall a woman by the name of Beverley.'

'She might have been in the same group of friends as John Seddon or she worked in the same section in Wylfa or she went to some of his parties.'

'It might be Beverley Tanner you're looking for. I haven't seen her for a long time.'

'Do you have any idea where she lives?'

'I think she lives in Amlwch somewhere with her family.'

Chapter 48

Drake didn't bother with the satnav. He knew the way to Amlwch easily enough. He barked instructions for Sara to contact Winder and Luned in the Incident Room. They had to get an address for Beverley Tanner. And they needed it without delay.

Sara took the call on her mobile as Drake was almost halfway to Amlwch, accelerating hard. Then she tapped the address into the satnav. 'That was Area Control with an address for a Mr and Mrs Tanner.'

Drake paid little attention to the view over to his left across to the port of Holyhead and the mountain looming over the town.

After skirting around the village of Cemaes he abruptly pulled the car into the verge and parked. 'Come on,' Drake said to Sara, 'something's been troubling me.'

He sprinted back for the junction they had just passed which led to the church and car park they had visited on the first day of the inquiry. He stopped and jerked a hand over towards a lane leading to a farm.

'That's where the van was seen.'

Sara looked confused. 'What's on your mind, boss?'

Drake turned to look up at the slight incline that led over a hill that dominated one side of the village. 'We know Jason Ackroyd left his house on the evening he'd been out on a pub crawl. He was drunk we know that.'

'He took his motorcycle. It was torched, boss.'

'It's not that, Sara.' Irritation now in Drake's voice. 'Why did he leave the house? Who called him?'

'Vicky Ackroyd did.'

Drake turned to her, an intense look in his eyes. 'Dead right. She rang him.'

'But there were two other calls that we haven't been able to account for.'

Drake ignored her and took two steps away and stared over at the location where the van had been spotted. 'And the eyewitness we have says that she spotted a woman in the speeding van.'

'We can't prove it was the same van.'

'What if it was Vicky Ackroyd,' Drake stepped towards Sara. 'She calls him, tells him she has to meet him, pretends she's in trouble. Anything to lure him out of the house.'

Sara began to develop the argument. 'And when he sees her on the road he stops. But she's not alone.'

'We need to talk to Beverley Tanner but in the meantime, we keep an open mind about Vicky Ackroyd.'

'It could have been another woman – somebody associated with the Haddock brothers. And if it was Vicky Ackroyd, she wouldn't be involved with the Haddock brothers, surely?'

Drake heaved the car door closed. Once Sara had done the same he sped away without answering her question.

The Tanners had a detached property built in the 1920s with attractive bay windows on the ground and first floors. A collection of garden ornaments filled the small concrete area at the front. Drake left the car and, as he made for the house, he called Winder, telling the detective to get to Anglesey with Luned – they might need backup.

Drake pushed open the gate, Sara behind him and he noticed movement downstairs, relieved that someone was home.

The consequences of any discussion he'd have that morning with Mr and Mrs Tanner might well have long-term implications, but his priority was finding John Seddon's son.

A man sporting a grey shirt and tie knotted precisely under a patterned sweater opened the door. He was clean-shaven and had an old-fashioned short back and sides.

Drake had decided that he needed to conduct this interview carefully.

'My name is Detective Inspector Drake of the Wales Police Service, and this is my colleague Detective Sergeant Sara Morgan.' Displaying both warrant cards had the desired effect of satisfying the curiosity on the man's face. 'We'd like to speak to Mrs Beverley Tanner.'

'What's this about?'

'Is Mrs Tanner in? Are you Mr Tanner?'

'Yes, I am. What's this about anyway?' Creases lined his forehead.

'It is a matter of some urgency.' Drake did his best not to sound demanding.

'Well, if you say so.' He pushed the door open and motioned for them to step inside. Then he called out to his wife. 'Bev, there's somebody to see you.'

Drake sat on a sofa in the sitting room and exchanged a worried glance with Sara. If this wasn't the Beverley they were looking for they had more work to do. The place had a dust-free feel to it, with ornaments and pictures all in perfect order.

When Beverley Tanner entered the room with her husband she gave them an innocent smile. Drake wondered how long it would last.

'This is a personal matter, Mrs Tanner.' Sara said using her best soft voice. 'It just concerns you. We would prefer to speak with you on your own.'

'Don't be silly. I haven't got any secrets from Malcolm. We've been married a long time.' She smiled warmly at him.

'If you're certain then,' Drake said, pleased that Sara had opened the interview. 'Do you have a son?'

'Yes, Paul. He's not in any trouble is he? Oh my God, what's happened to him?'

Drake raised a hand. 'I'm sure he's fine. And is he about twenty years old?'

'Look, Detective Inspector, what's all this about?' Mr Tanner now.

Drake looked over at Mrs Tanner. This was going to get uncomfortable. 'We have a lead in the inquiry into the murder of Jason Ackroyd. It has led us to a man called John Seddon.'

Mrs Tanner paled.

'Who?' Mr Tanner again.

'Mr Seddon worked at Wylfa as a contractor some twenty years ago. Is it true you had a relationship with him?'

Mrs Tanner stared at the floor. She must have been willing for it to open up and swallow her. Instead, her husband withdrew his hand from hers that he had been holding since the interview began.

'We have DNA evidence that conclusively proves that Mr Seddon was the father of the man who was camping near the cliff edge near a beach where the body of Jason Ackroyd was discovered.'

'Christ almighty, I have had enough of this rubbish,' Mr Tanner said.

Beverley started nodding her head. 'It was a long time ago.'

'What the hell do you mean? Paul... does he know?'

She shook her head.

'Where is your son?'

'At home,' Beverley said. 'I mean he has his own place, a flat.'

'We need the address. He could be in danger.'

'And does he have a girlfriend?'

'Zoe. My God, she's not in danger too.'

Drake and Sara got to their feet as soon as they had the information they needed. Paul's mobile number had already been punched into Sara's and she was out of the front door first, phone pinned to her ear. Drake hesitated for a moment as he saw the terrified look on Beverley Tanner's face. Behind her he heard her husband retching into the downstairs toilet.

Chapter 49

Drake jogged back to his car, reaching for his mobile at the same time. He almost yelled instructions for uniformed backup to get to Zoe's home in Cemaes. He couldn't be in two places at one time and he had decided that finding Paul was his priority. As he pulled away from the kerb, a message reached his handset from Winder confirming he and Luned were en route.

'I can't help thinking there was something odd about the interview with Bill Grant,' Sara said.

Drake flashed his headlights at vehicles ahead of him as he accelerated through the traffic and on out of Amlwch.

'He was a strange character.'

'He took the questioning about Norma Ellston's death in his stride.'

'As though he were expecting us?'

'That's right, boss.'

Once Drake was clear of the town he floored the accelerator as Sara inputted the postcode for Paul Tanner's address.

'There wasn't any shock in his demeanour,' Drake said, allowing the thread to develop in his mind. 'He's a professional. He should have been shocked that we wanted an explanation of his whereabouts near the home of a murder victim.'

'And he works in the court service.'

Drake fisted a hand against the steering wheel. 'Of course, of course, and he'd have access to all the documents in relation to the Haddock prosecution. And that would have included Norma Ellston's address.'

'And Vicky Ackroyd knew all about the evidence Ellston was going to give at the trial of the Haddock brothers. She could only have got that information from someone in the know.'

'And another thing – do you recall the way Marion Walker replied to us when we asked her about Vicky

Ackroyd's relationship? Sam Chandler wasn't the only man she was seeing.'

'Running a fish and chip shop isn't as posh as a civil servant.'

'And Vicky Ackroyd has plenty of money to bail out Grant.' Drake raised his voice. 'Damn. She was driving from Ellston's place when she was spotted on the cameras.'

'Either that or it was Grant or both of them.'

'And Bill Grant told us himself that his wife was taking sleeping tablets. All he had to do was double the dose and she'd be out of it all night. He could slip out without her knowing.'

The satnav announced they were within three minutes of their destination.

Drake wasted no further time – he called Winder.

'I want you to call at Bill Grant's home.'

'What do we do when we're there?'

'Arrest the bastard on suspicion of murdering Ackroyd and Ellston,' Drake said, the anger evident as he realised that Grant might well not be at home. As Grant's link to the martial arts group clicked into place, he added in a rush, 'We've missed a connection here. Grant got Jasper Heath to vouch for him. They are close...'

'And Heath is ex-military.'

'Damn it – get uniformed lads to pick up Jasper Heath for questioning. If anyone could have done that Russian omelette manoeuvre it would be him, ably helped by Grant.'

Beverley Tanner had described her son's flat as a converted part of a house by an old chapel. Drake pulled in off the road and parked. He and Sara left the vehicle and sprinted through the open gates along a cracked concrete path. At the end Drake spotted an open door and stopped. He motioned to Sara, telling her to be careful.

They stepped inside. The coats that had once hung on the hooks in the hallway were now strewn all over the floor. In front of Drake was a narrow, steep staircase. Ahead was a corridor leading to the rear of the property and immediately to his right a pine door opened into a small sitting room. The place had been well and truly trashed. Every cupboard had been emptied, every cushion ripped and torn.

He retreated out into the hallway and then through into the kitchen. The chaos there replicated that which he had seen moments earlier. It only took a few moments with Sara to visit the upstairs and examine the two minuscule bedrooms that had been ransacked too.

'Jesus, do you think he put up a fight?' Sara said.

Once they were back downstairs Drake called area control demanding a full CSI team be deployed. They'd look for signs of a struggle, blood deposits, torn fragments of clothing but he couldn't see any. Was it a good sign?

Maybe Paul Tanner had simply been overpowered quickly.

The image of Bill Grant in his martial arts clothing leapt back into his mind and knowing Jasper Heath's background and training Paul Tanner didn't stand a chance against them. They probably bundled him into the back of Jasper Heath's van, ready for him to be disposed of.

Drake's mobile rang and he snatched it from his pocket. 'Detective Inspector Drake.'

'Constable Thomas, sir, we've just been to the home of the girl Zoe. She's not here and her parents thought she was staying with Amy last night.'

Drake looked back into the house and a desperate feeling returned that both Paul and Zoe had been taken. Could he have done anything different? Could he have properly protected them?

'They gave us an address of an Amy, one of her friends where she stays occasionally.'

'Text it to me now.'

'And there is no sign of Vicky Ackroyd, sir.'

'Ask around the village. Somebody must know where she is.'

Drake finished the call before the officer had time to confirm. Drake turned to Sara. 'Zoe is not at home and her parents gave one of the uniformed lads the address of one of her friends. Let's get over there now.'

It was a short journey to Amy's home and when a young woman opened the front door Drake could see the surprise and apprehension on her face. She began to close the door in his face until he and Sara produced their warrant cards simultaneously. 'We are police,' he said simply. 'We need to contact Zoe and Paul.'

She kept the door firmly where it was, her body blocking out the view of most of the inside.

'Amy, who is it?' a man's voice called out.

Drake peered over her shoulder, willing it to be Paul Tanner. He could feel the waves of relief already developing.

A man emerged into the hallway behind Amy. He frowned when he looked over at Drake.

'Are you Paul Tanner?'

'Yes, who are you?'

'Detective Inspector Ian Drake of the Wales Police Service. We need to speak to you urgently.'

Then Drake, barged inside pushing Amy out of the way. Sara followed behind. Drake stood in the hallway. 'Is Zoe with you?'

'Yes, she's in the bedroom. We are just leaving.'

'What do you mean leaving?'

'We're leaving this place. There's nothing left for us here.'

Drake called out Zoe's name, adding, 'We need you in here now.'

He pushed Paul into the sitting room of the property, propelling him onto a sofa.

'We know it was you and Zoe camping in the field the night before Jason Ackroyd's body was found on the beach. And we know it was you that returned to the field with torches. What the hell were you doing?'

Paul blinked furiously. Zoe appeared in the door and Drake jerked his head for her to sit with her boyfriend.

'How did you know it was us?'

'Don't worry about that now. I want you to tell me what you saw that night.'

'Tell them,' Zoe said. 'Tell them. They can protect us.' She turned to look at Drake. 'You can protect us, can't you?'

'Of course, you're safe now. I want you to tell me everything you witnessed.'

Paul fumbled into his pocket and began scrolling through his mobile, not saying anything. It only took a few seconds to find what he was looking for and then he gave Drake the handset. 'I took photographs. There was a van and two men.'

Drake stared transfixed at the images.

Chapter 50

'Why the hell didn't you tell the police about the images before?' Drake couldn't contain his exasperation. 'These people are dangerous. You could have got yourself killed.'

'We were frightened,' Paul mumbled.

Drake shared the images with Sara. They provided a complete registration number for the van they were seeking. 'Get the reg number checked against the one owned by Jasper Heath.'

'Who did you say?' Amy said. 'My brother knows Jasper. They are in that martial arts group together.'

'And Amy told him about us,' Zoe said, the anger evident in her voice directed at her friend.

Drake fiddled with the images on the screen, trying to get a clear sight of one of the men. It didn't take him long to get an image that would stand up in court. The face of Bill Grant was unmistakable. Heath was more than just a hanger-on, he must have been trained and skilled and that meant he could easily have killed Ackroyd.

'We've just been to your place. It's been wrecked,' Drake turned to Amy. 'Your brother must have told Heath – that's why they knew where to find Paul. You were lucky you weren't there last night.'

Drake stood up nodding for Sara to join him.

Outside on the driveway Drake turned to Sara who was checking her mobile. 'Call area support. I'm going to speak to Gareth.'

'I've checked the reg number – it is Heath's van,' Sara said.

Winder answered after one ring. 'We've just been to Grant's property, boss. He isn't there and his wife is away with the fairies. She must be on something. She kept complaining she'd been sleeping for hours on end.'

'Luned has got the address for Jasper Heath. Get her to send it to me and I'll meet you there. Give me your ETA as soon as possible.'

Drake looked over at Sara.

She finished a call, confirming more support was on its way to Amy's home.

'Bill Grant isn't at home and Mrs Grant is high on something. Which might explain how her husband could slip out late at night without her knowing.' He tipped his head at the car. 'Let's go.'

Drake pulled up alongside the marked police car at the top of the lane to Heath's address. Drake marched over and met both officers as they left.

'We've been down to the property, but it looks empty.'

Moments later Winder arrived and he and Luned joined Drake and Sara.

'We need to be careful, sir. I learned more about Heath's background this morning. He's described as psychotic with a propensity for violence,' Luned said.

'Bloody hell,' Drake replied. 'Just the person to assist Bill Grant with a Russian omelette.'

'And I've done some preliminary research on Heath's property,' Luned nodded down the drive. 'Jasper Heath has a small cottage at the rear of a holiday home and what looks like a home gym from the images I've been able to find.'

'Good work. Let's get going, we haven't got time to waste,' Drake said before dictating detailed instructions of how he wanted the officers to approach and not to take any risks with their safety. One of the vehicles would block any possible escape by Jasper Heath.

Drake took the lead and skirting to the left of the main farmhouse pulled up in front of the cottage. Behind him Winder parked, blocking any escape route. Drake exited his car and yanked at the door handle of Jasper Heath's van. It was locked.

He made his way over to the main door of the cottage but no amount of shaking the handle opened it. He waved a hand for Winder and Luned to go around the rear and side.

He and Sara did the same, peering in through the windows but there was no sign of anybody. The place felt deserted.

He returned to his vehicle, which was parked at the front of the building, and made for the outbuildings Luned had mentioned. The first he tried was locked and the adjacent window was smeared with dirt on the inside. The second door eased open, and he stepped inside. He paused for a moment hoping he could sense movement, but he heard nothing. His brogues clattered on the wooden flooring as he ventured towards a door. On the other side of it was a small home-made gym. Free weights were stacked before a mirror in one corner. A rowing machine and static bike both of which were old judging by their wear and tear looked over at a television screwed to the wall.

'There's another door, boss,' Sara said pointing to a door in the corner.

He walked over and slowly grabbed the handle pushing it open. He shouted a warning. 'Police. Jasper Heath, we want to speak to you.'

Inside was more gym equipment.

Drake didn't have time to assess their age, his attention was taken by the body slumped against one wall. There was a single bullet wound to Jasper Heath's head. It meant he wouldn't be talking to anybody ever again.

Chapter 51

'I want an armed response vehicle deployed immediately,' Drake growled into his mobile.

Superintendent Hobbs sounded reluctant at first but once he heard Drake's explanation he was left with no choice. Any circumstances where a firearm had been discharged changed everything.

'Of course. I'll issue the order without delay.'

Drake stood for a moment with his team.

'Where the hell would Bill Grant have gone?' Drake said.

'We can't locate Vicky Ackroyd. We don't know where the hell she's gone either,' Winder said.

'I've already issued an alert for Bill Grant's car. He won't go far,' Luned said.

'Good, good.'

'And uniformed lads are with Paul and Zoe,' Sara said.

'Which means we've got the evidence to send Bill Grant down for a long time.'

Luned's mobile rang, and she took the call, mouthing the words 'road traffic'. Seconds later she finished and turned to Drake. 'They spotted his car speeding down towards Menai Bridge.'

'Let's go.'

Drake jumped into his car and once Winder had moved his, he raced up the driveway and on for Menai Bridge. He kept regular contact with the road traffic unit that had initially recognised Bill Grant's vehicle, but they had lost sight of him, and Drake cursed. The armed response vehicle wouldn't be with them for another twenty minutes.

He reached the Four Crosses roundabout at the top of Menai Bridge and decided that Grant wouldn't risk going over the Brittania Bridge where traffic police were more likely to catch him. So he took the exit down into the middle of the town and made for the suspension bridge.

At the next roundabout Drake slowed and cast his gaze

around. Winder was behind him. 'Tell Gareth to go down into the town, we'll go for the bridge.'

Sara did as she was told, and Drake saw Winder peeling off, indicating left. Drake powered on and reached the roundabout leading onto the bridge. He spotted Bill Grant's Audi approaching from the town centre. There was no mistaking the man's profile.

Drake switched on the headlights and began blasting his car horn, encouraging the vehicles ahead of him to get out of his way. Then he began to wave his arms as though it would magically move the vehicles in front of him. 'Call the road traffic unit and the ARV. Tell them we spotted him going over the suspension bridge.'

He managed to overtake two cars putting the fear of God into an oncoming vehicle whose driver waved a fist at Drake angrily. Grant had started to pull out into the middle of the carriageway, trying to force the vehicle ahead of him to pull over. He must have realised Drake was behind him.

It wouldn't be long before they were in Bangor. It was only a matter of time until Grant would have to slow for the traffic. He couldn't simply plough his way through red lights and pedestrian crossings. Over to his left Drake saw a motorboat ploughing through the waves of the Menai Strait.

Grant pulled out and bumped the car in front which crashed into the pavement. Grant sped on. Luckily the two vehicles ahead of Drake realised it was a police chase, so they pulled into the side of the road, mounting the pavement. But Grant had been able to gain a few valuable yards and he hurtled on.

Drake didn't expect him to turn left. 'What the hell is he doing? That's a residential area.'

Drake slowed the vehicle as he followed Grant. It was a neighbourhood of substantial detached properties near to the university buildings. Grant would have to pull up and make a run for it very soon.

Braking hard at the no entry sign should have been

automatic but Grant powered on down the one-way street. It left Drake with no alternative. He had to follow. As he did so a car travelling up the hill in the middle of the road flashed its lights, the driver waving a warning at Grant. The man had to pull into the side of the road and narrowly missed a collision with Grant's vehicle. Drake slowed a fraction as he followed.

'Where the hell is he going?' Sara said.

'This is a residential area that leads out of the city.' Drake said. As he finished the sentence he glanced over to his left and saw Bangor pier stretching out into the waters of the Menai Strait. 'Bloody hell, he's going for the pier, I bet you.'

More vehicles had been forced into the side of the road by the speed at which Grant was driving. Drake guessed he would turn left down towards the entrance of the pier. Moments later Drake pulled up behind him and watched as Grant left his car and run down to the pier. 'Tell the armed response vehicle where he is,' Drake yelled at Sara.

'Sure thing, boss.'

Drake set off in pursuit. Grant stretched his legs and sprinted for the end of the pier.

The pounding of Drake's brogues on the wooden decking would mean blisters he was certain and a tightness gripped his chest as he dragged in lungfuls of air. As he ran up the pier he yelled for the visitors to clear away. Some looked shocked, others ignored him, but most followed his advice and hurried away.

It was when he was over halfway that he noticed an expensive-looking craft slowing as it approached the end of the pier. The possibility Bill Grant was going to make his escape on some boat defied belief. Drake pressed on, increasing his pace, but it didn't make any difference. Bill Grant was much fitter.

He reached the end of the pier and scrambled to the top of a bench and then on to the railings near to a galvanised ladder down towards the sea.

Drake was nearing. He shouted, 'Police – stop! You're under arrest, Bill Grant.'

Grant turned to look at Drake and raised a middle finger in contempt, but as he did so he lost his footing and cracked his head against the edge of the ladder. Then he toppled over and fell headlong off the pier.

Drake climbed onto the same bench that Grant had used and peered down. There was no sign of Bill Grant in the murky waters of the Menai Strait. A few metres away Drake spotted Vicky Ackroyd on the open deck of her luxury motor yacht. As soon as she saw Drake, she went back into the wheel house and powered away, the water foaming as the propellers churned.

Chapter 52

The following morning the body of Bill Grant was washed up on the beach in Llanfairfechan. Vanessa Grant identified the corpse at the mortuary, but she didn't seem distressed or heartbroken and she certainly didn't play the grieving widow. Vicky Ackroyd's motorboat had been tracked easily enough using the latest satellite navigation to a small harbour on the Llŷn Peninsula. She had surrendered to the officers without argument.

The interview with her had been straightforward. No prevarication. No lies. She had admitted her involvement in murdering her husband and Norma Ellston. She blamed it all on the pressure she was under from her relationship with Bill Grant. He had been convinced that killing Ellston would be blamed on the Haddock brothers as well as the murder of Jason. She had become collateral in Grant's mind in his determination to get hold of Vicky's money and rid himself and Vicky of her husband.

And Drake didn't believe a word she said. But her admission to murder was enough to send her to prison for a long time. And after the minimum term she'd be on licence for the rest of her life.

It had been the same week that the case against the Haddock brothers had begun in the Crown Court. And by Friday the jury had been out for over twenty-four hours deliberating their verdict. Drake arrived a little before lunch and Myra Harrison, the King's Counsel, her junior barrister and Andy Thorsen sat in the room set aside for the prosecution. They managed weak nods of acknowledgement as Drake entered that reflected their downbeat mood.

'Is it a good sign the jury have been out for so long?' Drake sat by the table after pouring himself a coffee.

Harrison looked over at him. 'It's that old parlour game where we try to guess how a jury is thinking. It's impossible to say. I've seen juries acquit when I thought a guilty verdict was a slam dunk. The judge directed them before lunch that he'd accept a majority verdict.'

'I hear you had a satisfactory resolution to your two murder enquiries,' the junior barrister said.

Drake nodded. 'Mrs Ackroyd confessed but blamed it all on Bill Grant who conveniently is no longer with us.'

Myra Harrison smiled. 'And he's not around to contradict her. So the sentencing judge will have to believe her. Clever. It might reduce her minimum term but she's going away for a long time.'

Superintendent Hobbs entered, taking off his cap and placing it on the table whilst he helped himself to coffee. 'Has there been any indication from the jury?'

'None,' Thorsen replied. The senior Crown prosecutor was so monosyllabic and deadpan Drake wondered if there was any emotion to the man.

'And where is Tony Parry?' Drake said.

'He'll be back soon. I don't think he could stand waiting for the jury. He's walking around the civic centre.'

Another hour passed until an usher entered announcing the jury were ready to return. Tony Parry had arrived moments earlier, a haunted look on his face. If the Haddock brothers were acquitted, as seemed likely, he didn't envy Parry's task of explaining the outcome to the victims.

Within a few minutes everyone had gathered back in the main courtroom. Drake sat in a row of seats with Parry and Hobbs, looking out over the benches occupied by the lawyers in their gowns and wigs. The Haddock brothers in the dock still had that contemptuous grin on their face.

When the judge entered all present in the court stood up.

Then the jury filed in. The foreman was invited to read their verdicts. There was an audible gasp from the visitors' gallery at the first guilty verdict.

Then a shout – It's a fucking stitch up! – after the second guilty verdict.

Tony Parry's leg began to twitch.

Now Drake could see exactly where the jury was going. The third and final verdict was exactly like the first two. Drake could only imagine the relief coursing through Tony Parry's body.

He looked over at the Haddock brothers, their faces set hard with contempt.

'Stand up,' the judge directed as he glared over at the dock. 'These are very serious offences. The case against you was overwhelming and you have sought to inflict additional pain and suffering on your victims by having them attend court to give evidence. You will each be sentenced to ten years imprisonment with a minimum term of eight years. Take them down.'

Once the judge had left the court and the Haddock brothers had been removed from the dock after exchanging words of encouragement with their family in the visitors' gallery, Tony Parry doubled up in his seat putting his head in his hands. 'I don't fucking believe it.'

After leaving their seats Drake and Hobbs and Parry stood with Myra Harrison.

'That was a good result,' Hobbs said.

'Good work. You should all be pleased. And you can always rely on Hang 'em High Hughes.' Harrison shared a brief smile with the three officers before pacing away.

Drake left the building shortly afterwards delighted that for once he'd be able to get home early.

He had a lot to prepare before tomorrow, a lot to rehearse.

And he wondered how Annie would react.

Chapter 53

The 'few words' his mother wanted wasn't a speech of course, but it felt important. He had mulled over the right words, consulted Annie about the construction of each sentence, rehearsed each into a mirror until he told himself he really was obsessing about finding the right thing to say.

The Portmeirion Hotel was the perfect setting for a special occasion. As guests of the hotel they didn't need to use the usual tourist access and that Saturday morning the staff made his mother feel extra special. He had collected Helen and Megan in good time after the court case the previous afternoon. Annie had fussed over them that morning, making certain they looked the part for their grandmother's wedding.

Drake felt very proud his daughters had accompanied him and prouder still Annie was with him. Once they had been able to settle into their rooms at the hotel there wasn't much time before the ceremony itself. Helen had wanted to know if she could record everything on her mobile. Drake had been reluctant to agree without consulting his mother, who had smiled warmly, agreeing to her granddaughter's request.

The Town Hall building in the village had an arched roof that had been saved when the original house it belonged to had been demolished in the 1920s. The ceiling showed the trials of Hercules and he had shown his daughters the room on a previous visit not knowing then he would be here to witness his mother's marriage.

The ceremony was conducted with the minimum of fuss, and it was odd hearing the registrar asking his mother whether she would take Elfed as her husband. He glanced over at Susan who was blinking rapidly, choking away her tears. Drake smiled to himself. Nothing could remove the memories he had of his father and the loving relationship his parents had. He cherished his father's memory, but now his mother had fallen in love with another man and was going to spend the rest of her life with him.

Susan would have to support her mother as he had done. He feared his sister had her own problems, made plain by the absence of her husband George at the ceremony. Her two boys looked uncomfortable, not really certain they wanted to be present.

'I now pronounce you man and wife.' A spontaneous ripple of applause erupted from the guests. Was that the done thing? Drake joined in.

His mother beamed as she was escorted out by Elfed, arm in arm.

They walked down to the hotel and enjoyed pre-dinner drinks as they waited for the staff to announce their table was ready. Everything about the meal was a resounding success. The standard of the food impeccable and the service superb. He shared a warm smile with Annie who told him she knew it was as much of a success as he believed it to be.

There didn't seem to be a break in the conversations around the tables amongst the guests. He hoped his daughters would remember this day for a long time and his mother would value having her friends and family at this important event.

He reached a hand into his jacket pocket and pulled out the prompt card he had used to scribble the 'few words' he proposed to share with everybody. When the time came he cleared his throat and got to his feet. There was no going back now.

Half-jokingly he thanked Elfed for taking his mother on, suggesting he might not realise what a commitment it might be. It earned him a ripple of good-natured laughter. His mother smiled. So did Elfed, luckily. He reminded all the guests that family and friends were more important than anything and they shouldn't forget the memory of absent friends and family. But life is for living he added, looking over at Annie who beamed.

He raised his glass. 'I'd like to propose a toast. The

bride and groom.'

A chorus of voices joined in.

It was later, after dessert and coffee when the guests were mingling in the lounge, that Drake joined Annie on the patio outside the hotel, looking out over the estuary. She drew a shawl over her shoulders. He put a half-filled champagne flute in her hand and with the one he was still holding clinked the glasses together.

'This is quite the celebration,' Drake said threading an arm around Annie's waist. 'There's something I've been meaning to ask you.'

She looked into his eyes. And he knew then she knew exactly what he was going to ask.

'Annie Jenkins, will you marry me?'

Printed in Great Britain
by Amazon